MW01597953

Kansas City Heat

I think the older I get the more I like reading about older characters. I enjoyed "Dixon's Duty" and will be looking forward to the next book. ~ *The Blogger Girls*

KANSAS CITY HEAT
Volume One

Dixon's Duty

Peyton's Pursuit

JENNA BYRNES

Kansas City Heat Volume One
ISBN # 978-1-78430-205-4
©Copyright Jenna Byrnes 2014
Cover Art by Posh Gosh ©Copyright 2014
Interior text design by Claire Siemaszkiewicz
Totally Bound Publishing

Published in 2014 by Totally Bound Publishing, Newland House, The Point, Weaver Road, Lincoln, LN6 3QN, United Kingdom.

DIXON'S DUTY

Dedication

To Jude Mason, always.

Author's Note

While the Kansas City Police Department is definitely a real organization, the stories you will read in this series are complete works of fiction, with made up characters who are in no way based on actual persons. Likewise, some neighborhoods and locations are similarly fictional. The stories are simply born from a love of Kansas City, from the stockyards to Arrowhead Stadium, the Plaza to Legends Outlet Mall, and lots of things in between.

Chapter One

"Time of death was approximately ten to twelve hours ago. I'll know more when I get her back to the lab and can run specific tests." Abigail Walters, the medical examiner for the Kansas City Police Department, rose from her crouched position then stepped back from the corpse.

Detective James Dixon leaned in closer, studying the abrasions around the woman's neck. Her long blonde hair was splayed around her shoulders, but the reddish-purple marks on her skin were still visible. As were two round scorch marks on her breasts. "Strangled, just like the victim last week. Cigarette burns. Can't say I like where this is heading."

"Nope. Dix, check out her simple black dress and shoes. She doesn't look like a hooker, more like a business woman out for an evening on the town."

He glanced at the victim's left hand. "No indentations from a wedding ring, not that she'd still have the ring if she *was* wearing one." He looked in either direction down the alley they were standing in. "Who knows how many people were through here last night?" He turned to the uniformed officer who'd been first on the scene. "No sign of a purse or handbag of any kind?"

"No, sir." The officer shook his head.

"Let's keep looking. Have your team scour every inch of this area, including the dumpsters over there. Our perp may have taken what he wanted and ditched the bag."

"Look for cigarette butts, too," the ME added. "We might pull some DNA off them."

"We're on it," the man answered, then headed to confer with the others on his detail.

She made notes in a small book. "Very similar MO to the last vic, pretty, mid-thirties, long, light-colored hair. If it is the same guy, he's definitely got a 'type'."

Dix waggled his brows. "Better watch out, then. You just described yourself."

She tucked the notebook into her pocket while rolling her eyes. "Thanks, dude, but the 'thirties' door slammed on me a few years ago. And these gals had blonde hair, not shades of gray. Of course, the color *could* have come from a box. " She tucked a wispy strand that had fallen out of her ponytail behind her ear.

Facing her, he ducked his head and said quietly, "Your hair is a beautiful, shiny shade of silver, not gray, and I hope you never use bottled color on it. And as for the 'thirties' door being closed"—he shook his head—"well, Abby, you could have fooled me."

His gaze scanned up from her military-style boots to the unattractive navy jumpsuit she wore at crime scenes. It sported large KCPD letters on the front and back, and the boxy style successfully hid whether the wearer was male or female.

Abby laughed. "Dix, if I didn't know you were gay, I'd either have to jump your bones or bring you up on sexual harassment charges. Can't decide which would be more fun. I'd love to watch you squirm."

He grinned. "Which one of those two choices might make me squirm? Never mind, not sure my heart could take it. It's been a long dry spell since Raph left. You're starting to look pretty good to me, jumpsuit notwithstanding."

"You *are* hard up! Sexy beast like you shouldn't have trouble finding a man. Everybody loves shaggy brown hair that perpetually looks overdue for a trim and a three-day beard growth like yours. And those puppy-dog eyes have the tiniest little crinkles around the corners when you smile. Damn. Now I'm making myself horny."

He feigned a horrified expression. "Eye wrinkles? God, that is sexy."

"I said *crinkles*. They're *very* sexy on a man. A woman, not so much."

"Yeah," he grumbled. "Got those when that 'thirties' door slapped me on the ass on my way out." He glanced up as his partner approached.

"Got a witness who says he saw the vic coming out of a bar last night around midnight." He glanced at the ME. "Hey, Abby."

"Mac," she acknowledged. "If that's the case, this woman died shortly thereafter. Probably wasn't time to kill her somewhere else and dump the body."

"So she died here," Dix repeated. He glanced at Steve MacDonald, his partner for the past three years. "Want to let the unis know that? Might make a difference how they process the scene. You and I should take her picture to that bar and see if anyone recognizes her."

"Let's do it. I'll talk to the unit commander then meet you down at the end of the block. Bar's just around the corner."

"Sounds good." Dix watched Mac walk off before turning back to Abby.

"How's his wife doing?" she asked. "Last I heard she was starting chemo."

He nodded. "The doc thought he got all the cancer with her lumpectomy, but there was something about a suspicious lymph node. So yeah, chemo. It makes her sick as hell for a few days. Mac said this round is really kicking her butt."

"I'm sure it's rough, but it's the best option for a good outcome. I'll keep her in my thoughts."

He batted his lashes. "Me too?"

Abby chuckled. "Always. Go do your thing and let me finish up here. I'll text you when I have results, or phone you if we get lucky."

He kicked at a pebble in his path then headed toward the end of the alley. Over his shoulder he replied, "I won't hold my breath. I haven't gotten lucky in a *very* long time."

"You're due!" she called after him.

Dix grinned to himself and kept walking.

Mac was speaking with the captain on scene when Dix approached. His partner looked tired, with definite lines creasing his forehead and the skin around his eyes. Wrinkles, nothing that could be called 'crinkles'. *Worry lines. Lack-of-sleep lines.* Dix figured he could take his pick. He couldn't imagine caring for a spouse with cancer and counted his blessings that the disease hadn't touched his life. "Ready to do this?" he asked Mac.

"Yeah." They fell into step and headed around the next corner. "Place is named Last Call Bar and Grille. Ever heard of it?"

"No, but I don't frequent this neighborhood."

"Like I do." Mac rolled his eyes.

Dix grinned. His buddy's longish-blond hair and tweed jacket with patches on the elbows made him look more like a professor than a cop. Mac had three daughters, six granddaughters and a one-year-old grandson who was sure to be spoiled beyond belief. The family was a great support system for his wife Cecile, who'd been stoic since her diagnosis. Dix knew Mac would love to retire and spend more time with his wife and family, but police work didn't pay that well. He'd work the streets or shove papers around on a desk right up to retirement age, as would Dix, who had a few years longer to go than Mac.

He paused in front of the neat little sign identifying Last Call and checked it out. "Nice place. Not what I expected."

"Yeah," Mac agreed, opening the door. "Seems decent enough."

They stepped inside. The bar was dimly lit, but Dix could tell it was well-tended. "Pretty clean, too."

"Yeah. Could have fooled me, 'cause the neighborhood sucks."

Dix thought so, too. He hadn't figured the bar would be more than a dive, commonplace for the area. This place was no speakeasy—it seemed like more of a restaurant. And from what he could smell, a good one.

"Afternoon," the bartender greeted them. "Sit anywhere, as you can see we're not too busy today."

"That's no shit," Mac mumbled under his breath.

There were ten to twelve tables in the joint, and only one was occupied by a young couple eating burgers and fries. A lone man sat at the bar, thin with straggly gray hair. Dix wondered if the old guy was still breathing or if he'd kicked off and no one had realized it yet.

He couldn't help noticing the bartender, a handsome man about his own age with similar brown, shaggy hair. Something shined in his eyes, weariness for one thing, but Dix couldn't put his finger on what else. "Afternoon." He stepped up to the bar and flashed his badge. "I'm Detective Dixon and this is Detective MacDonald of the KCPD. We're investigating a murder that took place near here last night. Have you ever seen this woman?" He held up a photo of the deceased.

"Ugh." The bartender frowned. "Seriously? It's disrespectful flashing a photo like that around."

Dix smiled grimly. "It's not disrespectful for such a pretty, young woman to be lying in the morgue with no name? More than likely, someone out there is missing her right about now. Somebody is frantic that she didn't come home or show up at work today. You don't think those folks would want us to move heaven and earth to identify her?"

The man lowered his head. "I'm sorry, you're right. No, I don't know her."

Mac spoke up. "We have a witness who says she came out of this bar somewhere around midnight last night. Were you working?"

He sighed. "I'm always working."

"And you are—?" Dix prompted.

"Bryan Scott. I own the place."

"You're the only bartender?"

"No, I've got a couple part time guys, but they only work nights and weekends. Seems like I'm here more than not. Jack worked with me last night."

"Anyone else? Waitresses, cooks?"

"I have three waitresses, only Jaci worked last night. Three cooks. Mike was the only one here."

Mac glanced around. "Any of those people working today?"

Bryan shook his head. "As I said, most of my part-timers work nights and weekends. They have other jobs or are going to college."

"We need to show our victim's picture around, ask if they remember seeing her, noticed her talking to anyone or maybe leaving with someone."

"Jaci and Mike will be here tonight at six. Jack doesn't work again until the weekend."

Dix said, "We'll need his phone number, please. We can run this photo over to him and see if recognizes her. I can swing back by tonight and talk to Jaci and Mike."

"Whatever you need." Bryan pulled out his cell phone and looked up a number, then copied it down on a cocktail napkin. "Here you go. Anything else I can do for you, gentlemen?"

Dix glanced at Mac. "I could use a burger, how about you?"

"Sure. Hold the onion, extra cheese. Fries and a black coffee, please."

Dix smiled at the bartender. "Make that two. We can sit anywhere?"

The man spread his arm from one side to the next. "Take your pick. I'll put in your order and bring you that coffee."

Dix chose a close table so he could hear any conversations going on. He sat, keeping one eye on the man behind the bar.

"Something not feel right to you?" Mac followed his gaze.

"I dunno." He shrugged. "Maybe this place is busier at night. But if it was this dead last night, the bartender would have remembered seeing a woman as pretty as our vic."

"That's a point. He didn't seem thrilled to talk to us."

"Most people aren't, my friend." Dix added sugar to his coffee when it arrived, and continued his observation. A tall man with slicked back, dark hair appeared in the kitchen window. He was wearing a grease-spattered apron so Dix took him for the cook. The man talked to Bryan for a moment, cast a glance in their direction then disappeared again.

A blond-haired delivery man with a beer logo on his uniform shirt entered through a back door. He spoke with Bryan, and they went over what appeared to be an invoice. Bryan nodded and the man turned to leave. He took his time, glancing around the bar slowly.

"That's a muscular young man, right there," Mac commented. "Check out his physique."

Dix shook his head. "He's, like, twenty-five. Why would I want to check him out?"

Mac chuckled. "I was referring to his strength, and the size of his biceps. It takes a strong guy to strangle a woman to death. I wasn't suggesting you ask him out on a date."

"Oh." Dix felt his face flush. If he was going to admire anyone, it was the owner behind the bar. He was guarded, sure, but lots of folks were when the police came knocking. There was something else about the man, a hint of subtle sexuality. Whatever it was, it caused Dix's trousers to tent with the first erection he could remember in too long.

He tried not to think about the hunk behind the bar and turned back to the delivery boy. "Yeah, he looks pretty beefed up. Takes some heft to lift kegs and cases of beer, I suppose."

Still grinning, Mac said, "Your mind did *not* start out there, it went someplace totally different. How long's it been since that Italian stud of yours took off?"

"He didn't 'take off'," Dix said petulantly. "He moved back to Italy to be closer to his family. It's been six months."

"That's a long time to be celibate, man. Not for a married guy, because we get used to it. But for most guys."

Dix smiled. "I was married once. I remember what it's like once the kids start coming." He stopped talking as the owner approached. He tried not to look at the man's jean-clad body, but it was distracting.

Bryan brought two plates and a bottle of ketchup to their table. "Here you go."

"Smells great." Dix looked at his face. "Daytime cook leaves about what time?"

"My cousin Galen. He gets off between five-thirty and six."

Dix nodded. "How often do you get beer deliveries?"

Bryan folded his arms across his chest. "Don't miss a trick, do you?"

He smiled. "Wouldn't be a very good detective if I did. Just asking. You seem to have a pretty tight-knit little group here. Everyone looking out for one another. Seems like someone might have seen our girl coming in or going out."

"Someone did," Mac added. "Another customer."

Bryan shrugged. "Yeah, well we get a lot of patrons through the door. Some are regulars, many are not.

It's a sketchy neighborhood, we do watch out for our own."

"That's good," Dix agreed. "Beer deliveries? About this same time each day?"

The owner sighed. "Three to four times a week. His route varies, but it's usually early afternoon. Our vendor's just a kid, you probably saw him."

"We did." Dix looked at him. "Thanks for the information. And the food."

"Yell if you need anything."

"We will."

Bryan returned to the bar while Dix and Mac took the top bun off their burgers at the same time. Dix cocked his head at an angle and studied the meat and tomato. "Looks clean to me."

"Me too." Mac reached for the ketchup. "Always prefer to get our food *before* people find out we're cops."

"No shit." Dix took a bite. "Tastes good. We might have to remember this place."

"You can come back for dinner," Mac teased.

"I might do that."

His partner's face clouded over. "You don't mind coming alone, do you? I'd hate to leave Cecile."

"Course not. I might ask Abby to come with. She's got a keen sense of observation and might pick up on something."

Mac waggled his brows. "Abby, eh? You switch hitting these days?"

Dix wiped his mouth with a napkin. "We're just friends and you know it. I told my ex-wife she turned me off women for good."

"It's no wonder the two of you have such a good relationship," Mac teased.

He shrugged. "Don't have to see her anymore. Jared's twenty-five and lives half a world away."

"Marine Corps got a good one with that boy."

"Yes, they did." He glanced up when a young woman with a long blonde ponytail entered and walked straight to the bar. She barely looked old enough to drink. "Incoming."

Mac glanced at her surreptitiously. "Hope he checks ID."

Dix listened to try and catch their conversation.

"How you doing?" she asked Bryan.

"How's it look? Sl-ow," he drew out the word.

She glanced around the room. The other couple had finished and left. It was just their table and the old man at the bar. "Yeah, I see that. I was going to ask if you needed help for a couple hours, but I guess I got my answer."

Bryan shrugged. "Just me, old Pete and the cops."

Her gaze immediately darted to their table.

Dix looked at his plate, picking up a fry and popping it in his mouth.

"Cops?" she repeated. "Why are they here?"

"Eating lunch," Bryan replied.

"But they told you they were cops?"

He nodded.

"That's odd."

Mac spoke softly, not looking up from his food. "Most business-owners like having police patronize their establishments. Makes them feel safer."

"Unless they have something to hide," Dix agreed, one eye on the couple at the bar.

"Why do you think they're here?" she whispered, but it was loud enough for Dix to hear.

"Maybe they were hungry," Bryan whispered back.

She rolled her eyes. "You're no fun. Where's your sense of imagination?"

"Imagination gets people in trouble. I'd prefer to think they were hungry and heard we have good food, which we do. You want something?"

"Nope, if you don't need me I'm heading for the library. I have a paper to work on. See you later!" She leaned across the bar and kissed his cheek.

"Behave yourself," he called after her.

She glanced over her shoulder and winked. For a moment she locked eyes with Dix, and he saw amusement there. She winked at him, too, then flounced out. The place grew quiet again.

"College student, one of his waitresses," Mac observed.

"A waitress with benefits," Dix added. "She planted a kiss on him before she left."

"On the cheek."

"Do you kiss your boss on the cheek?"

Mac laughed. "Good point. Okay, waitress with benefits. She's a young one, though. Maybe Mr Scott is a dirty old man."

"He's not that old," Dix muttered. "About my age."

"I don't see you kissing twenty-year-olds."

"Another good point. You ready? I'll pay the check."

"I'm going to find the little boys' room." Mac stood. "Meet you out front."

"Yep." Dix pulled a twenty from his wallet and sauntered to the bar. "Food was great. I'll tell my friends, unless you don't want other cops coming around."

"Please. The more the merrier. As you can see, we could use the business."

"Kinda what I thought." He tossed the twenty on the bar. "Blondie one of your waitresses?"

Bryan paused from making change. "I'll bet you passed that detective's exam on your first try." He spread the bills and coins on the bar.

Dix grinned. "Damn straight. She just looked young, is all." He pulled back a couple of ones, leaving a five and some change for a tip.

"She *is* young. Putting herself through college. I like to give decent kids a break when I can."

He gazed into Bryan's eyes. "That all you like to give her?"

Anger flashed briefly in the owner's eyes, but it disappeared just as quickly. "She's a good kid, and she's twenty-one. Please leave her alone."

Dix shrugged. "Homicide investigation, you know. I have to go wherever it leads me. I noticed you didn't tell her we were here because of a murder."

Bryan studied him levelly. "I'm sure you'll take care of that when you come back tonight."

Dix nodded. "See you then." He went to the front sidewalk and waited for Mac. It was a decent spring day. The weather was warm but not yet hot. Summers in the Midwest made wearing a suit coat everyday feel like a sauna. He'd enjoy this weather while he could.

* * * *

Back at the station, they tacked photos and information up on an evidence board. Dix brought in materials from the first homicide just a week ago. Madison Ames had been found in another alley, a couple of blocks away from today's discovery. A married clerk in a ladies wear store, she was last seen leaving a restaurant after meeting friends, and was found strangled the next day. Evidence concluded she'd been raped, but no DNA was discovered at the scene. The half-dozen cigarette burns on her torso had been delivered ante mortem—preceding death.

This new case appeared to be eerily similar.

"I'll phone Madison's husband and see if she'd ever been to Last Call," Mac offered.

Dix nodded. "It may not be a connection, but at this point it's worth checking out. Something felt off in that place, though I can't put my finger on exactly what. *Yet.*"

Mac smiled and went to work.

When Dix's phone rang, he was pleased to hear Abby Walters on the other end of the line.

"We've got a positive ID. If you can believe this, her fingerprints were in the system. Donna Reitz worked as a secretary at the county courthouse. And of course, all government employees—"

"Would have fingerprints in the system," Dix finished her sentence. "Good job, Ab."

"You'll need to notify next of kin. Database says that's her mom and dad."

"We're on it. Mac and I went to the bar she was last seen at, but none of the same employees will be there until tonight. Food was pretty good. Want to go back with me after work, grab a bite and talk to a few people?"

"Let me guess, Mac doesn't want to leave Cecile and you hate to eat alone?"

"Something like that. I'll go by myself if I have to. Just thought it might be interesting to get your perspective on the place. Things don't seem quite right there."

"No, I'd love to check it out. Best offer I've had all week."

"Which is not saying much for your love life." Dix chuckled. "I'll call you later to firm up plans."

"I'll be here." She sighed dramatically, for his benefit, he knew. Abby was a knockout and she could have a man in her life if she wanted one. But like many members of the police department, sometimes it was easier to focus on work than to try and juggle the job and a relationship.

Until the right person comes along. Then the juggling is worth it. Dix smiled and went to find Mac. They had some bad news to deliver, and needed to get on with it.

Breaking the news of a loved one's demise was one of the hardest parts of Dix's job. Donna Reitz's parents took it hard, as they all did. They were close with their daughter but didn't know where she went on a daily basis after work and weren't sure if she frequented Last Call. Dix left his card with them and he and Mac returned to the station to continue digging.

"David Ames thought he and his wife may have been to Last Call once or twice, but it wasn't a place they went regularly," Mac told Dix.

"It might not be relevant." Dix tacked a newly acquired, pleasant photo of Donna on their evidence board next to the one of her corpse. "I might be reading too much into it."

"I trust your gut, always have. Hope you and Abby find something tonight."

Dix made a face. "Not sure what I want to find. "

Mac chuckled. "Same thing we're always after, my friend. Answers."

* * * *

Dix picked Abby up at her house shortly after six. She'd changed into black slacks and a silken red blouse. Her long, shiny platinum hair, usually pulled back, flowed freely around her shoulders.

He stepped out of his black Lincoln Navigator and opened the car door for her. "Wow, I should have run home and changed, sorry."

"Nah, you're working, it's cool. I always like to come home and rinse the pall of death off before going out."

"Understood." He climbed back in and drove to the Grille. "I'm not sure what's bothering me about this place," he admitted. "The owner's name is Bryan Scott. Seems affable enough, but he didn't really like talking to us. Thought the photo of the vic was disrespectful. That sort of thing."

"We got lucky with Donna. Most nice folks don't have prints in the system. Not sure there's an easier way to identify her than showing the least graphic photo we have."

"I agree." He parked and got out, then opened her door for her.

"Damn, Dix. A girl could get used to this." She took his arm as she got out.

He grinned. "Might as well go all out, put on a good show. Oh, and for the record, we try not to announce ourselves as cops until *after* we've gotten our food."

Abby laughed. "What, afraid someone will hock a loogie into your dinner?"

"Or worse. Just sayin'."

"Enough said, believe me. I've got it."

He led her inside and scanned the room. The bar was much busier. Most of the stools were filled. About half the tables were also full. For some reason, Dix was happy to see it. "This table okay?" He pointed to one up front.

"Sure." She allowed him to pull her chair out, and they both sat.

Dix glanced around but didn't see the owner. A young, red-headed man tended bar.

"Nice crowd tonight," Abby commented.

"There were a total of five people here for lunch, and I'm not sure the old guy at the bar was eating. At least he's gone. I was afraid he might be a regular fixture."

She chuckled, and they both looked up as their waitress approached.

Dix recognized the pony-tailed blonde from earlier.

Her eyebrows furrowed for a second as she seemed to question if she'd seen him before. Then she smiled. "Welcome. Menus are there on the table. What can I bring you to drink?"

"I'll have a Long Island Iced Tea, please," Abby requested.

"A virgin Bloody Mary," Dix added.

"Be right back with those. Would you like an appetizer tonight? We've got a great chip and dip sampler. There are other choices on the menu, onion rings, chicken strips…"

He glanced at Abby. "Shall we try the chips?"

"Why not?"

He nodded to the waitress. "Thanks."

"No problem." She walked off.

He winced. "I hate that expression. I never asked if it was a problem. Since when did 'no problem' replace 'you're welcome'?"

Abby laughed. "At some recent point, when you and I were busy avoiding the 'thirties door' hitting us on the ass."

"That's for fucking real." He picked up one menu and offered her another. They made small talk, and ordered steaks when the waitress returned.

"So where's this owner guy?" Abby glanced around. "Only people working here I see are children. Infants, really. That bartender has honest-to-God freckles on his face."

"Not here, unless he's hiding in the back somewhere."

"He was aware you'd be returning tonight?"

"He was."

"Curious."

"Yeah."

The steaks were as good as the burgers had been. Before long they'd polished off their food, and were enjoying a cup of coffee after the meal.

"This place is a diamond in the rough," Abby mused. "Not sure I'd come here alone, but the food was top notch and the drink was prepared well. Someone knows what they're doing."

Dix spotted Bryan entering through the back door, stopping to talk with the bartender. "*Someone* just walked in."

She glanced behind the bar. "Oh. My. Yeah. I see your dilemma."

Dix blinked. "Excuse me?"

Abby smiled. "Are we sure he's gay? If he's not, I might go after him myself."

"What the hell are you talking about?" Dix wasn't following.

She leaned back and crossed her arms. "I can see your hesitance in investigating this place. He's cute, Dix. Did you two share some sparks this afternoon?"

"You're out of your ever-loving mind. That thought *never* crossed my mind. He kissed our waitress, as a matter of fact. Mac called him a dirty old man."

"He's not that old, and I could get dirty with him. The waitress, huh? Definite competition. But either one of us could take her, hands down, in the maturity and experience department."

"Oh, sweet Jesus." Dix held his head in his hands. "You're off the deep end, Abigail. This is *not* why I brought you here."

"What? You always say I have a keen sense of observation. I'm telling you what I observed. The owner is hot. Smokin'. Don't even try to tell me you disagree. I've known you for too long, James."

He covertly studied the man from afar. *Cute doesn't begin to describe him. More like hot, sexy stud.* Dix shook his head to clear it. "We're working a case. He's potentially a person of interest until we can rule him out. Quit stirring the pot, Walters."

A wide grin split her face. "Man, are you flustered! You've gone from my nickname to my given name and now my last name. Confused about something, Detective? Because your face is turning red and I see a bead of sweat on your temple."

Confusion was an understatement. Dix wasn't sure what he was feeling, besides embarrassed. "You suck. We should go. Mac can come back and interview these people tomorrow."

She reached out and clasped his hand. "Take it easy, Dix. So what if the guy trips your trigger? He's not really a person of interest. More likely an innocent bystander. But you're not sure if he's gay? Talk to him."

His heart leaped into his throat at the idea. "And say what? I know I saw you kissing the waitress earlier today, but I was wondering if you might be gay?"

Abby smiled. "Um, maybe not quite that direct. You could bring up the case, let him know the victim's been identified. But you still need to ask if anyone saw her here last night."

"Which is exactly what I came here to do." He nodded, unsure why he suddenly felt like a school kid. He'd sensed something was up with the owner today. Could he have been projecting his own feelings into the situation? Mac had teased him about the beer deliveryman, and it had only taken Dix mere moments to acknowledge that guy hadn't been his type. He hadn't let his mind dwell on the owner. Of course not. *I was focused on my case.*

And now he was focused on Bryan's ass as he reached up to retrieve a bottle from above the bar.

When the man turned around, he spotted Dix, then took a moment to take in Abby. Setting the bottle on the bar, he approached their table. "Good evening, Detective Dixon."

"Mr Scott," Dix said politely. "This is Abby. Abby, Bryan Scott. He's the owner of this establishment."

"A pleasure." Bryan shook her hand.

"Thank you. Your restaurant is simply charming, Mr Scott. Our food was excellent and my drink was divine."

"So happy to hear it. May I bring you another?"

"Nope, one's my limit. And Dix is on duty, I'm sure you recall."

"Dix?" He glanced at them questioningly.

Dix waved him off. "You'll be happy to hear we identified our crime victim, so I have a much nicer photograph to show your employees." He pulled the picture of Donna from his jacket pocket and held it out.

"Better," Bryan agreed. "A very attractive woman. I'm sorry, I still don't recall seeing her in here last night. You're welcome to ask my staff."

"I'm afraid I'll have to do that. We appreciate your cooperation."

Bryan appeared thoughtful. "You have a very understanding wife, Detective. Most women wouldn't like their husbands mixing business with pleasure."

Abby laughed. "I'm not like most women, Mr Scott. And I'm not his wife."

Dix smiled at her. "Dr Walters is Chief Medical Examiner for the KCPD."

Bryan blinked. "Dr Walters? Oh, this is an honor. I've read about you in the papers."

"Don't believe everything you read," Dix teased.

She wagged a finger at him. "And don't believe everything he tells you, either. He's an ornery one. But he's a dear, even if he doesn't go for the female persuasion. Which basically means he and I sometimes go after the same guys." She winked at Bryan.

Dix wished he could disappear through a hole in the floor.

"Is that so?" Bryan's dark eyes flashed surprise for a second, before returning to something closer to indifference. Except he seemed amused. *Very amused.*

His smirk didn't ease Dix's discomfort.

The waitress returned with their check. Dix tried to focus because he needed to start questioning people about seeing Donna the previous night.

"Can I bring you anything else?" she asked pleasantly.

"No, everything was great." Dix inserted a credit card into the vinyl ticket folder. "I do need to ask you a question, though."

Bryan slipped an arm around the girl's waist. "Sami, this is Detective Dixon from the KCPD. A woman was killed near here last night, and someone said they thought she'd come from the bar before it happened."

Sami swallowed. "I didn't work last night."

Dix held up the photo. "Do you recall seeing her before? Might not have been yesterday. Could have been earlier."

She studied the shot. "She looks vaguely familiar, but not really. I don't think so." Sami put her hands on Bryan's chest. "She was killed near here?"

"In an alley a block over." Dix watched their interaction.

"I'm sorry, sweetie." Bryan kissed her forehead. "I didn't want you to find about it, but I guess you do need to know, so you can take precautions."

"What kind of precautions, Daddy?" She blinked.

Dix gulped. *Daddy?* He was her father?

Abby leaned back with a satisfied smile.

Bryan said, "Like, when you get ready to leave at night, you girls should walk out together. Or have someone walk you out. Right, Detective?"

Dix pulled his thoughts together. "Absolutely. Stay in groups of two or three—more is better. Have your car keys in your hand, you can use a key as a weapon in case of emergency. Carry your cell phone and maybe even some pepper spray. But be sure of what you're doing so you don't spray an innocent bystander."

She chuckled.

Dix heard his own words echoing back in his head. *Innocent bystander.* Abby had suggested that was what Bryan was. Had he got his vibes crossed earlier in the day? Had the niggling feelings of guilt and suspicion he'd sensed actually been something completely different?

Like *lust?*

Dix cleared his throat, and tried to calm his thudding heartbeat.

When their gazes locked, Bryan licked his lips.

Chapter Two

"There's been another murder."

Dix had gotten the dreaded call early the next morning. This victim had been discovered by someone she knew, so her family had found out at the same time as the police. It had made for quite a scene — distraught family members and a squad of police officers standing together in an alley off Baker Street.

He returned to the squad room and tacked a photo of Norma Lear on the evidence board. She appeared much like the other victims, twenty-five, with long blonde hair and happy blue eyes. The second picture he posted didn't show the happy eyes. Just a brutalized woman who'd been raped, burned and strangled. *Probably in that order.* Dix sighed.

"What do you think?" His captain, Rick Alvarez, leaned back against the nearest desk. "Same guy?"

Dix shrugged. "Not much to go on, but the similarities are striking. The victims were all Caucasian with long blonde hair. The killer's MO has been the same in all three cases. We're crazy if we don't think they're related."

"But no other connecting factors."

"Not yet. We're looking. Each of the women was last seen leaving a bar or a restaurant. No one remembers seeing them leave with any particular person, or even talking to someone who stood out. Mac's running down Norma Lear's final hours."

Alvarez touched the latest photo. "So we're looking for someone who doesn't stand out. Imagine that."

"Yeah. Go figure." Dix rubbed his face with his hands.

"Hey, Dixon," someone from the front of the office called. "You have a visitor."

He glanced up and saw Bryan Scott looking at him. His heart skipped a beat. *What the hell is he doing here?* Dix's mind went in several different directions, all of which caused the stirrings of another erection in his trousers.

He shook his head. *Don't be an idiot. He's here about the case.* He motioned for Bryan to come back and met him by his desk. "Hey. How's it going?"

"Pretty good." Bryan nodded. "I hope you don't mind my dropping in."

"Of course not. Have a seat." He motioned to the chair by his desk, then they both sat. "Is there something I can do for you?"

Bryan cleared his throat. "I, uh, wanted to let you know. I spoke with the rest of my employees. No one remembers seeing either of those two women at Last Call."

"There's three now." Dix leaned back and flexed his fingers together. "A third body found in another alley, last night."

"Oh, my God." Bryan appeared truly shocked. "That's awful."

"Yeah, it is." Dix stared at him and for a moment, neither of them spoke.

Bryan glanced down then back up again. He seemed nervous. "That's not the, uh, only reason I stopped by. It's about what your friend said last night." He glanced around surreptitiously.

Dix waved his hand. While he didn't usually conduct personal business in the squad room, everyone knew he was gay. It wasn't a concern. "Don't worry, it's cool. But please don't mind Abby. She thinks she's being helpful when she's actually not."

"It was helpful to me." Bryan smiled. "Dating since I came out as gay has been a lot harder than it was in high school when I dated girls because that's what guys were supposed to do. Unless you're at a GLBT rally or someplace like that, it's impossible to tell if people are gay or straight."

The words resounded in Dix's head. "Since you came out... You're telling me you're gay?"

Bryan's smile was more sheepish this time. "Yeah. I guess that's what I'm telling you. *Why* I'm telling you, well, I'm not exactly sure. My daughter kind of pushed me into it. Sami thought you were cute, and well, hell, I couldn't deny that."

Dix couldn't hold back his grin. "Sami, your daughter. I thought she was your girlfriend, the first time I saw her kiss your cheek."

"I remember."

"You could have set me straight." Dix realized his choice of words and when Bryan laughed, he did, too. "Okay, you know what I meant. You could have corrected my mistaken impression."

"Why would I want to do that? You were the suave, debonair detective with all the answers. I liked that you finally got something wrong."

Dix nearly choked. "Is that how I come across? Somebody should nominate me for a fucking Golden Globe, then. I sure as hell don't feel that way on the inside."

"Really." It wasn't spoken as a question, more of an observation. Bryan studied him for a moment. "I'd like to learn more about how you feel, Detective Dixon. I wondered if you'd like to stop by the place for dinner some night. Oh hell, I meant tonight. If you're interested, that is. And you're not busy."

Dix watched him just as thoughtfully. "I am."

"Busy?" Bryan's face fell.

"Interested. I'm always busy, but even cops make time to eat…and unwind a little bit."

"Great." His expression changed from disappointment to relief. He feigned wiping his brow. "Damn, I'd forgotten how much work that was."

Dix chuckled. "I hadn't. That's why I didn't make the first move. Well, that, and the fact I had no idea you were gay. Anyway, I'm glad you stopped by. Dinner sounds great. I should be done here by about six. That work for you?"

"Six would be fine." He rose. "Whenever you get there is good. I'll look forward to seeing you." He turned to leave.

"Oh, Bryan? Think I could get your cell number?"

The man faced him again.

Dix smiled apologetically. "First rule about being friends with a cop. Sometimes work gets in the way. I try not to let it, but you know." He nodded toward the evidence board.

Bryan glanced at the board but looked away quickly. "Understood. Sure, here, I'll write it down for you." He jotted the number on a piece of paper and passed it over. "Call anytime." He reconsidered. "Not to cancel, of course."

"Of course." Dix grinned. "If I had to, it wouldn't be *canceling*. It would be *postponing*."

"Cool. See you later." He walked off.

Dix watched his retreat. The man's jean-clad ass definitely gave credence to the old expression, 'hate to see you go but love to watch you leave'. His heart soared at the thought of the evening to come.

He turned back to the evidence and sighed. Miles to go before nightfall. Places to go, people to see. Homicide cases to solve. *With a little luck, and by the grace of God.*

* * * *

Shortly before six p.m., Dix removed his necktie and tucked it into his jacket pocket. The tie spent almost as much time there as it did around his neck. He usually kept one handy in case he needed it for work. But most of the day, an open collar sufficed.

Tonight, especially, he didn't want to look like a choirboy. He'd be more comfortable in jeans and a leather jacket, but didn't want to waste time driving home and back.

He strolled into Last Chance and glanced around. Another decent crowd—he was glad to see evenings were better than the one lunch he'd witnessed. *Maybe that was just a slow day.*

He wasn't sure, and *really* wasn't sure why Bryan's business concerned him. For some reason, it just did.

He wanted to see the man do well. But tonight, he just wanted to see the man.

Bryan was nowhere in sight. His daughter approached and smiled. "Good evening, Detective Dixon. My father said to give you a table and a drink. He'll be out shortly."

He smiled. "Hey, Sami. Thanks. I'll take you up on that drink. A vodka martini, please."

"You got it." She pointed to the corner. "This table okay?"

"Sure." He pulled out a chair. "So how was your day?"

"Not bad. Gearing up for finals in a few weeks."

"What's your major?"

"Restaurant management. My sister wants to be a chef. We're thinking maybe one day we can go into business together."

"Your sister?" He raised his brows. "Haven't heard about her yet. What's her name?"

"Kayla. She's twenty-four. She's a sous-chef at La Maison."

"Wow, impressive for someone so young."

"Daddy says she's a real go-getter. I'll be right back with your drink."

"Thank you." He watched her return to the bar. She seemed friendly and easy to talk to.

The longer he sat, the more his nerves kicked in. Dix truly hoped her father would be just as affable.

Sami brought his drink and Dix tried to nurse it, but had polished it off before Bryan ever showed up. It was nearly six-twenty when the man breezed in from the back, stopped to talk with the bartender then headed to the table with two drinks in his hands.

"Sorry I'm late." He set one of the drinks in front of Dix. "As you mentioned this morning, sometimes work gets in the way." Bryan sat opposite him and took a sip of his own martini.

"It does," Dix agreed. He glanced at the drink in front of him. "I usually keep it to one on work nights."

Bryan smiled. "Special occasion. One more won't hurt. Please accept my martini-bribe for making you wait."

Dix relented and picked up the glass. "No bribe required, you weren't that late."

Bryan tossed back half his drink, and as he set it down, his words tumbled out in a rush. "I swear, sometimes the kitchen staff is totally clueless. Galen's here all damned day and he does about half the prep work we need for an evening shift. The two night-time guys are on their phones as much as they are working. Texting, playing games, who knows what? They're worse than little girls." Another deep breath, then he polished off his drink and deposited the glass on its coaster with a *thud*. He looked at Dix and sighed. "Hello."

Dix grinned. "Hi there. Man, I didn't know restaurant work could be so grueling."

"What, you thought I leaned up against the bar all day?"

"No, I just..." He wasn't sure what to say. He'd honestly never thought about it.

Bryan waved a hand. "I'm kidding. It's nothing compared to your line of work, but it can get stressful. A different kind of stress, I guess."

"Of course it can. Every job has its good and bad points."

"That's right. Take this place, for instance. We're barely making ends meet. The bank is going to foreclose if I don't come up with an interest payment in sixty days. And people are dying after they come in here. But on the bright side, I met you. So it's not all doom and gloom." He smiled, but it didn't quite reach his eyes.

Dix set his jaw. "I'm sorry, Bryan. I had no idea. What am I saying? Of course I had no idea, I hardly know you. And 'people' is just one woman who may or may not have come in here. I hardly think her death can be attributed to your establishment."

"So that's another checkmark in the positive column. A woman died, but we're not blaming me."

Dix didn't know what to say. "Wow. You have had a bad day, or a bad week, whatever the case may be. Perhaps we should do this another time."

Bryan studied him. "I think we should get the hell out of here. I know I promised you dinner, but can we eat someplace that won't make me crazy?"

Dix saw anguish brimming in his eyes. The emotion looked like it could spill over into tears, and it wouldn't take much to set it off. "We can go anywhere you like, my friend. Hell, a drive-through joint would be fine, and we could just talk. Would you like to talk?"

"Maybe." Bryan chewed on his lower lip. "I'd rather do something else. Could I convince you to come to my place if we brought a bottle, maybe order a pizza?"

Their gazes were locked. While Dix's mind insisted that he didn't know the guy, and going *anywhere* with him would be crazy, his libido was telling him something else.

Crazy sounds fun.

Dix couldn't believe he was considering the invitation. The guy obviously had issues. Part of him said *turn and run* but a bigger part was curious to discover more about the sexy hunk. "I don't need a bottle. Pizza sounds good...for later."

Bryan breathed a sigh of relief. "Thank you. Here's my address." He wrote it on the cardboard coaster and pushed it toward Dix. "Want to follow me?"

Dix smiled. "For now. I may want to lead later."

Bryan stood and leaned in. "I just might let you. Come on."

They walked to the bar and Bryan told his daughter, "We're getting out of here. I'll be back later to close up."

"We can do it, Daddy," she insisted. "Carlos, Evan and I know what to do. Just go, and have a nice evening." She looked at Dix. "I never thought you should have dinner here in the first place. He needs to get away some times. I mean, Christ, he's always here! Open to close. He hates leaving responsibility to other people."

"Obviously." Dix smiled.

"I'm not sure—" Bryan was cut off by the man behind the bar.

"We'll take care of things and make sure Sami gets to her car safely. Go, and we'll see you tomorrow."

The owner finally nodded and turned to Dix. "I drive a blue Blazer. I'll pull around front so you can follow me."

"Sounds good."

Sami rolled her eyes. "Two cars. How romantic."

Dix wagged his brows at her. "Not leaving mine in this neighborhood." He glanced at Bryan. "Why'd you open your place here, anyway? Seems like you could have found better digs."

"My father opened Last Call in the seventies. It was a different area back then."

"Ah, gotcha." It did make sense. And Bryan's frustration with not making ends meet made even *more* sense. Letting the business his old man had started go down the tubes would play heavily on any man. "Let's go." To Sami he said, "Thanks."

"Have fun!"

He returned to his Navigator and started it up, waiting until he saw the Blazer moving slowly down the street. Dix pulled out and followed him on the ten minute trip to the man's house.

The house was in a good area, another five minutes and they'd be to Dix's own townhouse. *Fate.*

He pulled into the driveway behind Bryan, who motioned him to enter through the garage.

Dix followed and Bryan closed and locked the door behind them.

"Nice place." He glanced around the kitchen, which was neat if slightly cluttered.

"It's okay. Lived here with my wife before she died. It's been five years, but for the girls' sake, I never changed much."

They moved on into the living room and Dix saw what Bryan meant. Family pictures were everywhere. Bryan, two daughters and a pretty blonde-haired woman. One photo of them and the woman with *no* hair. He glanced at Bryan. "Cancer?"

"Yeah." He tossed his keys on the coffee table. "We'd just filed for divorce when she got the diagnosis, pancreatic cancer. It was pretty far advanced. I'd met someone else, a guy who'd done some remodeling work on the bar, and I'd finally come out to Elaine. But when we got the news, I just couldn't leave her and the girls. I broke it off with Tom and stayed with Elaine for the last few months of her life. It was horrible, and it was amazing, all at the same time."

Dix processed the story. "That's rough. I'm so sorry."

"Thanks."

"I'm curious. Did you ever go back and look up Tom?"

"Yeah. He'd moved on. He didn't value loyalty, which spoke volumes about the guy in hindsight."

"Yeah." Dix wasn't sure what to say. "My partner's wife has breast cancer."

"Sorry to hear it. I hope she's doing well."

"She's a fighter, and they caught it early."

"Makes all the difference." Bryan glanced around the room. "Jesus, I never realized what a shrine this place turned out to be. Not exactly a bachelor pad. Sorry."

Dix grinned and took a step closer. "For what? It's nice to see another side of you. We don't know anything about each other."

Bryan gazed at him. "Makes what we're doing here that much crazier. I'm generally not a fast and loose kind of guy. The most recent relationship I had— Oh, God, I can't even remember, it's been so long."

"Mine was just over six months ago. An Italian artist named Raphael, if you can believe that. He was quite a guy, but it was never going to last. I knew he'd be off to New York or L.A. or someplace more cultural than Kansas City."

"Where did he go? And why didn't you want to go with him?"

"Italy, actually." They both chuckled. "I just didn't. I wouldn't have gone to New York, either. I like the Midwest. I was born and raised here. My folks are gone, but I have a sister and some family. My kid's twenty-five, stationed overseas in the Marines."

"Just the one?"

Dix's heart thudded. *A loaded question and a sore subject.* But if he was going to get intimate with the guy, perhaps he needed to open up a bit. "We had a daughter, a couple years younger than Jared. She was killed in a traffic accident, on the night of her junior prom. The kid who was driving had been drinking, and of course he walked away from the wreck. My wife wanted to sue him and his parents, but I didn't see the point. It wasn't going to bring Julie back, you know? We just couldn't get past it."

"I'm sorry."

"Thanks." Dix tucked his fingers through two of Bryan's belt loops and pulled him closer. "Shall we count the number of times one of us has said 'sorry' tonight? We're a couple of pathetic sons of bitches."

Bryan's hands settled on Dix's hips. "That's no shit. What do you suppose we should do about it?"

"I have a couple thoughts." Dix cupped Bryan's neck and drew him in for a kiss. He paused when their lips were barely touching. "I'm clean, just so you know. But we should use condoms."

Bryan tightened his grasp on Dix's hips. "I'm clean too. Got some supplies in the nightstand drawer. Might have to dust them off."

Dix grinned. "We can do that. But first, we need to do this." He pressed their lips together.

The first kiss was electric. The feeling of another man's rough beard never failed to excite him. Dix opened his mouth so their tongues could explore, and sighed when Bryan obliged.

They batted tongues, groped and kissed until Bryan finally drew back for a breath. "Oh, God," he panted. "I want you. *Now*. Bedroom."

Dix let his mouth trail to Bryan's ear and whispered, "Lead the way. You have a preference, top or bottom?"

"I enjoy both. Your call."

"In that case, I'd like to fuck your nice, tight ass."

He actually felt the shiver that ran through Bryan's body. Dix grinned and gazed into his eyes. "What do you think? Would you like that?"

"I think—I'd *love* that. Come on." He grabbed Dix's hand and led him to the back of the house. "Forgive the mess."

Dix glanced around as he undressed. "Looks okay to me." The bed wasn't made and there were a few clothes on a chair in the corner. It was otherwise nice and neat, and clean enough for him. His own townhouse was probably messier, but well-kept underneath the clutter.

He unbuttoned his shirt and watched as Bryan undressed. "You look okay to me, too. Better than okay. Damned good."

They kicked out of their boxers at the same time and both erections sprang forth. Dix's mouth watered. Bryan's cock bobbed full and thick, more massive than his, if not quite as long. "Yeah, baby." He eyed the rod hungrily. "Lie down, face up, please."

Bryan opened the nightstand drawer and, reaching in, grabbed some condoms and lube then tossed them on top. He threw the covers off the bed and flopped onto his back. Grabbing his shaft, he gave it a slow tug. "See anything you like?"

"You know I do." Dix climbed between his legs. "I see plenty that I like. Lots that I want to taste." He began kissing behind the man's knee and worked his way higher. When he reached the apex, he switched legs and kissed his way up that side, too.

Bryan writhed under his touch. "Sweet torment," he muttered, his voice breathy.

"About to get sweeter." Dix blew on the shaft in front of him. It pulsed in response and hardened more when he licked from base to tip.

"God…please…"

He chuckled and continued his ministrations. As much as he wanted to continue the torment, he soon gave in and swallowed the length as deeply as he could.

Bryan gasped and groaned.

"Mmm hmm," Dix encouraged, his mouth full. He loved to hear his partner's reactions during sex. He pulled away just long enough to murmur, "Like that?" He drove down again, forcing the head to the back of his throat.

"Fuck yeah!" Bryan jerked his hips.

Dix bobbed with the motions, sucking until he couldn't breathe then backing off, licking with long, languorous strokes.

"You know the right moves." His lover ran both hands through Dix's hair. "I'm gonna come if you keep that up."

Dix squeezed his balls and gave one last, firm suck before releasing the tasty cock. "Nope, too soon for that. Just wanted to give you a little taste of what's to come, so to speak." He climbed on top of Bryan and rubbed their groins together. "Can't shoot yet. I've got more planned for you."

Bryan gazed at him, his eyes glassy. "Whatever you want to do. I'm putty in your hands right now."

Dix leaned in for a kiss that quickly deepened as they both opened their mouths. He sucked Bryan's tongue and rubbed their bodies together until he was sure he couldn't stand another minute of the beautiful friction.

He reached for the lube and squirted some into his palm. Using one finger, he felt between them and probed Bryan's anus.

Bryan gasped when the first digit slid in. Watching Dix's face, he said, "You know, when you came into the restaurant that first time, I wondered if you thought I might be the killer. You had a funny look in your eye."

Dix grinned, inserting another finger into the slick channel. "I had to check every lead out. You weren't overly thrilled we were there. I got the impression something was up with you."

Bryan's eyes rolled back as a third digit probed him. "Nothing was up but my cock when I saw you for the first time. Thought you were hot. What did you think about me?"

"I didn't know what the hell to think."

"Did you suspect me? Really? You can admit it. I won't kick you out of bed."

"Good thing, seeing as I have you in a compromising position. Three fingers up your ass and another coming in."

"Oh, God." Bryan shivered. "Do it."

Dix added the fourth and worked them from side to side. When he felt sure the hole was stretched sufficiently, he eased them out. "I never suspected you, I was just investigating the scene. Now I know it couldn't have been you."

"Oh yeah? Why's that?"

Dix smiled. "You're always working. You're too busy to kill anybody." He sheathed his cock in latex and stroked until it was covered with lube. Aiming the tip at his lover's anus, he pressed forward.

Bryan bucked at the same time, inviting him in.

Dix gritted his teeth. "I was wrong. You're killing me. Oh, God, you're killing me. I'm not going to last long." He planted himself as deep as he could go and paused to catch a breath. As he began the slow, in and out rhythm, he reached for Bryan's leaking erection and rubbed it, then licked salty pre-cum from his hand. "Yeah, baby. You're right there with me. A few strokes and we'll both be there."

"Do me." Bryan clutched Dix's thighs and squeezed. "Fuck me, yeah! Fuck harder, that's it."

They rode the frenzy together and when Bryan's cock erupted into the air and over both their stomachs, Dix let go, filling the rubber in his partner's ass. He thrust for as long as he could then slowed, resting lightly on Bryan, head on his shoulder.

"Perfect." Bryan kissed his forehead and everywhere he could reach.

"Very perfect," Dix agreed. "Wish I didn't have to move."

Bryan smiled. "Nothing saying we can't do it again."

Dix groaned. "I'll need a few minutes."

"A few minutes, what-the-fuck-ever. I'll need a half hour and some Red Bull. But you're worth it."

Happily, Dix closed his eyes.

Later, they ordered pizza and ate in the living room on the sofa.

"So, when did you realize you were gay?" Bryan asked over a slice of pepperoni.

Dix smiled. "When did I really know? Probably not for sure until about six years ago, when my marriage fell apart. I started dating again and discovered I wasn't looking for the same things in a mate that I once was."

Bryan chuckled. "We're so much alike it's scary. I was the same way. I haven't been 'out' for quite as long, and I can't say I like the dating process much. It's a different world than I remember."

"Things change," Dix agreed. "Good thing we decided not to date, and went straight to fucking."

A belly laugh this time. "A very good thing. Yep, one of us had a fantastic idea. Can't remember which."

"Pretty sure it was both of us." Dix looked at him thoughtfully. "What are you going to do about the bar? Or would you prefer I called it a restaurant?"

"It's definitely a bar. I added the 'Grille' part a few years ago, trying to bring in more business."

"The infamous remodel?"

"That would be correct. Anyway, I don't know what I'm going to do. If things don't turn around, I'll either have to sell the place or lose it to foreclosure."

"That would suck. Think you could sell it?"

He shrugged. "Dunno. Honestly, I haven't let my mind go there. I'm still hoping some kind of magic will fall in my lap and we can save the place."

"Sami tells me your other daughter is a sous chef."

Bryan rolled his eyes. "*Sous chef* is being generous. Kayla's an apprentice chef, two years out of cooking school. She's good, but not quite sous chef material yet."

"And Sami's going into restaurant management. Sounds like a theme running through the family."

"Yeah, my dream line up. Me, Kay and Sami running a nice restaurant, not a bar. Maybe something Italian. Kay could manage the kitchen, Sami would work front of the house and I'd be behind the scenes, managing the business end of it until they were ready to take that on."

"I love Italian food."

Bryan chuckled. "You would. Did the Italian stud cook for you?"

"No, he was no cook. He had other talents, though."

"I'll bet."

Dix chuckled. "What? He was a painter. Seriously, your dream sounds nice."

"Yeah." He set his plate aside. "You know what else sounds nice?" He dropped to his knees and moved between Dix's legs.

"I can only hope." Dix winked.

"You can do more than hope, lover."

"Is something magic about to fall into my lap?"

Bryan grinned. "Oh, yeah. If you help me with the zipper on those slacks."

Chapter Three

Dix forced himself to leave around midnight, with the promise of returning the following evening. It was Friday, and Bryan suggested he pack a bag so they could spend the weekend together. "Not a date, mind you."

"Just more fucking?"

"Lots more."

"I'm down with that. Or up for that. Whatever." He rubbed his face. "It's late, I'm beat. See you tomorrow."

Bryan pressed a kiss to his lips and for a moment, Dix didn't want to leave. He forced himself to go. As he drove home, he realized how much he was looking forward to the following evening, when he wouldn't have to go anywhere. Spending the night together sounded great.

He managed six hours of sleep then went for a run before he showered and dressed for work. He stopped to buy four cups of *good* coffee, and carried the drink holder to his desk.

"Morning," Mac greeted him. "How was your night?"

Dix could see his partner looked like hell, so he didn't expound about how great it had actually been. "Okay. How's Cecile? You guys get any rest last night?"

"Not much. She was pretty sick. Hopefully she's on the uphill swing today."

"I hope so, man." He handed over a coffee.

Their captain joined them and Dix handed over another.

"Thanks. What's the latest?"

The phone on Mac's desk rang and he snatched it up. "MacDonald. No." He closed his eyes and scrubbed his face with one hand. "Where was she found? Yep, we're on our way." He hung up the receiver.

"Don't tell me we have another one." Dix couldn't believe it. *One a day? Seriously?*

"Long blonde hair, strangled and burned dead woman in the alley off Jackson."

"Fuck!" Dix picked up his drink. "Guess ours are to go. I'll leave this one on Peyton's desk, whenever he gets his lazy ass in here." He set the last cup on their newest detective's desk. Nick Peyton had been assigned to help when the body count had hit three. Now that it was four, Dix wondered if his boss would call in more reinforcements.

The captain raised his brows. "He's here, he just ran down to the evidence room. I'll give him your regards."

Dix grinned over his shoulder. "You can leave out the 'lazy ass' part."

Mac grabbed his coffee and followed.

"Touch base as soon as you know anything," Alvarez called after them.

"Roger that," Mac replied, and they headed out.

"This guy is escalating," Dix muttered as they hurried to his Navigator.

"A vic a day is fucking nuts," Mac agreed.

"We need a break, and big time." He drove them to the alley where they met Abby and went over the scene.

"I see something." She squatted next to the woman's torso. "Looks like skin under her nails. She might have scratched the guy."

"That would be nice," Dix squinted to see the evidence. "You've got good eyes, Ab."

"It's all in the details." She smiled and nodded.

He glanced at Mac. "I guess we'll leave the minutia to the doc and start pounding the pavement."

A uniformed officer approached, holding up a matchbook in a clear plastic evidence bag. "May or may not be anything, but this was found a few feet away from her body."

Dix took the bag and studied the contents. "O'Malley's Pub." Handing the bag to Abby he looked at Mac. "That's about a block from here."

"Doubt anyone will be there this early. Let's take her photo around to some of the open businesses first. I'll bet the pub opens around ten."

"Let's do it." They canvassed the surrounding neighborhood and at ten headed to O'Malley's. "Morning," Dix told the middle-aged woman behind the bar.

"Is it? Looks pretty fucking much the same as last night when I closed this joint."

She had silver hair the color of Abby's, but the comparison ended there. This woman was probably in her sixties and looked as if she'd lived every one of those years. "So you worked last night..." Dix read her worn nametag. "Marge?"

"I did. You should have come in, sugar. Would have passed the time much more pleasant-like."

He smiled. "Sorry I missed it. I'm Detective Dixon and this is Detective MacDonald, with the KCPD. Unfortunately, a woman was found dead in the alley about a block away, just off Jackson. I wonder if you might remember seeing her?" He held up the photo.

"Hell yeah I remember! She was here for a few hours. First it was just her and a couple girlfriends. They met up with some fellas, lots of drinks flowing and some dancing. I'm not sure who left first, but one of the girls left with a guy." She looked to the ceiling, pondering. "Can't recall if I saw this one leave or not."

"So you didn't see her leave with one of the men?" Mac clarified.

She gazed at him levelly. "That's what I meant by 'can't recall if I saw her leave'."

He nodded.

Dix smiled. "You're sure it was her? She doesn't look her best in this photo, but it could be very important to the case if you saw her."

"I'm positive. One hundred percent, no doubt."

"And if we needed you to describe the men she was with, do you think you might be able to do that?"

"Probably, some details, anyway. Might be easier if you found her friends and asked them. They got a better look at the fellas."

"We're hoping to do that. You don't recall who paid the tab, do you? A credit card receipt would be amazing."

"We weren't that busy. I might be able to figure it out. Had to be one of them at that table. Sit tight, I'll go pull the records." She glanced up as a delivery man entered through the back.

"Hey, Marge. Finally Friday!"

"Like that means shit to me. I work the whole goddamned weekend. Gimme some extra longneck bottles, will you, Adam? The Royals have a three game away series this weekend, so we'll have a crowd."

"You got it." He glanced at Dix and Mac for a second before turning and leaving.

Dix looked at his partner. "Recognize him?"

"Our beefy delivery boy from Last Call the other day."

"Interesting."

Marge returned with some receipts.

"Hey, Marge, what company does your beer deliveries?" Dix asked.

"Wilson Beverage Distributors. Why?"

"No reason." He glanced at Mac. "You want to go through those with her? I'm going to step out and make a call."

"You got it." Mac turned back to the bar.

Dix moved to the front sidewalk and phoned Peyton at the office. "Hey, Nick, it's Dix."

"Hey there. Thanks for the coffee."

"You bet. Need some info, please. Wilson Beverage Distributors services O'Malley's Pub and Last Chance Bar and Grille. Both those places have the same route, driver by the name of Adam something. Blond curly hair, about twenty-five. Find out his route, and see if they service any of the other bars our vics were last seen at, would you?"

"I'm on it."

"Thanks, man." He ended the call and returned to Mac and Marge.

"Got a couple possibilities here," Mac told him. "Stephanie Marcus and Beverly Baldwin. One of them is either our vic or her friend."

"Excellent." They jotted down notes and thanked Marge before leaving the pub.

"You can thank me by coming back, sweetie!" She winked at Dix.

"You are trouble." He pointed at her, grinning. "I swore an oath I'd stay away from trouble if at all possible."

The woman was cackling when they walked out.

Mac shook his head. "Why do women always go for the gay guys?"

Dix shrugged. "I dunno, but you wouldn't want her to go for you, would you? Not exactly your type."

"You're right. My type has rapidly thinning hair and pukes at least three times a day. God, I love that woman." He patted his heart.

"You're a good man, Mac." They climbed in his Navigator and Dix drove back to the station.

Peyton met them at the door of the homicide division. "Hey, good catch on Wilson Beverages. Adam Reese happens to be the delivery driver for each of the four restaurants or bars our victims were last seen at."

Dix raised his brows. "Well, isn't that a co-inky-dink?"

Mac tacked a photo of the driver on their evidence board. "I don't think there's any coincidence to it. I suspected the kid right from the beginning. He's real beefed up, like he works out a lot."

Dix looked at Peyton. "He hauls kegs and cases of beer for a living."

Mac shook his head. "I don't think that's the only thing he hauls around. I say we go talk to Mr Adam Reese."

Peyton held out a slip of paper. "He'll be hard to pin down until about four-thirty. Here's the warehouse address. Reese drives a silver Dodge Ram."

Dix snatched the paper. "We'll plan to meet him there at four-thirty, then. Nice work, Nick."

"No problem. If you need anything else, just ask. Until then, I'll be behind my computer screen, going over every detail of these women's lives." He kept talking as he walked away. "Madison Ames worked out at Curves every day on her lunch hour. Donna Reitz went to Max Fitness three days a week after work. Norma Lear loathed exercise and seemed to maintain her nice figure by the grace of God. Those were her mother's words. She's Jewish, in case you couldn't tell."

"So no similarities there." Dix looked at the women's photos. "Were the other two Jewish?"

"Nope. One Catholic and one who didn't go to church."

"Okay, then, keep at it. I know it's tedious…"

"But important," Peyton agreed. "I know."

They all got to work, but Dix took a moment to call Bryan's cell.

"Hello?" The sexy voice sent a shiver down Dix's spine.

"Hey, handsome. How's your day going?"

"Better now! I was thinking about you, actually. Wondering what time you got off tonight."

Dix chuckled, and Bryan realized what he'd said. "I meant *from work*. Anytime you get off after that will be strictly under my control."

"Oh yeah? Sounds kinky. Well, usually five to five-thirty, but tonight we have to go talk to someone at four-thirty so I might be later. I can call you when I know for sure."

"That's fine. When I hear from you, I'll leave and meet you at my place. I thought I'd bring some food from here, if that works for you."

"Perfect. Have a good afternoon."

"You too."

"Not much chance of that. We're working the case of victim number four today."

"Ugh. Sorry. Catch the bastard, will ya?"

"That's the plan. Talk to you later."

"Yep."

Dix ended the call and thought about him for a moment. Bryan had said they were so much alike it was scary. Dix didn't find it scary, he actually found it amazing. And he couldn't wait to see where the relationship might go.

* * * *

Shortly after four, he and Mac drove to the Wilson Beverages warehouse parking lot and kept their eyes on the silver truck. Abby phoned his cell and he spoke to her while they waited.

"Stephanie Marcus is our girl. Her father and her friend Beverly just made a positive ID. I sent them over to your place, Peyton and the captain are going to interview them."

"Great. I'll touch base with them when we're done here."

"Dix, a couple more things. I definitely got skin under her fingernails, so she must have scratched the guy. Also, and this is new, there were traces of semen this time. Not much, so I suspect the condom broke or something like that. But we have the sucker's DNA now."

"Excellent. Nice work, Ab."

"Thanks. Last bit of business is kind of odd. The unis found a cigarette butt near the body. A Camel Non-filter. I ran the DNA and it belongs to Stephanie."

"So she was a smoker. Some people still are."

"Not according to her friend. But she smoked that one."

"You saying the perp made her smoke it before he burned her with the lit end?"

"That's what I'm thinking."

"This guy's getting stranger by the minute."

"I know it. Just hoping it'll all make sense when you catch him and the story unfolds."

"Easy as that. All right, then. Talk later."

"Yep." She disconnected the call.

He looked at Mac. "Perp left his DNA this time. Semen and he might have a scratch somewhere. Abby thinks he made this one smoke a cigarette before he burnt her with it."

"Weird-ass fuck wipe."

"Exactly what I was thinking. Vic was Stephanie Marcus. Peyton's getting ready to interview her dad and a friend."

Mac nodded. "We've got to stop this guy. He's out of control."

They both snapped to attention when their suspect approached his truck. "Here we go." Dix opened his door.

"Adam Reese?" They approached him cautiously. "KCPD. We'd like to talk to you."

Reese froze, his expression contorted in a mix of confusion and fear.

Dix glanced at the man's arm and saw three small scratches, parallel, as if they'd come from fingernails. As the facts sank in, Reese turned and ran.

"We got a runner!" Mac yelled.

"Take the car!" Dix tossed his keys to his partner. He ran daily and might have a shot at catching the younger man. Mac probably wouldn't.

"Got it, I'll call it in."

Dix took off, his partner's voice echoing behind him. "This is unit twenty-two, we have a suspect on foot in the thirteen hundred block of Adams, heading west. One officer in pursuit."

Reese had a block lead, and the kid showed no signs of slowing.

Dix's adrenaline kicked in and he closed the gap between them. "KCPD," he shouted. "Freeze."

The man glanced over his shoulder but kept going. He took a left at the first alley and disappeared.

Dix rounded the corner and spotted him again. The next intersection would be a busy street with lots of rush hour traffic. He wanted to stop the man before they reached it. A foot chase on a busy sidewalk would be hell. "Freeze!" he yelled again.

Reese looked back once more, and when he turned around again he ran directly into Dix's Navigator that Mac had just whipped in from the other end of the alley.

The kid rolled over the hood and landed on his back.

Dix and Mac reached him at the same time, weapons drawn. "Stay down," Mac ordered.

Dix holstered his gun and cuffed the suspect. He tried to resume normal breathing but had to gasp a couple of times to catch his breath. He finally muttered, "What the hell, man? We just wanted to talk to you. Now you're under arrest."

"I didn't do anything," Reese protested.

"Then why did you run?"

No answer, just a sullen stare.

Dix raised Reese's left arm. "How'd you get the scratches?"

"It was just an argument. I said I was sorry. Sent her flowers, even. I know she didn't call the cops."

"Stephanie Marcus? No she didn't, because she's dead. And we've got your DNA under her fingernails from this injury."

Reese's face went pale. "Stephanie Marcus? Who's that?"

"Your last victim." Mac took the suspect by the handcuffs and shoved him toward the patrol car that had just joined them.

"Victim? What?" Reese looked terrified as they guided him into the backseat of the vehicle.

"Read him his rights," Mac told the uniformed officer.

Dix rubbed a hand over the dent in the hood of his Navigator.

His partner returned to stand beside him. "Is it bad?"

"Nah. Nothing the body shop can't knock out."

"I should have held on to my '72 Ford construction truck. That puppy was made of steel, not fiberglass. Woulda taken more than a scrawny kid to dent that thing." Mac got in the passenger seat.

Dix climbed behind the wheel and glanced over at him. "No doubt. Were the floorboards rusted out so you could see the road beneath your feet as you drove? My old man had one the same way."

"Well, yeah, but a nice floor mat covered that up."

"Right." Dix chuckled and drove back to the Wilson Beverages parking lot. They waited for the crime scene unit to arrive and search the truck before impounding it. He drove them back to the station and glanced at his watch. Nearly six o'clock. "I need to make a quick call."

Mac nodded. "Me too." They went their separate ways.

Dix dialed Bryan's number.

"Hey, sexy," the man answered.

"One word of advice. If anything happened to me, and someone wanted to notify you, they'd use my phone to call."

Bryan chuckled. "Oh, shit. Point taken. Second rule about being friends with a cop?"

"You could say that. But I think we're quickly moving past the 'friends' business, don't you? I haven't stopped thinking about you all damned day. Well, except for that time I was chasing a suspect through an alley. My mind was kind of occupied then."

"You chased a suspect? Oh, my God, Dix, are you okay?" His tone sounded amazed and terrified, all at the same time.

Dix was touched. "I'm fine, but I'm pleased that you asked."

"You got him, then?"

"We have a suspect in custody, yes, which is the reason for my call. I need to question the man. I'm not sure tonight is going to happen."

"Oh, it's going to happen all right. Just might not be the schedule we'd outlined. Call me when you're done, I don't care what time it is. I'll wait up for you."

His heart filled with warmth. "Sounds nice. I've gotta go, but I'll check back when I can. And Bryan? Thanks."

"Don't thank me, I haven't done anything. *Yet.*" His voice grew husky. "Later, you can thank me. I know I'll be thanking you."

Laughing, Dix ended the call. He met Mac in the hallway outside the number one interrogation room, which had a large two way mirror. Peyton and the captain were there, studying Reese, who was handcuffed to the single table in the room.

Alvarez looked at him. "Abby wants this guy's DNA ASAP to process it and see if we have a match. Instant test results aren't conclusive, but should be enough to hold him if we've got a partial match."

Dix nodded. "Is there a CSI tech around to do the swab?"

"Yes. You get him to agree, and we'll send one in."

"Okay." Dix straightened his jacket. "We'll start there." He entered the small room. The mirror took up a good portion of one whole wall. The others were bare. He looked at Reese. "I'm Detective Dixon. I'll remove those cuffs if you promise to behave yourself."

"I know who you are. And I haven't done anything," Reese insisted.

Dix unfastened the cuffs and dropped them in his pocket. He sat in the chair opposite the suspect. "If that's the case, why did you run? Innocent people don't usually take off like that."

Reese sighed. "I panicked. I got pulled over by the Sedalia police a few nights ago for suspicion of DUI. I didn't get a ticket, they just gave me a warning."

"DUIs are bad, but if it's your first you wouldn't do jail time."

"I drive a truck for a living. My boss has a zero tolerance policy. One DUI and my job is history."

"So you thought we were coming to talk to you about your traffic stop? Seriously?"

He shrugged. "I didn't know. Like I said, I panicked."

"Well, Adam, we're investigating a string of serial rapes and murders around the neighborhood you work in. Four victims to date, all of them last seen leaving a bar or restaurant that you happen to deliver to."

"That's ridiculous! I'd never do anything like that. I have a girlfriend, and we spend most of our time together."

"Were you with her last night? We'll need to talk to her. We'd also like to get a DNA swab from you. It's painless and will only take a minute."

"I'd rather not involve her. And I don't think I want to give you my DNA."

Dix pushed away from the table and stood. "All right, then. I hope you're prepared to be our guest for a while. Funny, you were worried enough about losing your job that you ran from us. I wonder how long you'll be employed once your boss finds out you've been arrested for rape and murder."

Reese jumped up and pounded on the table. "I didn't rape anyone, and I sure as hell didn't kill them, either!"

Dix gazed at him levelly. "You need to sit back down, son. One more move like that will get the cuffs back on."

He sank into the chair. "I'm sorry. I just can't get anyone to listen. *I did not do this.*"

"Then prove it. Let us take the DNA, and tell me your girlfriend's name. If she's truly a friend, wouldn't she want to help clear your name?"

Reese scowled. "Her father doesn't know about us. I'm a little older. She doesn't think her dad would approve."

Dix shrugged. "Your call, kid. Sit in jail, or make an effort to prove yourself innocent."

"I'll take the test," he finally said.

The technician was in the room and the swab taken before Reese could change his mind.

When it was just the two of them again, Dix folded his hands on the table. "Now, what about the girlfriend? If she's your alibi, we need to talk to her."

"Is there any way her father can be kept out of it?"

"Of course. We'll need to talk to her, not her dad."

Reese glanced down then up again. "The thing is, you know her, *and her dad*. I'm dating Sami Scott."

Dix's heart lurched, but he remained calm. "Is that so? Guess that's why you were scrutinizing the dining room at Last Call the other day. I assumed you were checking out the patrons."

"I was looking for Sami. She told me she might be working the lunch shift, but I guess when she got there it was pretty quiet so she didn't stay."

"I remember."

Reese tapped his fingers on the table. "She said you went on a date with her old man."

"We're friends. It was definitely not a date." *According to the rules Bryan and I jokingly established.*

The suspect stared him down. "I was just thinking, maybe *you* could help me get out of this. Sami told me her old man's gay. Since you went on a date with him, by process of elimination I'd guess that makes you gay, too. If you'd like me to keep that bit of information to myself, then why don't you help me shake loose? I promise, I did *not* do what you're accusing me of. Honestly, if I did, why would I choose women from the territory my route is in? I'm not that stupid."

Dix smiled. "Glad to hear it. Just so you know, there's a bunch of detectives, our unit captain, and possibly, by now, a district attorney on the other side of that mirror watching us. If everyone didn't already know I was gay, you just outed me."

Reese glanced at the mirror and back quickly. His face fell.

"See, Adam, blackmail works better when nobody else knows the secret. But you knew that, because you're not stupid, right?" He stood and went to the door. "And if I wasn't going to tell Sami's father, you can sure as hell bet I'll be telling him now. I hope your alibi checks out, kid, or you're going to be real popular in prison." He walked out and closed the door with a thud.

Reese ran to the mirror and pounded on it. "I didn't do anything! Let me out of here!"

Mac shook his head, trying not to smile. "Way to rile him up, Dix. Now I get to go back in there and calm him down." He picked up a bottle of water and went into the room.

Dix watched him order Reese to be seated. He handed over the bottle and cuffed one of the suspect's hands to the table before walking out again.

Alvarez frowned. "He looks scared. Makes me think he could be innocent. Frankly, I'm not sure he's smart enough to have pulled these murders off and not left a shit-load of evidence."

Dix replied, "Hopefully what he left this last time will be enough to convict him."

"You know his girlfriend? We need to get her in here."

Peyton joined them. "Your mouth to God's ear. Sami Scott and her father are here, asking for Detective Dixon."

"Good news travels fast," Dix muttered and stomped into the bullpen.

"Where is he?" Sami rushed to his side. "Can I see him?"

He gazed at her incredulously. "Are you kidding me? He's our number one suspect. He won't get visitors till he hits Sing Sing."

"You can't do this! Adam is innocent. I was with him all last night."

"All night?" Her father didn't look pleased.

Sami frowned. "Look, I don't question who you spend the night with, and I'd appreciate the same courtesy." She turned back to Dix and pounded his chest. "And you, how can you do this? It's not fair!"

He grabbed her hands and held them firmly, speaking in a low voice for her and Bryan to hear, "Sami, I'm sorry. I had no idea you were dating the guy. I have a duty to uphold the law, and Adam popped up as a prime suspect. The latest victim gouged her attacker. Adam has fresh scratch marks on his arm."

"I gave him those! We had a fight, and we shoved each other around a little. But we made up. He never left my place last night. He sent me flowers to apologize today."

Bryan looked at Dix. "Book him."

"I'm working on it." Dix squeezed Sami's hands one last time. "No guy should put his hands on a woman. If the douche bag doesn't know that, you're better off without him."

"I hit him first," she spouted defiantly.

Bryan tried not to smile.

Dix scowled. "Works both ways, kid. Women can be douche bags, too. Ask me about my ex sometime."

She relaxed her hands and leaned against him. "I know I was wrong, I was just pissed off. It wasn't a big thing, or I didn't think it was, anyway. Who knew the cops would get involved?"

Her father brushed a lock of hair from her eyes. "I think you better get used to that."

Dix smiled. "Rule number three about being friends with a cop. Prepare yourself for the fact that we're always going to be involved."

He released Sami and she stood on her own. "I need to interview you in one of the rooms." To Bryan he said, "You'll need to wait out here."

"He can't come with me?" She sounded younger than her twenty-one years.

"No, but if you want him to observe, he can stand outside with the homicide captain and watch."

She nodded. "That's fine."

Bryan kissed her cheek. "Just tell the truth, honey."

"I will."

Dix led them to the second interrogation room and showed her inside. He told his captain, "This is Sami Scott's father, Bryan. Bryan, this is Capt Alvarez."

The men shook hands.

"He's going to wait out here while I question his daughter."

"Cup of coffee?" Mac asked Bryan.

"I could use one."

Mac went to get the drink.

Dix glanced at Bryan, a hundred different thoughts going through his head. The only thing he could say in front of the captain was, "You sure you want to hear this?"

Bryan nodded.

Dix entered the room. He sat opposite Sami. "Did you want a bottle of water or anything?"

"Bottled water is bad for the environment."

"It sure is. All righty, then, I guess we'll get started. How long have you been dating Adam Reese?"

She folded her arms across her chest. "Are you asking this as a cop or as a friend of my father's?"

He rolled his eyes. "If you feel I have a conflict of interest, I can recuse myself and send someone else in to question you."

Sami studied him for a moment then sighed. "No, I like you. It's okay. We've been dating about five months."

"You see each other pretty regularly?"

"Every day. We have our own places, but he stays over at mine most nights." She glanced at the mirror and looked away quickly.

Dix realized this was a safe way for Sami to tell her father about the relationship without fear of his getting angry. He wondered how upset Bryan would actually be, and whether she had a legitimate reason for keeping the secret from him.

He continued the line of questioning. "Adam says he was with you last night between the hours of ten and six a.m. I'd assume you were sleeping some of that time. Is there any way he could have left and come back without your hearing him?"

"No. My apartment door squeaks. Daddy was going to put some grease on it, but I realized I like hearing when it opens and closes. Same with the door locks. I have three, and they're noisy. I wouldn't sleep through them being opened."

He nodded thoughtfully, wondering about his next line of questioning. *Tread lightly.* "You told us you put the scratch marks on Adam's arm. What was the argument about?"

Sami hesitated. "I'd rather not say."

He started to reply when the door opened and Abby stuck her head in. "Preliminary DNA is back, Dix. Adam Reese does *not* match the samples found on Samantha Marcus."

Chapter Four

Sami grinned and jumped up. "It's not him! I *told you* it wasn't him!"

Dix groaned and stood. Before he realized what was happening, Sami grabbed him around the neck and hugged. "I knew it!" she repeated. "Can I take him home now?"

He walked her out to Bryan and the captain. "Cut him loose?" he asked Alvarez.

"Cut him loose," the captain agreed. "Thanks for coming in," he told Sami and Bryan.

She clung to her father, smiling ear to ear. "It's all going to be okay."

He looked at her skeptically. "We'll see about that."

Dix cleared his throat. "You two riding in one car?"

She nodded. "Mine's at the bar."

He turned to Bryan. "Why don't you ride with me? Let Sami take Adam, they can swap vehicles and leave yours at the bar. We'll pick it up later."

"Okay, but why?" Bryan asked.

"Because I don't think you need to see the young man right now. Let them go tonight. You can talk to them later, maybe this weekend or next week. Give it some time."

He sighed. "You're sure he isn't the guy you were after?"

Dix nodded. "Sometimes the clues point in the wrong direction. It's all a part of police work. Not the best part, but something we deal with."

Bryan handed his keys to Sami. "I'd rather you leave my car at home. Park it in the driveway. We'll talk about things some other time."

She hugged her father and turned back to Dix expectantly.

"Give me a minute." He went back into the first interrogation room.

Adam had beads of sweat running down his temples. "What's happening?"

Dix leaned over and unlocked the handcuff. "You're free to go. DNA evidence does not match. But hang on. Sami and her father are here. I'm gonna do you a favor and take him home first. Sami can drive you over to the impound lot and they'll release your truck to you."

Adam rubbed his wrist. "Bryan can't be mad at me if the evidence says I didn't do this."

"You think? Bryan's upset because you and his daughter got into some kind of tussle and she put those marks on your arm. That's the main thing right now. Let's not even go into the fact that you've been sleeping over at the girl's house most nights for the past five months."

"He knows that?"

"We all know, kid. So cool your jets for a couple more minutes. I'll get him out of here. My partner will come back in and sign you out, and explain where impound is located. Got it?"

He nodded. "Thanks, Detective. And hey, I'm sorry about what I said earlier. I wasn't really trying to blackmail you. I was scared and desperate."

Dix sighed. "I know. Look, this won't go on the record as an official arrest, so your job should be okay. But you've got to get this domestic violence crap under control. Bryan and I are going to be watching you like hawks. The next time Sami turns up with the smallest bruise, we're gonna find out about it. You got that?"

His words came out in a relieved rush. "I do. I promise, nothing's going to happen. I love Sami, and she loves me."

Dix nodded, and headed out of the door. For some reason he believed him. Stopping at Mac's desk, he said, "I'm going to take Bryan home. Will you sign out the kid and tell him where to get his truck out of impound, please? Sami will drive him over."

"Can do. Have a good weekend. Hope I don't see you."

"You too. Hugs to Cecile. Hope I don't see you either." He returned to Bryan and Sami.

"Hope I don't see you?" She raised her eyebrows at Dix.

He flicked a strand of hair off her shoulder. "If there's another murder, we'll both be called in to work this weekend."

She nodded. "So you hope there's not another murder."

He smiled. "Yeah, even if it would put us out of our jobs. We can only hope there won't be another murder. *Ever.*"

"Got it." She gave him a quick hug. "Thanks. I don't like 'Dix'. What's your real name?"

He gazed at her patiently. "James."

"Ooh, can I call you Jimbo?"

"Not more than once."

She made a face. "Jim? Jimmy?"

He shook his head. "That's ex-wife territory."

"James?"

"I could live with James. But the first time it gets shortened, I search your record for unpaid parking tickets."

Sami smiled. "Thank you, James. Have a nice weekend." She turned to her father. "Bye, Daddy."

"See you, princess."

Dix grinned and grabbed a couple of things off his desk before heading out. "Nothing spoiled about that kid."

Bryan fell into step on their way to the parking lot. "Eh, it's our little joke. I only call her 'princess' when she's gotten away with something and she knows it."

"Got it." He unlocked the Navigator and they both climbed in. Dix paused and looked at him. "So how pissed are you about this thing between her and Adam?"

Bryan shrugged. "I'm more upset that they got into a physical fight. That can't keep happening. As far as the relationship goes, I dunno. I always thought he was okay. He is a bit old for her."

"You're not unhappy they've been sleeping together? I figured that might set you off."

"I've known for a long time Sami's not a virgin. There was a pregnancy scare back in high school... Let's just say we squeaked by on that one. Her mom got her to a doctor and on birth control. Since then, I've had this 'don't ask, don't tell' thing going on."

"Yeah, I probably would, too, if Julie had lived longer. I escaped that particular horror. It's different with a son, for some reason."

Bryan smiled. "Two daughters. I suppose it would be, but I don't really know."

"I gotta tell you something, and I hope you don't think I was presumptuous. I told Adam we were going to be watching him like hawks, so he'd better treat Sami right."

"Thank you. That was very cool."

"Got to thinking maybe I overstepped my boundaries."

"Not a bit."

He exhaled with relief. "Great. Then I'm hoping it won't be presumptuous to suggest that I'd like to get on over to your place so we can fuck our brains out."

"Not in the slightest. That's always been the plan, if you'll recall." He glanced at his watch. "We're just about three hours behind schedule. Are you hungry? We could drive through some place."

Dix started up the car. "Only hungry for one thing. After that's been satisfied, we can discuss dinner." He drove toward the house.

Bryan ran a hand over Dix's thigh. "I like the way you think. And I *loved* watching you work tonight. Got me very excited, seeing you all police-like."

Glancing sideways, Dix waggled his brows. "Oh yeah? Maybe I should bring in my cuffs."

"Maybe. But you're not going to need them tonight, stud. I'm ready for whatever you have in mind."

He pulled into Bryan's driveway and parked. "First thing I need is a quick shower. There are some days, you just gotta take a rinser and get it washed off, you know?"

"You bring your overnight bag?"

"I did."

"Perfect." Bryan led him inside, locking the door and turning on lights as they went. He set out some clean towels. "Help yourself to anything you need. Take your time."

Dix started to strip. "All I need is about five minutes to clean up. Then I need you, with a rubber and some lube, to join me in the shower. You up for that?"

Bryan rubbed his lips over Dix's. "I told you, I'm up for anything you suggest, handsome. Your five minutes start now." He drew his tongue across lightly then pulled away and left the room smiling.

Dix peeled out of his clothes then reached in and turned the shower on hot. He climbed in, allowing the water to flow over him before washing his hair with the fresh-smelling shampoo Bryan had on the ledge. As he was soaping up his body, the curtain parted and Bryan looked in.

"Ready for some company?"

"Damn straight. Been thinking about you." He glanced down at his rampant erection.

"Um, good thoughts, I hope." His lover climbed in and closed the curtains. He jumped when the spray hit him. "Damn, that water is hot!"

Dix chuckled. "Sorry. I'll cool it down."

"Just a little."

"Just a little," Dix repeated and adjusted the knob. He reached for Bryan's waist and drew him close. "Just for you."

They gazed into each other's eyes. "Do you know how happy this makes me?" Bryan finally asked.

"Yeah. As happy as it makes me. It's nice to have someone to come home to. Did you mean it when you said seeing me at work got you excited?"

"Oh, yeah." Bryan ran his hands over Dix's back. "Definitely. I wish I had a more interesting job, so you could say the same. Not sure offering someone a Whiskey Sour ever got them hot and bothered."

"Someone with an alcohol problem, maybe. But don't be so hard on yourself. You're more than a bartender, you own the place. Not that it matters to me. I'd still want to fuck you if you were the janitor."

Bryan smiled. "Because janitors can be pretty hot."

"You're hot no matter what you're doing. Face it, man. Seeing you breathe gets me excited."

"Aw, that just earned you dealer's choice tonight. Care to give or receive?"

Dix grinned, rubbing their groins together. "Both. But I'll give, first. Turn around and assume the position. Hands on the wall."

"Oh, yes, Officer." Bryan did as ordered, spreading his feet and placing his hands on the steamy tile.

Dix reached for the lube and foil packet they'd left on the rim of the tub. After squirting the lube into his palm, he used a finger to ream his lover's ass until the man squirmed. "Mmm, and that's just one. Wait till I get four in there."

"Four? Holy shit! Who has time for that? Do two and call it good. I want your cock inside me, and your hands everywhere they can reach."

Dix inserted a second digit into the warm channel and stretched from side to side. "I love it when you're hot for me. I could tease you a while longer, see how hot you can really get…"

Bryan jutted his ass backwards a couple of times. "Don't even joke about that. I'm as ready as I'll ever be. Fuck me, baby, and fuck me good."

"Don't need to ask me twice." He removed his hand and greased the condom covering his shaft. "Here we go. Ready or not."

"Ready," Bryan groaned, one fist pounding the wall. "So ready."

Dix inched his cock forward until he was balls-deep. He sighed for a moment at the glorious tightness, then drew out slowly and began the thrusting rhythm he knew they both loved.

"Good. Yes, that's it."

"You're good," Dix muttered through gritted teeth. "I could fuck you forever."

"Gonna hold you to that. Grab my cock and jerk me off. Won't take much."

Dix rested his forehead against one of Bryan's shoulder blades. He curled his fingers around the full, throbbing shaft and for a moment, he wished he could see it…taste it. But he was more than satisfied with his current position. Tightening his grasp, he thrust and tugged in motion with his fucking.

"Damn, yeah. Oh, God. Told you it wouldn't take much."

"Shame to waste that sweet cum, but you're gonna have to spray the wall this time, lover. Wouldn't miss this fuck for the world."

"Come on, then. Do it like you mean it!"

Dix groaned at the good-natured coaxing and quickened his pace. Bodies melded, he applied just the right amount of pressure to the pulsing shaft he could only envision… They both shattered. Moans filled the room as they came in unison. Dix stayed with him as long as he could then had to stop and catch his breath.

Bryan rested his head against the wall. "Fuck, fuck, fuck," he muttered.

"Again? So soon?"

He chuckled. "Maybe. You bring out the best in me, man. I think I might be able to go again with you in charge."

Dix kissed all over his lover's wet back and finally, regretfully, pulled out. He chucked the condom into the nearby trash can then adjusted the water temperature to make it warmer. "Gotta turn it up, babe. We're cooling off fast here."

"Not me." Bryan sighed as he turned to face Dix. "I'm still cranking at a hundred degrees Fahrenheit." He grabbed Dix's face and planted a loud, sloppy kiss on his mouth. "Damn, baby, it just gets better every time. That was amazing."

"Yeah, it was. You're amazing." Dix kissed him back, open mouthed, as hungrily as he'd ever kissed anyone. When he pulled back for air, he murmured, "I am totally, completely infatuated with you. I don't care what else happens. If I died tonight, I'd be the happiest man on earth."

"After me, that is. I'm fucking giddy as a schoolgirl. But let's not test out that dying thing. I'm not finished with you, yet."

Dix smiled. "Really glad I don't have to leave tonight. I think we're gonna have one hell of an evening."

"And it's off to a very good start. What do you say we rinse off real quick then throw on a couple robes? I'll whip us up something to eat. I make a mean stir-fry—it's fast and tasty."

"Sounds like a blow job. Just kidding. I'd love it. But I didn't bring a robe."

"I've got a robe for you, and I might have a blow job, too."

Closing his eyes, Dix stuck his face under the water. He pulled back and shook his head to clear the droplets. He smiled at Bryan. "That settles it. I'm never going home."

* * * *

The weekend flew and by Sunday, Dix *really* wished he didn't have to leave. He and Bryan had gotten very comfortable, sharing more in common than either of them could have guessed. They went to his townhouse to pack another *bigger* bag, and ended up making love in the whirlpool tub.

"Damn, this is nice." Bryan leaned back against the edge. "I could enjoy one of these."

Dix sat between his legs, his back to Bryan's chest. "You're welcome to use this one anytime you want."

Bryan nibbled his earlobe. "Then what are we doing packing your stuff to go to my place?"

Dix grinned. "Yours is closer to work. I guess we figured the shorter commute would give us more time in bed each morning?"

"I guess." Bryan ran his hands over Dix's chest. "We may have to rethink that decision at some point. Because this is *very nice.*" He glanced around. "The whole place is. Did you live here with your wife?"

"No! I bought it after the divorce. She's never been here."

Bryan chuckled. "Doesn't sound like there's much love lost between you two."

"Not anymore. We were friendly for a while, but she lost it when she found out I was seeing other men. Got really nasty. It wasn't pleasant. I think our bickering was part of the reason Jared enlisted in the Marines and moved so far away."

"Did he take sides, or was he cool?"

"Definitely not cool. He didn't actually 'take sides', but he's his mother's son. Let's put it this way, he calls her once a week and I hear from him regularly—once a year on my birthday."

"Ouch." Bryan hugged him. "That hurts."

Dix shrugged. "It did, but I'm over it. I love him and he knows it. How he chooses to treat me is totally up to him."

"I know, but still." Bryan kissed his temple. "Sorry, babe."

"Thanks. Hey, I just realized the station hasn't called all weekend."

"This is a good thing."

"A very good thing. I hope it keeps up."

"Me too, for your sake. And for the people of Kansas City, of course. I want everyone to stay safe, but especially you. I have a newly vested interest in you."

"You do, huh?" Dix rolled over so their stomachs touched. He pressed his lips against Bryan's, and their kiss was slow and passionate.

Tongue batted against tongue as desire increased. He rubbed his groin against his lover's and felt both their cocks respond.

"Mmm." Bryan drew back for air. "So soon? You think we're up for that?"

"You kidding me? We're forty-five, not ninety-five. Besides, my sexual appetite has quadrupled since I met you."

Bryan grinned. "Yeah, me too. Ain't it great?"

"Very great. So come on. My turn to play."

They dried off and raced to the bed, flopping on top of the comforter. Dix didn't bother to pull it back. He crawled between his partner's legs and eyed the erect cock he found there.

Bryan patted the mattress next to him. "Flip around so I can play too."

"Good idea." He did as directed and moaned when the man touched his shaft. "Very good idea."

Chuckling, Bryan continued to stroke the length before his mouth took over.

Hips thrusting, Dix followed the movements on Bryan's cock. Rubbing turned to licking then all out sucking. He deep-throated as long as he could then pulled back and sucked the head, running his tongue through the slit.

He nearly exploded when Bryan did the same thing. Before long they were each on their sides, both sucking with all their might. He felt his lover's balls draw up and knew release was close. When Bryan grunted, "Now" with his mouth full, Dix allowed himself to relax and let go.

Both of them shuddered, shooting at the same time. Intense pleasure soared through him as he came, then he continued sucking to make sure his job was done.

Bryan pulled back. "God, Dix. That was... Words fail me."

He chuckled. "Me too, babe. All I know is I loved it."

"Love. Yeah." Bryan let the word hang there.

Dix knew what he meant. It was too early, but they both felt it. *Love.*

* * * *

He rose and showered at Bryan's place the next morning. Bryan didn't have to go in as early, so he lay in bed and watched Dix dress.

"I was thinking it's time you met Kayla. I thought this might be a good week to plan something since we won't be so busy. How about dinner one night? I'd invite Sami too, of course. And maybe that boyfriend of hers." He made a face.

Dix smiled. They'd talked more about Sami. He knew her father was getting used to the idea of the boyfriend. "Why won't you be as busy?"

"Spring break for most of the schools. Some of them stagger the schedule, but most are off this week."

"Spring break?" Dix mulled the thought over in his head.

"Guess you don't have to think about it when you don't have kids in school anymore."

"Yeah." His mind continued to race as he stood in front of the mirror and adjusted his tie.

"You look swell. I could use that necktie to drag you back to bed and have my way with you."

Dix leaned over him for a kiss. "That sounds like loads of fun, but I can't be late for the Monday morning briefing. I promise you can have your way with me tonight, how's that?"

"I suppose it'll do. One more kiss." He parted his lips and the kiss was sensual and passionate.

Dix pulled back regretfully and smiled. "Later, sexy." He headed out of the room.

"Hey, you never gave me an answer about dinner!"

He called over his shoulder, "Whatever you want is fine with me. You plan it, I'll be there."

"You always going to be this agreeable?"

Dix winked and left.

* * * *

The homicide briefing offered little new in his case, or the couple of other cases various detectives worked on. Dix spoke up. "I wonder if there's anything to the fact that it's spring break vacation for many of the schools around here, and we haven't had a new victim since Thursday night."

"Spring break?" Capt Alvarez mused. "Might be a coincidence, might not. The suspect could be in school, or have ties to one of the local institutions.

Problem is, there are too many colleges in the area to go at him from that angle."

"True," Dix agreed. "It's even possible the suspect could be a big high schooler. That opens up the possibilities even more."

"Something to keep in mind," Alvarez concurred. "For now, let's enjoy the break and put our noses to the grindstone. It'd be excellent to catch this whack job before he strikes again."

They filtered back to their desks and Mac approached Dix. "Interesting thought, tying the suspect to spring break. What triggered that?"

He shrugged. "Bryan happened to mention it. His daughter has the week off from school."

Mac grinned. "*Bryan* did, huh? Did you see *Bryan* this weekend?"

Dix felt the heat of a blush but wasn't really embarrassed. "Maybe. Probably. Well, yeah. Only when my eyes were open."

His partner laughed. "Good for you. Seems like a nice guy. The daughter was okay, too."

"She's the one who encouraged him to ask me out. Quite a change from my own family dynamic."

Mac scratched his chin. "Yeah, but once the kids are grown, their opinions shouldn't matter all that much."

Dix shot him a look. "Shouldn't, but they still do. You and I both know that."

"Maybe so. All I'm saying is, don't go head over heels for this guy because he's got a supportive daughter. That's not the main quality you want in a life partner, all right?"

"Probably not, but it doesn't hurt. What are you getting at, Mac?"

He held his hands up. "Never mind. None of my business."

"It is if I asked."

He seemed to think about that, then replied, "Just seems maybe you're moving kinda fast with this one. You only met him the other day, and now you're spending twenty-four seven together?"

"No we're not. We both have to work." He tried to smile his way out, but Mac wasn't buying it. Dix understood what his partner was saying, and suddenly, in the harsh light of day, he felt the same way. "You're probably right. I don't know much about the guy. Besides the fact that we have *a lot* in common."

"Wouldn't hurt to check him out."

"I'm not going to do that," Dix scoffed. "He's a perfectly decent and respectable guy."

"That's what they said about Ted Bundy. *'What a handsome young man!'* You think serial killers all have swastikas carved into their foreheads?"

"No, I do not, and I don't think Bryan is a serial killer, either. But I'll check him out just to make you happy."

"Thank you." He returned to his own desk.

Dix sat and fired up his computer, running some searches and printing out whatever he could find about Bryan Scott.

He was relieved to discover there wasn't much. The only 'record' the man had involved a couple of parking tickets years ago. The rest of the info that came up when his name was searched were permits to acquire a liquor license, and other business-related activities.

Dix read the reports and felt increasingly embarrassed. He'd known Bryan had nothing to hide. He should have trusted his gut. Now he felt like a total shit.

Before he could decide what else to do, he ran his own name and printed out the report on himself. He tucked both sets of paperwork away and tried to put Bryan out of his mind. He found it tough to do when he wasn't busy.

He went to Mac's desk and folded his arms.

"Anything?" his partner asked.

"Of course not. I knew there wouldn't be."

"Good. I'm going over employee records from the restaurants and bars the women were last seen in. Care to help?"

"Yes. I need something to do."

Mac smiled. "Have a seat, my friend."

* * * *

When Dix left work he texted Bryan and they met at the man's house, arriving at the same time.

"Hey there." Bryan spoke to him from the garage. "Come in this way."

Dix followed and closed the doors behind them.

Bryan tossed some mail on the counter and turned to face him. "How was your day?"

Dix shrugged. "I've had better."

"Another murder?"

"No, thankfully." Dix's gut churned. He didn't want to admit what he'd done, but he had to. "This was all my own doing."

"You don't look good, buddy. Everything okay?"

"You might have to tell me. I think I screwed up, big time."

Chapter Five

Bryan eyed him levelly. "Let's grab a couple beers and go sit down. First, I need to be greeted properly." He moved in front of Dix and smiled.

Dix didn't want to kiss him, because once he started, he knew he wouldn't want to stop. He needed to come clean before anything more happened between them. If Bryan was going to throw him out, it best happened sooner than later. He gave him a quick kiss then pulled away.

"Well, gee. That was sweet." Bryan went to the fridge and retrieved two bottles, then headed into the front room. He took a seat on the sofa and set one of the bottles on the table next to him. "What's up?"

Dix sat beside him and tossed the sheaf of papers toward Bryan. "I fucked up. I panicked, and I blew it." He reached for the beer and twisted it open.

"What's this?" Bryan started to read. A slow grin spread across his face. "Damn, who knew those parking tickets would hang around so long?" He glanced up. "So does this mean we're through?"

"I feel like an ass. This weekend was go great, but once I got back to work—to the real world—I started thinking about how fast we were moving and it got to me. Before I knew what was happening, I did a search. I'm sorry, Bryan. It was a shitty thing to do. I'm sorry."

Bryan continued flipping through the reports. "What else is here? This is about you."

"Yeah. I printed my own record out of guilt. Figured it was the least I could do."

"A speeding ticket twenty years ago? Wow, I'm surprised they allowed you on the force. Thought they would have vetted their officers better than that." He tossed the papers aside.

"Maybe they were desperate." Dix took a drink from his bottle. The cold liquid burned going down.

"I *am* surprised that stuff is still on our records from so long ago. I thought minor violations went away after a few years."

"They do, on your official driving record. Police have access to more information than others."

"So I suspected." He leaned back and sipped his beer. "Actually, I thought you might check me out. Figured you'd have done it before our first dinner. Guess I thought that was rule number four about being friends with a cop. They're going check into your background, just to be safe."

"Let's call it like it is, shall we? We're not just friends anymore. We're dating. Okay, maybe not 'dating' as much as fucking, but we're seeing each other. Right?"

Bryan smiled. "I sure hope so. Look, James, if you thought I was going to be mad, don't worry. I'm not. I don't blame you for wanting to be sure. I had more of a clue that your record would be clean since you're a detective, right? But in this day and age, any sane person with access to that information would be reckless not to look at it."

Dix breathed a sigh of pure relief. "Thank you. I felt so guilty after I did it. I thought you might not want to see me anymore."

"Think again. I definitely want to see you. *All of you, all the time.* You're the only thing I seem to think about these days. Whether our relationship is right or wrong, too fast or just fucking crazy, I don't know. But we're in this thing, man. And I'm not ready for it to be over."

"I feel the same way. Crazy and reckless, maybe. But it feels good to me. Honestly, nothing has ever felt better."

Bryan tossed back the last of his beer and set the bottle down. "We're in total agreement. So what do you say we seal the deal with a quickie before dinner?"

Dix polished off his drink and grinned. "Have I mentioned that I like the way you think?"

Bryan scratched his chin. "Oh, maybe once or twice."

Standing, Dix reached for his lover's hand. "Think there'll ever come a time we decide to eat dinner *before* we fuck?"

"Probably. But I don't see that happening for a long time." They kissed and groped each other, and without separating, made their way slowly to the bedroom.

* * * *

Wednesday evening Bryan put a sign in the front window of the bar which read, 'Closing early for private party'. He told Dix that Galen had offered to cook for them when he'd found out Bryan was planning a family get-together.

The station had been quiet all week and Dix arrived shortly after five.

"Come in." Bryan unlocked the door for him. "How was your day?"

"Strangely calm. We all feel it. Kind of like we're waiting for the other shoe to drop."

"Maybe it never will. What if all the murderers in Kansas City packed up and went to Canada? You might have to switch to traffic patrol."

"I'd do it. It'd be worth the trade-off." He grinned and they kissed. Dix's heart soared. He'd never felt happier.

Bryan was a refreshing change of pace from the people he worked with all day. Nice folks, but serious, solemn and focused on the job at hand. *Great qualities for cops.* Fortunately, Bryan wasn't a cop. He also wasn't serious or unsmiling like half the detective force. Bryan knew there was a time for business and a time for pleasure. *Lots of time for pleasure.* Dix's cock pulsed pleasantly at the thought.

"So come on over, I want you to meet Kayla." He motioned to the tall, slender woman standing next to the bar. Her hair was light brown, not dark like her father's but nowhere near as blonde as her sister's. "Kay, this is Dix. James Dixon." He looked at Dix. "This is my beautiful daughter Kayla."

Dix extended a hand. "Pleased to meet you. I've heard good things."

"So have I!" She smiled, her greeting genuine. "Sami talks about you all the time. Daddy would too, if she'd let him get a word in edgewise."

Dix grinned. "Sami's a good little cheerleader. Not sure what I did to make her like me, but we seemed to hit it off."

"What's not to like?" Bryan went behind the bar and poured a mug of beer. He slid it across and winked.

"Right back atcha." Dix picked up the drink and sipped it.

"It's awful about those women," Kayla said. "Do you have any leads, besides Sami's boyfriend?"

He set his stein down. "No one that looks as good as Adam did. He had circumstantial evidence pointing at him like crazy. Fortunately, the DNA has come back and definitely cleared him. We're not giving up, though. We've got leads coming in through hotline tips every day. One of them is going to pay off. They almost always do."

"I hope so." She glanced up. "Hey, there."

Dix followed her gaze. Sami and Adam entered through the back door.

"Hi, everyone!" Sami breezed in with her ever-present upbeat attitude. She kissed her father's cheek then gave Kayla a hug. Turning to Dix, she smiled widely. "Hi, James! Good to see you." She hugged his neck.

He chuckled and patted her back. "Hey, Sami." When she pulled away he looked behind her. "Hi, Adam. How's it going?"

Her boyfriend nodded. "Okay. Pretty good, I guess. Still have my job, anyway."

"Of course you do." Dix tried to be friendly and supportive, realizing he could have had a hand in the kid *losing* his employment.

Sami went back to Adam's side and looped an arm through his. "He's doing great. He may even get a promotion."

Bryan raised his brows. "Promotion, eh?"

"A bigger route, basically, in the downtown area. I'd make more money on commissions. It's not a done deal yet, but I'm hopeful."

Bryan teased, "What are you going to do if you can't stop in here regularly and pretend you're *not* looking for Sami?"

"That part will be tough. I might have to convince her to move in with me permanently."

"Sorry I asked." Bryan turned his back on them and rolled his eyes toward Dix.

"Doesn't sound that bad to me," Dix whispered so only Bryan could hear.

His lover grinned, then turned back around. "All right everyone, let's have a seat. I've got a bottle of wine I'd like to pour, to celebrate the family getting together tonight."

"I'll help," Sami offered.

"Sit down, I'm serving tonight. You're a guest." He went behind the bar and retrieved some wine glasses.

Dix removed his jacket and hung it on the back of a bar stool. He moved next to Bryan and said, "I'll help. You've been serving people all day."

Bryan smiled. "Never gonna turn down help from you."

Dix bumped hips with him before pausing to wash his hands, then picked up two glasses of wine.

Bryan followed him to the table, carrying the other three.

Sami accepted hers. "Haven't *you* been serving people all day too, James?"

He chuckled. "So to speak. It's been pretty quiet this week."

"Spring break, I'm telling you," Bryan offered. "This guy is somehow affected by the school schedule."

Dix nodded. "We're looking into that. But I don't want to talk shop tonight. I'd like to propose a toast." He raised his glass, and the others did the same. "To Bryan and his lovely family, Kayla and Samantha. Thanks for welcoming me here. I think I can speak for Adam in saying we're glad to join you tonight, and hope we can share many more dinners like this."

Adam agreed. "*Salud.*"

They toasted and drank the wine, then chatted about Kayla's job.

"Next time, I'd like to cook for you," she said. "I'm learning some wonderful Italian dishes. I've got my veal parmigiana recipe nearly perfected. I'm working on risotto next."

"I've heard that's complicated," Dix agreed.

"The timing has to be perfect. It's a challenge."

Galen appeared in the window and nodded to Bryan.

"Looks like our dinner is ready. It won't be veal parmigiana, but Galen's a good cook, and I think you'll enjoy it." He stood.

"I'll help." Dix went with him. "Should we invite Galen to join us? He's your cousin, after all. I hardly know him."

"I asked him, but he declined. He pretty much keeps to himself." He paused. "Galen served several tours of duty overseas. He saw some action over there, and it was tough on him. He's been treated for PTSD. He's okay now, his wife Rae says he's doing fine. He just prefers a solitary lifestyle. We try to respect that. As you know, he's a great cook and a real asset to the grille."

"Whatever works. I just thought I'd ask."

"You're such a nice guy, wanting everyone to feel included." Bryan gazed at him admiringly.

"Yeah, that's me, Officer Friendly." They moved into the hallway between the bar and the kitchen, and he took the opportunity to draw Bryan close for a passionate kiss.

"I think you're very amiable," Bryan said when they came up for air. "And I intend to show you how chummy I can be in return when we get home tonight."

Dix studied him for a moment. "That sounds good."

Bryan smiled. "Getting chummy?"

"That too." Dix laughed. "I meant the 'home' part."

"Doesn't it sound nice?" Bryan clasped his hips. "It's nice having someone to go home with."

"And come home to. Very nice." They kissed one more time, then Dix regretfully pulled back. He took a moment to compose himself before they headed into the kitchen.

"Hey, Galen," Bryan said cheerfully. "You remember James Dixon. He's been here a few times."

"Love the food," Dix added.

Galen didn't crack a smile. His hair was slicked back as usual, and he looked much older than Bryan, even though Dix knew them to be the same age.

Bryan cleared his throat and picked up a tray of savory meat. "We'll just take this on out. Galen made Kansas City Barbecued Ribs. I thought we'd serve family style."

"Smells great," Dix observed.

"I'll take this, if you'd grab the cheesy potatoes." Bryan walked out.

"Will do." Dix noticed Galen had fixed himself a plate. "I wish you'd come eat with us. It's just family."

The cook gazed at him levelly. "It's not *just family*, now, is it?"

Dix bowed his head. "Point taken. I guess it's not. I was just saying, it'd be nice to have you join us."

"I'm fine." He turned his back.

"Suit yourself." Dix picked up the large bowl of potatoes and returned to the dining area.

"Sit down." Bryan removed the dish from his hands and placed it on the table. "I'll grab the green beans and rolls, and be right back." He went to the kitchen again.

Dix sat. "Galen's an interesting man. I invited him to eat with us, but he insisted he was fine in there."

Kayla screwed up her face. "He's weird."

"No he's not." Sami rolled her eyes. "You're just too critical."

Adam shrugged. "He seems okay to me, but I don't know him that well. I see him a few times a week when I make deliveries."

Kayla scowled again. "His son is definitely an oddball. No one can dispute that."

Sami chuckled. "Howard is a little goofy. I'll agree with that."

Bryan returned with the last of the food. "Who's goofy?"

"Howard." Sami nodded toward the kitchen.

Kayla spoke up. "I said he was weird. I think Galen is strange, too."

Her father frowned. "We don't talk about people that way, especially family. You were raised better than that."

The girl clammed up, but her expression indicated she didn't agree.

Bryan sat and began passing food platters. "Let's enjoy this great meal. Galen outdid himself."

"It looks wonderful," Dix agreed. He watched the faces of the family for a moment. Galen was obviously a source of dissention amongst them. *What's up with that?* He'd ask Bryan later when they were alone.

The meal tasted as good as it looked. Food slowly disappeared as they ate, talked and laughed. Afterwards, they carried their plates to the kitchen and loaded the big dishwasher.

"I'll do that," Galen offered, but everyone continued to load their own utensils.

Adam slipped away and when Dix went to look for him, he spotted him smoking in the alley out back. "I didn't know he smoked," he murmured.

Galen answered, "Sami does, too, when she's with him. They go out back and puff away. It's a filthy habit."

Dix glanced at him. "Is that so?" The information surprised him. He'd never smelled smoke on her.

Galen had turned his back again so Dix returned to the front of the bar, mulling the smoking over.

Kayla stepped in front of him. "Well, Detective Dixon, I wasn't so sure about Daddy seeing a cop, but you're okay. You seem like a stand-up guy, and I like the way my father looks at you. Just don't break his heart."

He smiled. "I'll try not to."

Sami moved between them and patted his chest. "We're not worried. You've got the same expression on your face when you look at Daddy. I think you've both got it for each other, bad. Besides, it might come in handy to have a cop in the family. Someone to fix my parking tickets."

"Are you kidding?" Dix blinked. "I'd throw you in jail first. Don't think I wouldn't do it."

Adam bobbed his head. "I believe you."

They all chuckled.

The sound of shattering glass outside was followed by the blaring of a car alarm.

"What the—?" Dix raced for the door. Outside, he cringed when he saw the back window of his Navigator had been smashed. The lights were flashing and the horn honking. Reaching for keys in his pocket, he pressed a button and quieted the noise.

"What the fuck?" Bryan surveyed the damage. "Who would do this?"

Adam muttered, "Well, shit."

Dix looked up and saw him standing next to his Ram truck with a similar broken window. "Your truck, damn."

"Yes. Fuck! I only have liability insurance."

"This is awful." Bryan shook his head. "I'm going to run out back and make sure our cars are okay." He looked at his daughters huddled on the sidewalk. "You two, stay here."

They nodded.

Dix called for a patrol officer to come file a report.

When Bryan returned he said, "Our three cars in the alley are fine."

Dix glanced at Adam. "You came in through the back with Sami. Why did you park out here?"

"There were no more spaces in back. There's only room for four cars to keep the alley open for deliveries. I parked here and walked around to meet her."

"So the family's cars are fine." Dix recalled the cook's comment. "Is Galen still here?"

"No." Bryan shook his head. "He left once he started the dishwasher. You don't think he had anything to do with this?"

Dix frowned. "Just wondering if his car was okay." *That wasn't what I was wondering at all.*

The police car arrived and two officers took their statements. An hour later, Dix, Bryan and the others had the glass swept up from the street, and out of the backs of the vehicles as best they could.

"I'm sorry about this." Bryan sighed.

"It's not your fault." Dix looked at Adam. "I'll call a glass guy in the morning and see when he can take care of both of us. Don't worry about the cost."

"Thank you so much." Adam appeared relieved.

Bryan frowned. "This happened at my place, I'll take care of it." He waved a hand toward Dix. "Just get them fixed and give me the bills."

Dix raised his brows. Suddenly, there was tension in the room.

Sami gave her dad a hug. "Thanks, Daddy." She hugged Dix next. "Thank you, too. I was just kidding about the parking tickets, you know. But if anything worse ever happened, I know you'd have my back, right?"

He gazed at her for a moment. "Of course." *What a strange thing to say.* "You okay?"

"Yeah. Just tired. We're going now. See you all later."

"Good night." He glanced at Adam. "I'll call you tomorrow."

"Thanks." Adam slipped an arm around Sami. "I'll walk you to your car and you can drop me off back here."

"Yep." They started to leave.

"Hang on," Kayla called. "I'll walk with you." She hugged her father and waved shyly to Dix. "Night. Thanks for dinner, Daddy."

Bryan nodded, strangely quiet.

"Night," Dix offered and watched them go. "Well, that was quite an evening."

"Started out so well, too." Bryan sighed.

Dix tucked two fingers through Bryan's front belt loops. "I'm the one whose car is fucked up. Why are you in such a bad mood?"

He scowled. "This kind of shit is bad for business. I'm fully aware your car is 'fucked up'. I hate like hell that it happened."

"Take it easy." Dix drew their hips together. "It's just a car. It can be fixed. Why don't we get out of here and see if your mood can be improved."

"I'm still pissed," Bryan muttered.

Dix pressed their lips together in an insistent kiss. His lover finally relented and opened his mouth, just enough for Dix to slide his tongue in. The kiss quickly deepened and both men groaned. "We need to go home and get out of these clothes," Dix suggested.

"Let's go. I'll lock the front door behind you and meet you at the house."

Dix patted his ass on the way out of the door, and smiled. Bryan still didn't look happy. He hoped he could change that once they got in bed.

The ride home was breezy with no back window, but at least the weather was clear, and he didn't have to worry about rain. In Bryan's driveway, he removed everything of value that he could, since the car wasn't able to be locked. He entered through the garage and set his stuff on the kitchen counter. A thought niggled at him, and he had to get it off his chest. "I was thinking about something."

"Does it involve a can of whipped cream and some chocolate sauce in the bedroom? Because that's what I was thinking about."

Dix grinned. "No, but I could definitely be persuaded to go there. I just have to ask you about

Galen. He made a comment to me before dinner, and it's bothering me."

"What kind of comment?"

"I saw he'd fixed a plate and was eating alone in the kitchen. I invited him to join us. I said something about it just being family. He gave me a funny look and replied that it wasn't *just* family, now was it? I didn't think much about it until later, when the only two cars damaged belonged to the 'not quite family'."

"That's ridiculous! You *do* think Galen was behind this. Why didn't you tell the other cops then?"

"I don't have anything to go on. You know how my mind works. I'm just running different scenarios through it."

"With my cousin as the villain."

"I never said that. I was just trying to be nice to the guy, and he couldn't have been more the opposite to me."

"I told you he has PTSD. He likes his privacy."

"He could have just said 'no thank you'."

Bryan stomped around the room. "I wish everyone would back off and leave Galen alone. Yeah, he has issues, but he's family. His father and mine were very close brothers. I promised my dad I'd watch out for Galen. It was hard after what Howard did, but I kept my promise and intend to keep doing so."

"What Howard did? Howard is Galen's son, right?"

Bryan sighed. "Yeah. He's a little older than the girls, close to thirty now. A few years ago, when Sami was still a teenager, sixteen I think, we caught Howard taking pictures of her. When his mom started snooping around, she found a scrapbook full of photos. All of Sami, at different ages. We kept it of course. My wife wanted to call the police, but I talked her out of it. Nothing had really happened, he'd just been watching her. It was creepy, but it was over. We all moved on."

"Which explains why the girls think Howard is weird. Strange, Kayla seems to dislike him more than Sami."

"Kay was older and understood the creepiness factor, I guess. Sami kind of shrugged it off. She's my easy-going one."

"I'm not so sure you should have let it go the way you did. Stalking leads to worse crimes when you have an unbalanced mind."

Bryan frowned. "You don't know anything about my cousin or his family, so I'd appreciate you not calling them 'unbalanced'." He headed toward the back of the house. "I'm tired. I think I'll just go to bed."

"You want me to leave?" Dix called.

Bryan paused but didn't turn around. "No," he finally said, "of course not."

Dix smiled and went after him.

* * * *

In the middle of the night, he woke to find Bryan lying on his side, staring at him. "Hey." Dix rubbed his face.

"I'm sorry."

"For what?"

"For getting pissy and going to bed without making love first."

Dix smiled. "It's fine. Despite what you might think from my behavior the past week, I honestly don't *need* sex three or four times a day. It's been great, but I knew it couldn't last forever."

"It should last longer than a week. The bloom isn't off the rose quite yet. I guess I'm just sensitive where my cousin is concerned. You see, Galen was smaller than the other kids in school. He used to get picked on all the time. My brother and I tried to watch out for him. We weren't always successful, but we did what we could."

"I'm sure he appreciated you."

"Maybe. Not always. It was harder in high school. We played football, Galen was a nerd who read a lot. We weren't there for him as much as we should have been. But we did try. My uncle and my dad were happy after graduation when Galen enlisted, they figured it'd be good for him. Not sure it worked out the way everyone hoped."

"You're a very good cousin, still watching out for him."

Bryan shrugged. "Both our fathers are gone, and my brother lives in St. Louis. There's only me and my family, now. I feel the need to do what I can."

"You're a good man, Bryan Scott. I knew that from the day I met you."

He moved closer. "I feel the same way about you. I just need to learn how to show it. I haven't opened up to anyone in a long time, so I'm out of practice. But I want to let you in, rather than push you away. Does that make sense?"

"Of course it does." Dix wrapped his arms around him and they kissed. Both had gone to bed in T-shirts and boxers, so it only took a moment to shed the clothing. He reached between them and clasped both their erections in his left hand.

Bryan groaned, thrusting into grasp.

Lips pressed together, Dix mumbled, "This is going to be short and sweet. Morning's going to come much too early."

"Nothing short about you, big guy," Bryan murmured back. "Stroke it, yeah, that's it. Stroke it good."

Dix tugged their shafts in unison, the friction and pressure almost more than he could bear for long. "You feel so fucking perfect in my arms. At times like this I never want to let you go."

"Then don't." Bryan drove back into the kiss, tongue probing as deep as possible. His hand covered Dix's thrusting one, squeezing balls and rubbing lightly.

"Fuck yeah," Dix groaned. "I'm close."

"Right there with you, babe. Come on." He placed his hand over Dix's and they pumped together then exploded in one burst. Warm, sticky cum covered their hands and torsos. It was several minutes before either of them slowed their thrusts, and eventually they lay quietly together.

"Thank you," Bryan whispered in the dark. "If I tell you I love you, will you say it's too soon and I'm crazy to feel this way about a man I barely know?"

Dix's heart soared. "Yeah. And then I'll tell you I love you, too. If we're crazy, we'll be that way together. Because I'm happy right here and I never want to leave your arms."

Bryan kissed him again. "How about I slip away just long enough to grab a warm washcloth and clean us up? Then I'll be right back."

Sated and full of joy, Dix smiled. "Works for me."

* * * *

Dix reached a mobile glass guy the next morning, and both his and Adam's vehicles were repaired before noon. He gladly paid for the quick work, and didn't plan to say anything about the bill to Bryan. It wasn't his lover's fault. Merely thinking of the sexy stud had Dix smiling. He did that so often these days, he could have sworn his jaw was sore from the unusual activity. *Of course it could be all the blow jobs.* Either way, he was a happy man.

When his phone rang at one-thirty, he was pleased to hear Bryan's voice on the line. "Hey handsome. I've been thinking about you. 'Course, that's nothing new."

"James, Sami didn't show up for work today. I've been trying to call her, but it goes straight to voicemail."

"Is that unusual for her?"

"Well, yeah. She always calls when something comes up. She knows we only schedule one waitress during the noon shift. I've been so busy, this is the first chance I've had to call."

"Have you phoned Adam? He might know where she is."

"No, you were the first person I thought to call."

"That makes me happy, but in this case, I think Adam might know more than me. I've talked to him a couple times already today. We got both cars fixed first thing this morning."

"Wow, that was fast!"

"Yeah, he seemed to do good work, too. I'm pleased. Anyway, I'll call the kid and get back to you. Don't worry, I'm sure she's fine."

"Thanks, Dix."

"You bet. Talk soon." He ended the call and punched up Adam's number. "Hey, me again. Three times in one day, people are going to start thinking we're best friends."

Adam chuckled. "After the miracle you pulled off with getting my window fixed so fast, I'll happily call myself your friend. What's up?"

"Bryan just phoned, he said Sami didn't show up for work today. Any idea where she is?"

"What? You're kidding me. She never misses work. I don't have a delivery for them today, so I haven't seen her since this morning."

"You saw her before work, though, and she was okay?"

"Sure. I left about seven-thirty, same as usual. She was still in bed since there's no school. Did he try to call her?"

"Went straight to voicemail."

"Hmm. I'm not too far from there. Let me finish this delivery and I'll swing by."

"Thanks, Adam. Oh, and call me back, okay? Bryan's busy today and me...not so much."

"That's a good thing, right? Will do. Bye." He hung up.

Dix put down the phone, wondering what could have caused Sami to miss work. He didn't know enough about her daily routine to speculate. He stood and stretched, then walked to the coffee pot to pour himself a cup.

Back at his desk, he pushed papers around, trying to keep his mind occupied. About thirty minutes had gone by when his phone rang back, and he recognized Adam's number. "Dixon."

"Dix, it's Adam." The words tumbled out in a rush. "Something's wrong. Sami's car is here, but she's not."

"Okay, slow down. Could someone have picked her up? A girlfriend, someone like that? Maybe they went out for lunch."

"Without her purse and phone?" His voice screeched. "And her favorite pair of shoes is still by the door."

Dix forced himself to remain calm, refusing to let his thoughts get carried away. "She's a woman. Surely she has more than one pair of shoes."

"Of course she does, she has like twenty. But only one she wears daily, and she kicks them off by the door when she gets home. She carries the one purse, and never goes anywhere without her phone." His breathing became jagged. "That's not the only thing. The apartment is messed up, like maybe there were signs of a struggle. I don't know. I'm hyperventilating. I can't think."

"Take it easy, Adam. Give me the address, and I'll be right there."

"Three fifty-five Jacobs, apartment three. Main floor on the right."

"Okay, listen. I'm on my way. Don't touch anything more than you already have. Find a place to sit and catch your breath. I'll be there in ten minutes."

"Thanks."

Dix ended the call and stood, pocketing his cell phone. He grabbed his suit coat and went to Mac's desk. Once again, he forced himself to remain calm. "I need to go take care of something."

"What is it? You look like you just saw a ghost."

"Nah, it's just—well, you know Sami, Bryan's daughter? She didn't show up for work today. Her boyfriend says their apartment looks trashed, like there might have been a struggle. Her car and phone are still there, but she's nowhere in sight."

Mac stood. "Sami, the pretty little thing with the long blonde ponytail?"

Dix froze. His gaze locked with Mac's and both of them turned to the large evidence board across the room. Four other women with long blonde hair stared back at them with vacant eyes. Those women were all dead. "Oh, my God." Dix thought he might hyperventilate, too.

"Come on." Mac shoved him toward the door. "I'll drive."

Chapter Six

"I need to call Bryan." Dix fumbled for his phone as Mac drove to Sami's address.

"You need to hold up. Let us have a look around, see if we need to call the unis before we go off half-cocked. Hell, she might be home by the time we get there."

"I hope so." Thoughts of Bryan's daughters flitted through his mind. Kayla was nice, but calm and reserved. Sami had spunk and personality to spare. She reminded him of what his own daughter might have been like, had she lived. A tear formed in the corner of his eye and he brushed it away.

Mac glanced at him sideways. "She's not Julie, Dix. I know you've become attached to the kid, but don't let things get out of control in your mind. She's not your daughter."

"I know that," he snapped, then took a breath. When he spoke again his voice was calm. "But she's sweet and affectionate and, God help me, she's starting to feel like one."

"I know that, too," Mac said softly. He pulled into the parking lot of the apartment complex.

Dix spotted the beer truck taking up several spaces on the end. They climbed out and he led the way. "Apartment three, on the right," he said.

"Right behind you."

Dix pulled gloves from his pocket and slipped them on. He nudged open the door to number three and peered in. "Adam?"

He appeared in the doorway. "Thank God you're here. I've been frantic, imagining all kinds of awful things."

They stepped in cautiously, looking around. "You haven't thought of any place she could be? Anyone you could call?"

"I phoned her friend Trina, but she's at work and hasn't seen Sami for about a week. I couldn't think of anyone else. She has lots of friends from school, but most of them are gone this week."

"Yeah." Dix went in farther. The apartment was small but tidy, until they reached the bedroom. Sheets and a comforter were strewn across, hanging halfway onto the floor.

"Purse and phone here." Mac pointed to the dresser. He slipped on some latex gloves and picked up the phone. "Last call out was yesterday, to her dad. Ten missed calls today, from him and the boyfriend. No unknown numbers."

Using two fingers, Dix gently lifted the covers off the bed and peered under them. "Well, shit." He tossed them back part way. "Blood."

A small spot, the size of a jagged quarter. He looked at Adam. "You notice if that was there before?"

"It wasn't. She just did laundry yesterday, including the sheets. I heard all about it last night."

Dix smiled. "Look at everything I do for you?"

"Yeah, sort of. 'It's my vacation and I spent the whole damn day doing laundry.'"

Nodding, Dix glanced at Mac. "We need to get CSI over here. A couple unis to canvass the neighbors."

"I'll do that. The call you have to make won't be so easy."

He nodded and they went into separate rooms. Dialing Bryan's cell, he rehearsed his words before the call connected.

"Yeah, Dix? Anything?"

"Bryan, Mac and I are at Sami's place with Adam. Her car is here, but she's not. We've also got her phone and purse. And a certain pair of shoes Adam says is all she wears these days."

"Oh, my God, Oh, my God." Bryan gasped. "Where is she, Dix? What does this mean? Why doesn't Adam know where she is? Does he know she got home last night?"

"Buddy, listen. She was fine this morning when he left for work. There's probably a logical explanation for this, and we're going to laugh about it after we scold her up one side and down the other."

"I'm coming over."

"No! Look, you won't be allowed in until the techs have processed the scene. Don't waste your time."

"Why did you call techs? What do you mean, 'scene'?"

"Sweetie, I need you to calm down. It looks like there might have been a struggle here. We'll know more once the CSI unit arrives."

"Oh, my God!" Bryan's voice was frantic.

"I'm going to stay here and work the case. You need to sit tight, and I'll call as soon as we know anything. Bryan, I mean it. I will call you. Don't come here."

"Is she dead, Dix? Is that why you don't want me there?"

His gut roiled. Memories of the phone call he'd placed to his wife after Julie had died rushed through him. He handed the phone to Adam, who'd been listening to his end of the call. "He thinks she's dead, and her body's here."

Adam grabbed the cell. "Oh, no, sir! Sami was fine the last time I saw her. She's just not here now. The blood spot is tiny, really. I don't know if she's on her period or not, we didn't, um…last night."

Dix held his head until the wave of nausea left him. *Perhaps it wasn't the smartest idea to hand the phone over.*

"Okay, yes. We'll call you. I will. Bye." He ended the call and glanced at Dix. "You all right?"

"I think so. Thanks."

"He's calmed down a little. He believed us. I can't understand what's going on, though. This is not like Sami."

Dix pocketed his phone and glanced up as uniformed officers arrived. "You're going to have to tell your story again. Just do it until they're satisfied, then you might want to think about getting that beer truck back to the warehouse. The neighbors might not like you taking up so many spaces in the lot."

"Yeah, right."

A female officer entered the bedroom. "Dixon, what's homicide doing here? Somebody jump the gun? I didn't think we had a body, yet."

He scowled. "Anderson, I'm here because I'm a friend of the missing girl. This is her boyfriend. We don't have a body, and we pray to God there won't be one." He brushed past her and murmured, "Some tact would be appreciated."

"Sorry." Anderson seemed genuinely embarrassed.

Dix didn't care, he just needed to get out for a few minutes. "I'm going to look around the block," he told Mac as he walked by.

"CSI is on the way. Ten minutes, tops."

"Thanks." Dix kept walking. If he was going to be sick, he wanted to be outside, far away from everybody. He'd never thrown up at a crime scene, not in his early days, or even covering the grisliest murder. But the thought of Sami Scott being referred to as 'the body' was the most sickening thing he'd heard in a very long time. He was very close to losing it.

* * * *

Shortly after five, he texted Bryan.

No news. I'll be there soon. Mac dropping me off.

A minute later came the reply.

ok.

"You sure you don't want to go get your car?" his partner asked.

"Nah, it's better off at the station than here. Bryan can take me later. Thanks."

"Sure. Sorry we don't have any news for him. On the bright side, this doesn't fit the MO of our case, so it's probably not related."

"Yeah." Dix could only hope, but he wasn't at all convinced. "See you tomorrow."

"I'll fill the captain in. See you."

He exited the car in front of Last Chance and hurried inside. There were no customers, which was probably a good thing, as Bryan made a beeline for his arms.

"God, I've just been beside myself." He hugged Dix tight.

"I know. I'm sorry. There just wasn't anything to report." He inhaled the scent of Bryan's hair and hugged back with all his strength.

"What are we going to do, Dix? I mean, what's the next step? How far out are the police canvassing?"

"Let's sit down." They chose the two closest chairs. "The problem we've got is that with adults, they usually need to be missing at least twenty-four hours before police can do anything. Because I got involved, we started the process earlier."

"I don't understand. My daughter is missing. The cops need to *do something*."

"She's not a minor, and adults sometimes go off by themselves. Nothing against the law there. And yes, her bedroom was messed up. But not *really* bad, like no broken lamps or anything."

"So there has to be a murder before anyone will take it seriously?"

"I didn't say that. We're taking it very seriously. There just isn't much we can do, yet. First thing in the morning we'll put out an APB—an All Points Bulletin. That'll alert other law enforcement to be on the lookout for her."

Bryan frowned. "I want them to be looking for her *now*. Not tomorrow morning."

"I understand. I do, too. But you'd be surprised how much money these things cost, and how many times the person turns up the next morning. Drunk, hung over, whatever, but all completely unaware anyone was looking for them. I've put out some feelers, Bryan, so local precincts are aware we're looking for her. But officially, it has to wait until tomorrow."

"So back to my original question. What are we supposed to do now? I can't just go home and pretend like nothing's happened."

"I don't know, babe. Have you spoken with Kayla? Maybe she heard from her."

"Yes, and no she hasn't. She's at work, but she'll leave if we need her to."

"No reason right now. I'm afraid we're going to have to give it some time."

"This sucks. I mean it really sucks." He stood and paced. "This whole day has been awful. We were busy at lunch with no waitress or cook. I finally got a hold of Mike and he came in to cook for me. Luckily, the rest of the day's been quiet."

Dix stared at him. "Why no cook?"

"Galen called in sick."

He stood and went to Bryan. "And you didn't think that was worth mentioning?"

"Why would I?" He studied Dix's face for a moment then shook his head. "Oh, no. Don't start this shit again. Galen sounded like hell when he called, coughing and hacking."

Dix couldn't believe his ears. He tried to remind himself that Bryan was a trusting man, and not jaded by years of police work. But it was hard to keep calm. "Let's you and me take a run over to Galen's house right now. We'll just stop in to see how he's feeling."

"No! That's absurd."

"Really? Your daughter is missing. I wouldn't think any lead would be too crazy to follow up."

"Well, this one is. But okay, whatever. Just to shut you up, let's go. I'll close the place and send Mike home." He locked the front door and turned the 'Open' sign to 'Closed'.

Dix hated to piss him off, but he didn't see Galen through the same rose-colored glasses Bryan obviously did. It wasn't even Galen that worried him as much as Howard, the son with the fetish for Sami from years ago. People didn't always get over stuff like that. Sometimes, it festered.

Bryan sent Mike home and turned off the kitchen lights. He locked the back door and they climbed into his car. "Galen lives close to here. This won't take long. Maybe when we're done we could go wait at Sami's. I still don't feel like going home."

"We'll see." Dix wasn't as convinced that they'd be 'done' so soon.

Galen and his wife lived in a rundown house in an older neighborhood. There were no lights on at all. Dead plants in flowerboxes lined the walks. "Guess Rae hasn't planted anything yet this season," Bryan mused as they approached the front door.

"Place looks pretty rundown." Dix peered in a window.

"Yeah, well, he doesn't make a fortune." He rang the bell and when no one answered, knocked loudly.

"Strange. If he was so sick, shouldn't he be home in bed? Or at least on the sofa watching TV?"

"Yeah, yeah." Bryan pulled out his cell and dialed a number.

Dix could hear it go to voicemail. "Do you have his wife's number?"

"Yes." Bryan punched a few more buttons.

"Put her on speaker, will you?"

Bryan did. When a woman answered he said, "Rae? It's Bryan. How are you?"

"Hello, Bryan. I'm doing well. Mother is better, too. She should be released from the hospital in a few days. It's been a long battle."

"I'm sorry. I didn't know she was in the hospital. Doesn't she live in Atlanta?"

"Yes. Good grief, I assumed Galen would have told you. I've been here for three weeks, now."

"Three weeks? Really." Bryan glanced at Dix.

Dix was doing mental math. The first murder had occurred about three weeks earlier.

"Rae, Galen called in sick today. I stopped by the house to make sure he was all right, but he's not here. Have you spoken with him?"

"Not since yesterday. He sounded fine then. What's wrong? I hate to think of his being sick."

"Just a cold and cough, I think. I'm sure it's nothing. I was just worried about him is all."

"You're such a good friend to him, Bryan. Thanks for checking up. You might call Howard, maybe he went to his house for a while. Do you have his number?"

"No, could you give it to me please?"

Dix pulled a pen and paper from his pocket and wrote down the number she gave.

"Can you remind me of Howard's address, please? I know it's over in Raytown somewhere."

"Yes." She told him the address and Dix jotted it down.

"Thanks, Rae. Good to talk to you. Give your mother a hug from me."

"I will. Good night, Bryan."

He ended the call and stared at Dix. "I'm getting a funny feeling about this."

"Welcome to the club. Let's get over there before Mom calls Howard and lets him know we're coming."

"She wouldn't do that."

Dix gazed at him skeptically.

"Okay, how the hell do I know what anyone would do anymore? Let's go."

He drove quickly to the small, even dingier house than the parents lived in. "I don't see Galen's car. He drives a silver Mercury. About twenty years old."

Dix followed Bryan to the front porch. Once again Bryan rang the front bell, then knocked.

A pudgy man with a badly receding hairline and fringes of light brown hair around his ears answered the door.

"Hey, Howard. How's it going?" Bryan glanced over the man's shoulder nervously.

"Hey, Bryan. It's okay. I'm in the middle of a *Star Trek* marathon, actually."

"Cool. This is my friend James. We were looking for your father, heard he was feeling sick. Have you seen him?"

"Nope. Haven't talked to him." Howard fidgeted from one foot to the other.

"Can we come in for a minute?" Dix asked, pushing his way forward.

"Um, I was just getting ready to eat dinner. And like I said, I'm watching movies right now. The *Wrath of Khan* is on. It's almost to my favorite part."

Dix pressed Howard lightly in the chest to back him up. "Go ahead and pause it, if you like. We might be a few minutes." He stepped inside and glanced around.

"Hey, what are you doing?"

"Looking for your dad," Bryan followed Dix in. "I talked with your mom. She thought he might be here."

"No, I told you I haven't seen him." He glanced back and forth between the men, unable to watch both of them at once.

The house smelled like cheese and something sour Dix didn't want to identify. It was messy, but something on the coffee table caught his eye. Sticking out from under the edge of a video game magazine, he spotted a photo and got a glimpse of blonde hair. He grabbed the picture and discovered it was a shot of Sami. *A recent shot.* "What's this, Howard?"

"Hey, you can't go through my stuff!" Howard grabbed for the photo, but Dix pulled it back.

"I wasn't going through anything, it was lying right out there in the open." He picked up the magazines and found four more photos of Sami and other blonde women. He scrutinized them carefully, but none were photos of their murder victims. "What do we have here?"

"Those are none of your business!" Howard dove for him.

Dix sidestepped and the heavier man tripped and landed on the sofa. While Howard was still down, Dix turned to Bryan and offered the photos.

Bryan's face reddened. "Son of a bitch! Where is she, you little bastard?" He took three giant steps and was over Howard, grabbing him by the collar.

"What? Who?"

"You know who! Where's my daughter?" Bryan balled up a fist and drew back.

Dix grabbed his arm and stopped him. "Bryan, no. This isn't the way. Let me take him to the station and interrogate him there."

Fury blazed in Bryan's eyes. It took a moment before he relaxed and dropped his arm. "Okay. But we need to check this place to make sure she's not here."

"You're right." Dix reached behind him and pulled out handcuffs. "Sit up, Howard. I'm cuffing you for your own protection. He won't clobber you if you're restrained."

"Why do you have those? Who are you?" Howard blubbered.

"Oh, sorry." Dix showed his badge. "I'm a detective with the KCPD. And you're going in for questioning on the disappearance of Sami Scott." He worked Howard's hands behind him and cuffed them together.

Howard shot scathing looks but didn't say another word.

Dix looked at him. *That speaks volumes.* He recalled Adam jabbering the whole time about how innocent he was. *Innocent people are scared. Guilty people are wily, and tend to clam up.*

"Keep an eye on him," Dix said to Bryan. "I'll call for a patrol car and search the house."

"I want to search the house too!" Bryan's frustration was showing.

"Then go through the police academy and get a badge. Until then, you're my lookout."

"Whatever." Resigned, Bryan folded his arms and stared at Howard.

Dix made his calls then moved warily though the house in case they weren't alone. There were no signs of other people, no basement and no more evidence at first inspection.

The patrol car arrived and Dix turned Howard over to the officers. Peyton and his partner Laura Evans showed up, and he left them to continue searching the premises. He hated to call Mac after hours unless something truly broke open. Then he wouldn't hesitate.

They watched the patrol car leave and he told Bryan, "Take me to the station so I can question him, please? My car is there so you can just drop me off." They got in.

Bryan spoke as he drove. "Where the hell am I supposed to go? What do you think I'm going to do?"

"I'm sorry, babe. There's just no reason for you to be at the station. I can't let you witness the interrogation. You'd have to hang out in the waiting area. I figured you'd rather go be with Adam or Kayla."

"I don't want to be with anyone but you. You're going to find Sami. I need to stay with you."

"I'm going to try." He reached over and squeezed Bryan's knee.

Bryan glanced in his rear-view mirror and changed lanes. "It's times like this when I wish I still smoked."

Dix chuckled. "I know the feeling. I quit when I joined the force at twenty-one. How about you?"

Bryan smiled. "When Kayla was born. At twenty-one."

Dix eyed him affectionately. *We have so much in common.* He recalled something from the night before and said, "Did you know Sami smokes?"

"No!" Bryan almost drove off the road. "Why do you think she does?"

"Galen mentioned it last night. Adam slipped outside for a cigarette after dinner. I casually mentioned that I didn't know he smoked. Galen said Sami does, too. She goes out to smoke with Adam when he makes his deliveries."

"Well I'll be. That's news to me."

"Not sure it's relevant, but curious. I never smelled smoke on her."

"Me either. That's why I wonder if she really does, or if he was just stirring the pot."

Dix raised his brows. "So you agree maybe Galen wasn't being the nicest guy last night?"

Bryan sighed. "Yeah, I do. I didn't want to see it then. Now, it keeps jumping out at me. I wish I could figure out what the hell is going on."

"Give me some time." Dix squeezed his knee again. "We're working on it."

* * * *

He left Bryan in the waiting area and went to the hallway outside the interrogation room.

Alvarez was there, studying Howard through the window. "You like this guy for the murders?" The captain cut straight to the chase.

"Not sure. Right now we've got a missing girl with blonde hair and a ponytail. Howard Scott is Samantha's cousin once or twice removed, not sure about that. Anyway, a few years ago, Howard had a thing for Sami. Their parents found a scrapbook he made full of her photos. She was a minor at that time. She's twenty-one now, and while the family thought his obsession was over, we're not so sure it is." He pulled the photos from his pocket. "These were found on Howard's coffee table. I don't know the other women, but this is Sami Scott."

The captain handled the photos by the edges and dropped them into plastic evidence bags. "Peyton just checked in. He found more pictures of blonde haired women on Howard's computer. Some of them pretty nasty, and some of them not fully grown women. Glad we got that search warrant."

Dix frowned. "Ugh. So he's a pedophile, we know that much. Our serial killer goes for adults. We'll have to keep digging to make this fit."

"Talk to him. See what he knows. He's sweating pretty good already. Might not take much to scare him."

Dix loosened his tie and glanced over his shoulder as he headed for the room. "He's pissed to begin with. We had to pull him away from a *Star Trek* marathon."

"Which movie?"

"*The Wrath of Khan.*"

"I'd be pissed too. That was the best one."

"*The Voyage Home* was pretty good."

"With the whales?" Alvarez smiled.

"Yeah." Dix chuckled. He took a breath then went in. The small talk gave him a chance to clear his head before interrogating a suspect. It was tricky business, and he needed to be sharp. He closed the door and sat. "Hello, Howard."

"What am I doing here? I've done nothing wrong."

"If you tell us where Samantha Scott is, we can see about getting you out of here."

"I don't know where she is. I haven't seen her in forever." He looked around the small room. "I'm hungry."

Dix ignored the comment. "The picture on your coffee table was pretty recent. Did you take that one, or did someone else?"

Howard set his jaw.

"It was a good shot. She wasn't wearing a coat so it had to be within the past couple weeks, since it warmed up. Where was she at, Howard? Did you follow her on campus, or to work maybe?"

"I didn't follow her anywhere."

"Who did? Who's the photographer? I might want to use him to get some pictures taken."

Howard stared at him.

Dix slapped his hands on the table between them. "Okay, then, if you don't want to talk, I'm going to get out of here. It's getting late, and I'm ready for dinner. Think I'll have a nice, juicy steak and a baked potato. I wonder what's on the menu in jail tonight?" He checked his watch. "Oops, you've missed dinner. You might get a snack, some graham crackers and juice. Breakfast comes at eight."

"Jail? Why would I go to jail? I haven't done anything! I told you, I haven't seen Sami."

"Yeah, you told me, but I'm not sure I believe you. *You had her pictures.* You also had photos of a lot of other women—and girls—on your computer. Some of them weren't very nice. *Or legal.* Child pornography is against the law, Howard." He stood and leaned down to the man. "Don't worry, though. You'll get along fine in jail as long as no one knows you're in there for kiddie porn. Funny, the worst criminals, the most murderous biker thugs and gang members, for some reason they don't like guys who prey on children. They'll rough you up pretty bad when they find out what you're there for."

"I didn't do anything! That stuff doesn't belong to me! I swear it."

Dix slapped the table again. "It's on your computer! Who would you let keep shit like that on *your* computer?" It dawned on him at that moment, and he saw in Howard's eyes that they both knew. "Oh, my God. Those pictures belong to your father, don't they?"

Howard set his jaw again. "I'm not saying another word."

"Your dad couldn't keep stuff like that at home because your mother would find it. So he used your computer, and your house, to look at his filth. Was he the one who took the pictures? The scrapbook of Sami from five years ago—was that your father's, Howard?"

His face fell. "He made me take the blame. I didn't want to do it. Everyone looked at me funny. Everyone except Sami. It was almost like she knew I didn't do it."

Dix studied him, taking it all in. Sami hadn't been too hard on Howard the night before. Perhaps somehow she did know. "So your father made you take the blame back then. Tell me, Howard. What do you think would have happened if Sami's mother had called the police like she wanted to? Do you think your dad would have spoken up, or would he have continued to allow you to take the punishment that was rightfully his?"

Tears formed in the man's eyes.

"Yeah, pretty much what I thought. And what about now? Is your father here to bail you out? Or do you think he's going to allow you to take the heat this time, too?"

"I can't go to jail," Howard blubbered, tears falling freely now. "I'd never survive."

"It'd be hell, that's for damn sure. You'd be someone different's bitch every night. I hope you're up for that, Howard."

Something flashed in the man's eyes. "My father has a thing for Sami. He has for years. He was trying to get her out of his system by dating other women that kinda look like her, but it didn't work. He wanted her worse than ever."

"*Dating other women?* Is that what he calls raping and murdering them?"

Howard's jaw slacked open. "He did that?"

"We think so." Dix heard a knock at the door and went to open it.

Alvarez met him. "We got a DNA match from the Howard's house to the fourth vic, Stephanie Marcus. A hair. A greasy black hair."

Dix blinked. Howard's hair, what was left of it, was short and light brown. "Galen."

Alvarez nodded.

"Fuck me," Dix muttered. It felt good to have a match. It felt lousy that the match belonged to Bryan's cousin. He sighed and returned to Howard.

"Well, buddy, we just matched some DNA evidence to a strand of hair found in your house. A black hair."

Howard's eyes widened.

"We know it wasn't you, Howard. Your father's the man we're after. Tell us where he is, and we might be able to get you out of here tonight."

"To jail?"

"No, home. If you're telling the truth, and all the evidence belongs to your dad, we can probably let you go. But you have to help us. Where is he?"

Howard chewed his lip nervously.

"I think you know where he might be. He's not at home, and he's not at your place. Where would he go? Where would he take Sami if he had her?"

"If I tell you, you won't find a way to spin it and send me to jail, will you?"

"Not if you had no part in the crimes. If you were part of them, then all deals are off."

"I had no part of any of it! I swear to you, I didn't know he was killing anyone. He told me he was dating them."

Dix frowned. "He's a married man. You thought that was normal behavior?"

Howard shrugged. "He's my dad. I figured he knew what he was doing."

"Yeah, I can see that. So do you have an idea where he might be?"

"Yes." Howard nodded slowly. "We have a hunting cabin out by the lake."

Dix's heart leaped. "Of course you do. You think he might be there?"

He nodded again.

"Does Bryan know where this cabin is?"

"He's been there plenty of times. He should."

"Thank you, Howard!" Dix raced from the room.

"Can I get some Burger King?" Howard called after him.

Alvarez was already talking to Bryan. He told Dix, "Let him drive, so you can text Mac and me with the coordinates. When you get there, wait for us. I mean this with every fiber of my being. If you so much as set foot in that cabin, Scott, I'll have you arrested for obstructing justice and everything else I can think of."

"I hear you." Bryan grinned, and they headed for the door.

Dix called back over his shoulder, "Have someone get Howard some Burger King, will you? I'd say he's earned it."

The drive to the cabin took twenty-five minutes. Dix texted Mac and Alvarez the location and Mac replied they were about ten minutes behind with a squad of SWAT team members and police.

Bryan pulled off the road by the long driveway and turned off the car.

They crept toward the cabin. "Lights are on," Dix observed.

"I'm going to kill the son of a bitch. I took care of him, I championed him, gave him a job and every courtesy my family had to offer. If he's harmed one hair on my daughter's head, I will fucking kill him."

Dix grabbed Bryan around the waist. "No, you will not. We have orders to wait for backup. *I have to* follow orders."

"You may have to, but I don't. That's my daughter in there, Dix. I can't sit here and twiddle my thumbs."

"You *can,* or I'll handcuff you to that tree over there. I'm as worried about Sami as you are, babe. She's very important to me. But I won't lose you. If you go in there and do something stupid, you'll go to prison. I'm not going to let that happen. I love you, remember?"

Bryan tensed and paced. "I know, damn it. I just don't know what's going to happen if I find out he's — hurt her. I might lose it, Dix. I really might."

"Then we're staying right here. I won't take the chance of losing you. Mac and the captain will be here any minute." He wrapped his arms around Bryan and they held each other until the crackling noise on the drive indicated the others had arrived. When SWAT team members began creeping forward, Dix handed Bryan off to one of them. "This is the girl's father. He needs to stay back. Far back."

"Roger, sir." The agent took Bryan by the arm and led him away.

Bryan locked gazed with Dix. "Love you," he mouthed.

Dix nodded and put on the bullet-proof vest that Mac handed him. "Seen anything?"

"Nope. I've been busy trying to keep Bryan from killing the ass-wipe."

"I pray to God she's okay," Mac muttered, securing his vest.

"I've been doing a lot of that myself. I just hope we're not too late. It'd kill me to know we've been out here waiting when we should have gone in."

Alvarez, Peyton and Evans moved in behind them. "You had orders not to go in without backup," the captain said. "You did the right thing, Dix. Now let's go. SWAT team is in place."

They surrounded the cabin with Dix and Mac on either side of the front door. Dix counted and nodded. "Three, two, one. Now!" He battered the door and it cracked and broke open. "KCPD! Freeze!"

Sami, clothing torn, was tied to a straight back chair. Her face was bruised and she looked like she'd been beaten. But she was alive.

Galen stood in front of them, a .38 Special gun in his hand.

"Drop it, Galen," Dix ordered. "We've got you surrounded. We've got your DNA. This is over."

He didn't speak, just slowly raised his weapon.

"Death by cop," Mac whispered.

"I said *drop it!*" Dix yelled. He saw what his partner did. A suspect who couldn't escape often made a threatening move so the police had no choice but to shoot him. He *did not* want to be the one to shoot Bryan's cousin. "Galen, don't be fucking stupid. This is over."

Dix saw resignation in the man's eyes. "Yeah, it is." He lowered his arm then just as quickly, raised it again and shot himself through the mouth. Blood sprayed out the back of his head and his body slumped to the ground.

Sami screamed.

Dix and Mac winced. "Damn it," Mac swore, moving to kick the gun away from the suspect, just in case.

Dix grimaced. Mac needn't have bothered. He hurried to Sami's side, knelt and began untying her. "Hey, princess. Good to see you. Just so you know, this would be a great time to hit your dad up for a new car or something. He's right outside. Think big."

She grinned through her tears, and when her hands were free, she flew into his arms. "I knew you'd find me. I kept telling myself that, the whole time he was..."

Dix groaned. "God, baby, I'm sorry. I'm so sorry this happened to you."

"I'll be okay." She nodded, wiping her filthy face. "Galen was whacked out, though. Honestly, I think he figured it would end this way. I don't see how it could have gone in any other direction, given the things he did." She looked in Dix's eyes. "He *told me* about all of it, in detail."

A shiver ran down his spine. "I'm sorry. That had to be terrible." They'd need to get Sami some therapy when all was said and done.

"Did he tell you why?" Mac asked over Dix's shoulder.

"Something about my dad having everything, and him having nothing. I didn't understand all of it. He was drinking pretty heavily, and taking some kind of pills."

"Never a good mix." Dix shook his head. "Stupid son of a bitch. Your dad did everything he could to help him."

Mac said, "Some people just need to blame others for the shitty way their lives turned out."

Dix accepted a blanket from someone behind him. He helped Sami stand and wrapped the blanket around her. He nearly wept when he spotted the burn mark on the upper edge of her cleavage. "Damn it, no."

She smiled sadly. "Cured me of the smoking habit. I'll never touch another cigarette." She glanced at the pack on the table next to her.

Dix looked down. Camel Non-Filters. "Sick bastard." He put an arm around her. "Can you walk?"

"Yeah. I just want to go home."

"Sorry, babe. You've earned a trip to the hospital first. I expect they'll want to keep you overnight. Then we're going to have a ton of questions for you. It won't be easy, and it doesn't have to be me. If you'd prefer to talk to a female detective, I'd understand."

She clutched his arm. "I'd rather talk to you. I trust you. For some reason, I have since we met."

Glancing at her, he cocked his head. "Did you have a premonition that something might happen? What you said to me the other night...it was strange."

"I don't know. I felt something in my gut. I can't explain it."

"Maybe you oughta be a cop."

"Nah. I'll leave that to you. You're the best."

He smiled. "Thanks, kid. And just so you know, while anything you tell me is confidential, it might be tricky keeping things from your father. You see, I love him. And he loves me."

"I know. I could have told you that a week ago. And no, we won't be keeping anything from my dad." She tightened her grip. "Not from either of my dads. I want you both to know what happened, so you can help me get over it."

He kissed her temple. "That's a promise."

They walked out of the cabin and Dix saw Bryan standing back with some SWAT team agents. When he spotted them, relief flooded his face. He broke into a grin and began running.

Epilogue

The grand opening of *Buono Mangia* was a roaring success. It had taken nine months to pull it together, and Bryan lovingly compared it to birthing a baby. Once the Last Call Bar and Grille had sold, Dix had come up with the other half of the capital, and they'd found the perfect building in a bright, downtown location. Kayla had convinced the chef at La Maison to come work for them and continue training her. He was so much in love with her, he'd have done anything she asked. But what he'd *admitted to* was excitement at the new opportunity.

Sami had assumed the role of assistant manager under her father, who eventually hoped to retire and leave the place to his kids. Adam had taken to bartending with great aplomb, and they all agreed he was perfect for the job.

"Thank you, everyone." Bryan raised his glass of champagne in a toast. His family and close friends who surrounded him did the same. "You all know, this past year has been one of ups and downs for us.

There were some awful low points, but also some very bright spots." He smiled at Dix, standing next to him.

Dix raised his glass and nodded.

Bryan continued, "My family and I believe that *Buono Mangia*, or Good Eats, is the start of something exciting for all of us. We appreciate your being here to begin this journey with us. To all of you we wish — let's see if I can get this right. Excuse my Italian! *Vivi bene, ridi spesso, ama molto e mangia italiano.*"

Dix grinned. "That means live well, laugh often, love much and eat Italian."

Everyone cheered and drank their champagne.

Bryan took a sip, then slipped an arm around Dix and kissed his cheek. He whispered, "I intend to love you as much as I can, handsome. Well and often."

"You already do, stud. If it gets any better than this, I might collapse from exhaustion."

"Keep that in mind when we get home to the townhouse. I think a soak in the whirlpool might be in order."

They smiled at each other then separated when guests filtered up to speak with them.

"So…" Mac glanced around the place. "With a cushy berth like this, I can't see why you'd want to keep your day job."

Dix chuckled. "What would I be, the janitor? No thanks. I like my 'protect and serve' gig. I'll come here for dinner at night. And I hope you and Cecile will join me as often as possible."

"Count on it." Mac's wife gave Dix a hug. Her hair had finally grown in enough that she didn't need a wig. She had color in her pallor again, too.

Dix squeezed her hand. "You look great."

"I feel great. Better than I have in months. Tonight was just what I needed."

"Me too!" Abby Walters joined them. Her hand was tucked through the arm of a tall, dark-skinned man in a stylish suit. "Everyone, this is Dr Rylon Taylor, Chief of Emergency Medicine at County General." She introduced her friends.

"Pleasure to meet you." Dix shook his hand.

Bryan added, "We hope to see you around the restaurant often."

"Absolutely. It's just what this neighborhood needed. You're going to have a raving success on your hands."

Bryan raised his brows at Dix. "Hope we can live up to those kind words."

Dix waggled his brows in return. He had no doubts. His friends sauntered off and Rae Scott stepped forward.

"The place is very festive," she remarked.

"Rae! I'm so pleased you could make it." Bryan gave her a hug.

"You're very kind. I wanted to say goodbye. Howard and I have packed up the last of our things. We'll be leaving for Atlanta in the morning."

"I'm glad. A fresh start will be good for you both."

She looked around. "I hope this fresh start for is good for your family, too. And that Sami is doing okay."

"Sami's great. No worries. She still sees a therapist occasionally, but even he is amazed at how well she came through everything."

"Good." She tried to smile, but her sadness showed through. "I love the Christmas decorations. You fit right in with the Plaza."

"It's a nice time of year for the opening," Bryan agreed. "A month earlier wouldn't have hurt, but we're happy to be open a few days before Christmas at least." He squeezed Rae's hand before she turned to leave.

To Dix he said, "The Christmas decorations do look great. I'm actually looking forward to celebrating this year."

"It's going to be a great holiday." Dix felt it in his gut.

Bryan glanced at the door and said quietly, "Maybe greater than you realized."

"Hmm?" He glanced up to see a man in uniform walking their way. "Oh, my God. Jared?"

The Marine smiled. "Hello, Dad. It's good to see you." He glanced at Bryan. "Hello, Mr Scott." They shook hands.

"Please, call me Bryan."

Dix tried to keep his jaw closed as he looked at his lover. "You knew about this?"

Bryan shrugged. "We've talked a couple times. Jared was coming home for a visit anyway. He agreed the time was right."

His son faced him. "I've missed you, Dad. We have a lot to talk about. I have some apologies to make."

"Nah, you don't." Dix drew him into a hug. "It's just so good to see you again."

The hug was returned in full force. "It's good to see you, too. I love you, Dad."

"I love you too, son." Dix tried not to bawl like a baby, but one tear managed to escape. When he pulled back, he wiped it away quickly.

Bryan reached for his hand and squeezed.

"Oh, he's here!" Sami's squeal filled the room. She and Kayla descended on them and were hugging Jared before he ever knew what hit him. "We've always wanted a brother!"

Jared laughed as the girls held his arms.

Bryan grinned and pointed. "Kayla. Sami. Jared."

"We know!" Sami clung to his uniform sleeve.

"Take it easy," Bryan told her. "Don't overwhelm him."

"It's fine." Jared grinned. "It's been too long since I had a sister to torment. Really looking forward to it."

"Two of us. Double trouble," Kayla agreed.

Sami hugged Jared's shoulder. "This is so great!"

Dix slipped an arm around Bryan's waist. "Yeah, it is, isn't it?"

His lover grinned and winked.

PEYTON'S
PURSUIT

Dedication

To Cyndi, Paul, and Eddie, wherever you are.

Author's Note

While the Kansas City Police Department is definitely a real organization, the stories you will read in this series are complete works of fiction, with made-up characters who are in no way based on actual persons. Likewise, some neighborhoods and locations are similarly fictional. The stories are simply born from a love of Kansas City, from the stockyards to Arrowhead Stadium, the Plaza to Legends Outlet Mall, and lots of things in between.

Chapter One

"He's dead?" The distraught widow's eyes rolled back in her head as she crumpled to the floor.

Detective Nick Peyton scooped her up before she hit. Calling over his shoulder, "A little help here," he glanced around for the nearest chair.

A uniformed officer who appeared to be about twelve—and very green around the gills—joined him. "Is she okay?" He seemed flustered and unsure what to do.

"Here." Nick's partner Laura Evans positioned herself on the other side of the woman, helping him ease her onto the sofa in the spacious living room. She eyed the boy in blue. "She just found out her husband is dead, for Pete's sake. No, she's not okay. Get her a glass of water, please."

He stammered, "I—uh—I'm not supposed to touch anything until CSI gets here."

Nick turned to the young officer. "Very carefully open a cabinet, get a glass, and bring Mrs Wilson some water. If they find your prints when they dust, we'll vouch for you."

"Yes, sir." He hurried off.

Laura smirked. "What a noob." She tucked a strand of her long brown hair behind one ear.

"We were all new once." Nick shrugged. He remembered his first homicide case as a patrol officer. It wasn't something most cops forgot. He expected the kid would feel the same way, whether or not this was his first. Judging by his expression, it very well might be.

He returned with a glass of water, his face still a mask of concern.

"Thanks," Nick handed the drink to his partner and read the kid's name tag. "Jones. Good job. Go wait for CSI by the front door, will you?"

"Yes, sir." Obviously relieved to be dismissed, Jones hurried away.

"Mrs Wilson?" Laura patted the widow's cheek. "Have a sip of this." She held the glass to the woman's mouth.

A small drink, then she opened her eyes. She glanced around warily. "What happened?"

Nick moved in front of her. "It appears to be a home invasion, ma'am." He eyed the woman, fiftyish, matronly, with a shade of blonde hair that could only come from a bottle. *Terror-filled eyes.* He needed to tread lightly. "I know it's a rotten time, but I need to ask you a few questions."

She hesitated, then nodded.

"Your husband was home alone?"

"Yes. I was in Springfield with my mother. She just had surgery, so I spent a couple of nights."

He jotted notes on a small pad. "When's the last time you talked to him?"

"Last night, around nine o'clock." She sniffed. "How was he killed?"

Nick inhaled. *This part of the job is the worst.* "He was shot, Mrs Wilson."

Her eyes filled with tears. "Did he—suffer?"

He hesitated, then offered, "No, I'm sure he went quickly. He probably didn't feel a thing."

The woman's sniffles turned into choking sobs. "I think I'm going to be sick."

"Let me help you." Laura assisted the widow as she stood, and followed Mrs Wilson down the hall. She made a face over her shoulder at Nick.

He smiled and mouthed, "Thanks."

"Nice having a female partner," someone said from behind.

Nick turned to see the Medical Examiner, Abigail Walters. "Sometimes. Other times we butt heads, 'cause she can be a real pain in the ass."

"Like you can't?" Abby smirked.

Feigning shock, he placed a hand over his heart. "What? Me?"

"Yeah, yeah. Choirboy, I know your type. So where's Dixon today? I thought he'd catch this case."

"Dix took off for a couple days. His son's getting some kind of commendation from the Marine Corps, and he wanted to be there."

She nodded. "Nice."

He thought about her question, and furrowed his brow. "You don't think I can handle this? I realize Laura and I are the newest detectives in the homicide bureau, but both of us have years of experience on the force. We didn't get our badges out of Cracker Jack boxes, you know."

"I never thought you did." A smile flickered across her face. "But you just lied to that woman. How do you know her husband went quickly? Are you a doctor now?"

Jenna Byrnes

He glanced toward the hall and back at Abby. "What would you have had me tell her? 'Well, ma'am, your husband lay on the floor alone and gasping for hours before he finally died.'"

She bowed her head slightly. "Of course not. I'm just letting you know that I won't falsify the report. If my findings are different from what you just told her, she may read about it if she requests a copy."

He shrugged. "So sue me. I suspect she won't remember much of today when asked about it later. This whole event will be one long, bad nightmare."

"I'm sure you're right. And I probably would have told her the same thing. I'm done here. They'll be taking the victim's body soon. I'll have my report on your desk asap."

"Thanks, Abby." He watched the silver-haired ME walk away. She knew her job backwards and forwards, no doubt about that. And no one would *ever* question her integrity, or think that she might falsify a report. He knew enough to recognize that fact.

She and Dixon had worked many cases together— Nick knew they were friends. A senior homicide detective, Dix often took the lead in high profile cases. But he was away, and Nick was more than capable of handling this one. He was sure of it, and would prove it to anyone who might doubt him.

Laura returned holding Mrs Wilson by the arm. "Is there anyone we can call for you?" she asked.

"My sister lives here. I should call her."

"Have a seat." Laura got her settled. "Would you like me to phone her?"

"I can do it. I just don't know what to say. What am I supposed to do next?"

Nick stepped forward. "You might be more comfortable staying with her while the crime scene techs go through your home today. Tomorrow, we'd like to walk through with you and make a list of the property you know is missing. You'll need to give it some thought. The big stuff is obvious." He motioned to where a TV probably used to sit, atop an empty stand with nothing but cords and dust bunnies covering it now. "The little things will be harder to remember. Jewelry, electronic devices, that kind of stuff."

Mrs Wilson nodded blankly.

He could tell she was slipping into shock. The whole concept had to be totally overwhelming. He squatted next to her and touched her hand. "Call your sister. We'll wait here until she can pick you up. You don't need to do anything else right now."

She looked at him with sad gray eyes. "What about—? Do I need to call someone to take care of...Roger?"

He squeezed her hand. "Just let us know which funeral home you'd like to use. Once the Medical Examiner's office is through, they'll make the initial arrangements for you. The funeral director will call once he's got Roger, and set up an appointment with you."

Mrs Wilson's expression was more grateful this time. "Thank you. This is all too much to bear."

"I understand. One step at a time, that's all you have to manage. Call your sister now." Nick rose and walked to look out of the window.

"You're good with people," Laura commented from behind him, while Mrs Wilson placed her call.

He turned to look at her. "All part of life in the Homicide Department."

She smiled sheepishly. "Sometimes I think I'm better with the dead bodies, doing the digging, finding out the whys and the why nots. I don't always do so well with the ones left behind."

He grinned. "You do fine. That's what makes us such a good team."

"That, and the fact you don't date women. My last partner never knew where to draw the line. His conduct bordered on sexual harassment. I was always on edge with him. It's a relief not to feel that with you."

Nick cocked an eyebrow. "Even if we go after the same guy sometimes?"

She laughed softly. "Dibs on the straight ones."

* * * *

Back at the station, Nick pinned crime scene photos on a large evidence board. The few pictures barely filled a corner of the board. Some cases spread out across the entire blasted thing. He hoped they'd solve this one before it spread any further.

"What do we think?" His captain, Rick Alvarez, studied the photos. "Home invasion gone wrong?"

"Looks that way. Roger Wilson, age sixty, was home alone last night according to his wife, who was in Springfield taking care of her mother. Evidence bears that out. Roger got Chinese takeout and rented some DVDs."

"Anything kinky?"

Nick shook his head. "Action flicks, Rambo type stuff. Wilson owned a dry cleaning store. Nothing on his record suggests he wasn't totally above board."

"So why this man, this house? Do we know what the perps took?"

"Most obvious thing was a big TV. Wife was pretty distraught. We're going to meet her there tomorrow to walk through and establish a better list. Figured that'd give her time to compose herself, and give CSI a chance to finish with the house."

Alvarez nodded. "We'll want to touch base with the Property Crimes guys, this is bordering on their area."

Nick looked at him. "Until a man got killed. Now it's our case."

"Agreed, but they have more experience with the stolen goods end of things. Get a list and we'll start working it from that angle, pawn shops and such. Might not get us anywhere, but it's worth a shot. Until we have a better idea who wanted our dry cleaner dead."

"Yes, Captain." Nick kicked at a smudge on the floor and wandered back over to his desk.

He slapped one hand on the hard surface before dropping into his chair.

Laura glanced up from her desk, surprised. "What's bugging you?"

Nick tried to cover. "Dead body. Duh!" He waved his hands.

She shook her head. "This is the Homicide Department, man. Takes more than a dead body to shake us up. Spill it."

He frowned. "Alvarez wants us to get with the Property Crimes guys to work this case. I'd really rather not."

She scratched her chin. "Property Crimes? I know somebody over there, what's his name? Cameron, that's it. Don Cameron."

"Dean."

Laura raised her brows. "Dean Cameron, yeah. I guess you know him, too. He's pretty cute, if I recall."

He rolled his eyes but didn't meet her gaze.

"Oh, you call dibs on that one?"

"Not exactly. More like 'been there, done that'. Dating other cops is a *really bad idea*. Not sure how he'll take to seeing me."

"Did you break his heart or something?"

Nick rolled his eyes again.

"You did! You devil. Okay, I'll deal with Detective Hottie—er—Cameron. He shouldn't have a problem working with me."

"He *shouldn't* have a problem working with me, but I guess we'll see about that."

She waggled her eyebrows. "I guess we will."

* * * *

Nick found out how Dean Cameron was going to react about an hour later when the handsome blond detective showed up in Homicide.

"Hey." His blue eyes were still crystal clear. "Long time no see."

Nick tamped down a stirring in his gut. "Kinda figured that was the way you wanted it."

Dean lowered his voice. "Why would you think that? You were the one who ended it between us."

"Which is *almost* how I remember it, but not exactly." Nick recalled walking in on Dean and another man in bed. He'd been pissed off at the time but nowhere near heartbroken. They'd only been seeing each other a few weeks and he wasn't convinced it would have lasted much longer.

After a night of hard drinking, he'd gotten over Dean pretty quickly and had decided it was better to find out the guy's true colors sooner rather than later.

Dean smiled. "Maybe we can have a drink sometime and catch up."

"Yeah, maybe." Nick had no intentions of following through, but didn't admit it. He needed to make things easier, since it appeared they might be working together on this latest case. He broached the matter in an effort to change the subject. "Sounds like our recent homicide may have been a home invasion gone wrong."

"That's what we're thinking over in Property Crimes. Except for the murder, the MO on this case is the same as six recent home invasions."

"Six? You're fucking kidding me. Is that normal for you guys?"

The cop chuckled. "Eh, we try to nab 'em before they get this many under their belts. But yeah, sometimes we have multiples like this one. We actually have some info I'd like to share with you and your partner."

"We're going to walk through the house tomorrow with Mrs Wilson. Hopefully we can compile a list of what was taken. Could we get together after that?"

Dean frowned. "Tomorrow? Why wait?"

Nick folded his arms across his chest. "The woman just lost her husband. She's in no condition to do it today. We spoke with her and her sister. They're going to think about it tonight. She'll be better prepared to make the list tomorrow."

"I suppose." Dean's frown didn't waver. "I should be there. We have tips and techniques for helping people remember things they might not otherwise."

"Feel free to join them." He made a decision right there on the spot. "Evans is meeting Mrs Wilson at ten a.m."

Dean raised an eyebrow. "You're not going?"

Not now that I know you are. He shook his head. "She can handle it. But I'm sure your tips will be welcome."

Dean cast one more curious glance his way. "We should compare notes once we have the Wilsons' list. I have contacts at some of the local pawn shops, but there are several more we need to reach out to. We just don't have the manpower to get it all done."

"Evans and I can definitely help."

"Good, we can use you. We've got a lot of stolen property to track down."

Nick eyed him levelly. "And *we* have a homicide to solve. That's our first priority."

"Of course it is. You've got your job and I've got mine. Doesn't hurt to be up front about our priorities, but it seems we do have a common interest." He winked then turned to leave.

Nick wasn't sure he was still talking about the case. Dean appeared much too friendly for his liking. He hoped their history wasn't going to be an issue.

* * * *

Nick sighed. The Wilsons' walk-through had taken most of the morning and the Property Crimes briefing had used up the better part of the afternoon. He and Laura had a couple of hours left of the day, and he wanted to hit at least two of the pawn shops on the list Dean had given them.

"Cameron was good," Laura admitted on their drive to the first shop. "They have an extensive list of jewelry and items that crime victims might not think of. It was interesting to watch him work. I'd never given it much thought, but if someone robbed my place, how much would I be able to remember about what was taken?"

"Probably not everything. We don't think to take pictures, either."

"Yeah. Some of the stuff she came up with had been tucked away in drawers or her jewelry box, and she hadn't looked at it in ages."

"I don't know what's to stop people from making shit up. My house got robbed? Yeah, I had five Rolex watches and six pairs of diamond cufflinks."

"Cameron said the department doesn't worry about that too much. It's the insurance companies who really care about fraud—they're the ones who have to pay out. They go to great lengths to prove property existed. Generally, if people have nice things, they also have a photo or two of them, wearing the cufflinks at a wedding or whatever. That's what some of these pictures are." She leafed through the stack in her hands.

"I guess." He glanced at the sign on the building he'd just parked in front of. "Hewlett Pawn. This would be our first stop."

She studied the face of the store. "Nice little place. Looks clean and organized."

He gave her a look. "We'll see about that, won't we?"

Chuckling, Laura exited his silver Ford Explorer and fell into step beside him. "Know what you're going to say?"

"This ain't my first rodeo. Of course I do."

"Just askin'."

He smiled sideways at her and held the door open so she could enter first.

She nodded, and went ahead.

Nick glanced around the small shop. It was neat and well organized. They had nice stuff on the shelves. He suspected there might be junk somewhere, but he didn't spot it right off.

A man behind the counter acknowledged them. "Afternoon. Can I help you find anything in particular?"

Nick glanced at the clerk, and every coherent thought in his mind went dormant. About his height, the man had straight brown hair pulled into a ponytail, and sported a mustache and a close beard. He appeared muscular and fit in his tight black T-shirt. Nick could only see the waistband of his jeans from the opposite side of the counter. *Probably a good thing.* If the fit was anywhere as tight as the shirt, Nick would need the sheaf of papers Laura carried to cover his tented trousers.

"Can. I. Help. You?" the hunk repeated, an amused smile crossing his perfectly shaped lips.

Lips. Nick forced his mind not to go there. He could spend precious long moments imagining exactly how those lips would feel, and just how they might taste. For a brief moment he envisioned the gorgeous pink lips wrapped around his cock, giving him the blow job of his life. *The rough tickle of the mustache.* He shook his head to clear it, then pulled his badge out and flashed it. "Yeah. I'm Detective Peyton with KCPD Homicide. This is Detective Evans. We'd like to ask you a few questions."

The handsome man's smile faded. "Homicide? What the hell would you have to ask me about?"

Laura leaned against the counter. "Don't look so worried. If you don't have anything to hide, we'll get along just fine."

He scowled, his eyebrows furrowing. "I don't have anything to hide and I don't appreciate the inference. Now, what is it you wanted?"

"Let's start with your name."

"I suppose not telling you would imply that I had something to hide?"

"Pretty much." She gazed at him expectantly.

Nick wanted to kick himself. Her brash manner had gotten them off on a shaky start. But she wouldn't have said anything if he hadn't suddenly became all tongue-tied. *Tongue.* He pictured kissing the stud, their tongues batting together, each seeking dominance.

His erection perked up. *Damn it!* He needed to get his mind back to business, but the sexy beast before him wasn't going to make that easy. *He might not even be gay.* Nick tried to convince himself. *Most likely he has a gorgeous blonde wife and two cute little kids waiting at home for him. I'll bet he drives a minivan.* Nick cleared his throat. "I'm sorry — let me make our intentions clearer. We're investigating a burglary in which the home owner was shot and killed. I understand the Property Crimes division usually brings around lists of stolen goods and photos in an effort to track down the items."

The Greek-minivan-driving-god nodded. "Yeah, we've worked with them in the past. I knew there'd been a rash of thefts lately. I hadn't heard about the murder. I'm sorry. I'm Rob Hewlett. My brother and I own this place."

Nick found himself checking the man's left hand. *No ring.*

His scrutiny hadn't gone unnoticed. Rob followed his gaze and grinned.

Nick glanced away quickly. "Nice store. Your brother and you, huh?" He turned away to compose himself.

A group of framed photos on the back wall caught his eye. Nick wandered over to them and studied the pictures. Rob and a big, burly biker-type fellow, standing in front of a Harley-Davidson cycle. The man was completely bald but sported a full, bushy beard. Another photo of Rob and the biker showed them with two children, a boy and a girl who looked to be about ten years old. Nick swallowed. *There's the family.*

A third picture had him puzzled. Rob standing behind a smaller motorcycle with a different driver. This man appeared somewhat younger, with closely cropped blond hair and lots of tattoos on his exposed arms.

"My family," Rob confirmed, over Nick's shoulder.

"I figured. Cute kids."

"Oh, *those* aren't my family. I mean, they *are*— they're my niece and nephew." He pointed to the bald biker. "That's my brother Danny. Max and Celia are his kids. The picture's old, they're grown now."

No more photos. He said this was his family, yet he hadn't mentioned a wife or kids of his own. Nick's curiosity was piqued. "Who's the other biker?"

Rob chuckled. "Wannabe biker. That's Randy, my late ex."

Nick's heart leaped, but he tried to tamp down the excitement. He should *not* be happy, he needed to show sympathy. "I'm really sorry, man."

A slow grin spread across Rob's handsome face. "Why? He was late everywhere we went so I booted his ass out the door. That, and the fact that I caught him in the sack with one of our supposed 'best' friends. I heard the relationship between him and that louse didn't last, either. I'm not sure it ever works out when someone has an affair. If he cheated on me, why in the hell did the other guy think he wouldn't cheat on him?"

Nick was speechless, and for a moment all he could do was shrug. He finally muttered, "I know, right? Go figure." Thoughts and even naughtier thoughts were floating around in his head. He finally managed to get out the question that had been plaguing him. "If you kicked him out, why keep his picture on the wall?"

Another wicked grin. "It's a conversation starter. I mean, I suppose I could wear a rainbow pin or something that indicated I was gay, but I don't want to advertise it to just everybody."

A rush of desire flooded Nick, but he strained to keep it in check. "Yeah, me either. The police department is cool, and so are most of my co-workers. But it's not like I can add the label to my badge or anything."

Rob's eyes flashed and for a moment, he rubbed his chin thoughtfully. He finally smiled again, and this time it wasn't just wicked. It was downright *lustful.*

Nick thought he might come right there on the spot.

"Good to know." Rob allowed a slight nod. "But as interesting as that is, I guess it's not what you came to talk about. Did you have a list, or some pictures you wanted to show me?"

"Um, yeah. Sure." Their mutual love of men was exactly what Nick wanted to discuss, but he figured he'd better get busy and do his job. Laura had been nosing around the shop, and before long she'd be close enough to hear their conversation. She didn't need to hear *anything* he'd been thinking, and he couldn't promise some of the thoughts wouldn't slip out of his head and onto his tongue.

He turned to her. "Can we show him the photos, please?"

"Of course." She went to the front counter and spread them out.

Rob moved to stand beside her.

Nick bit back a groan. The store owner's ass looked as fine in well-worn jeans as he'd imagined it would. He stepped behind Rob, close enough to feel heat generating from his muscular torso. He actually did groan that time, but covered it with a cough.

Rob studied the photos. "I haven't seen any of this stuff yet, but it's early. Can you leave me copies of these pictures? I'll be on the lookout."

Laura scooped them up. "These are copies—you're welcome to keep them. Does your brother do any of the buying? Perhaps you should ask him, too."

"I'll do that. Jewelry is generally my area, but he can look at these just in case."

"Thanks." She nodded. "Sorry to come across so harsh. The first few days after a murder are critical. The trail grows colder with each day that passes."

"Of course. I understand." Rob smiled at her. "I'm sorry to give you a hard time. The cops we usually get in here are arrogant and unpleasant. I get a little tired of defending myself and my shop."

"As you should. Nobody has the right to give you a hard time for no reason. It's boorish and unprofessional."

"Absolutely," Nick chimed in. Laura was laying it on a bit thick. Maybe she was thinking the same thing that he was. *This guy is hot.*

Rob seemed amused. "Thank you both." He looked at Nick. "Do you have a card? In case any of this stuff shows up?"

Before his business card was out of his pocket, Laura waved hers in Rob's face.

"Here you go," she offered.

"Thanks again." Rob gazed at Nick, still amused.

Nick extended his own card. "Call any time." He motioned to the door and Laura headed out before him.

Rob took both cards and studied them. "I will."

Nick stood in the doorway after Laura had gone out. He wasn't sure what to say, but felt like he needed to add something. "I'll, uh, see you."

"I hope so." Rob's eyes flickered.

Nick saw appreciation there, and something more powerful. *Pure, unadulterated lust.* The same raw emotion he was feeling himself. The only emotion strong enough for him to lay his heart on the line with someone he didn't know. "I do, too. Like I said, call any time."

"What if I called tonight about nine p.m.?"

His heart raced. Headed into unfamiliar territory, he couldn't seem to rein himself in. "I'd probably have to answer that call. Maybe even meet you somewhere for a beer... For starters."

"For starters." Rob grinned. "I like that. I'll be in touch, Detective Peyton."

Nick nodded. "Mr Hewlett." He cast one last glance over the man's physique before stepping out.

Laura waited by his Explorer, seemingly lost in her own thoughts.

He couldn't believe she hadn't felt the heat between him and Rob. It was all he *could* feel.

She climbed into the passenger side and, as she fastened her seatbelt, remarked, "Man, he was good-looking. I wouldn't mind if he called, whether he had a lead or not."

Nick glanced over at her and smiled. "Dibs."

Chapter Two

Nick stopped at one more pawn shop before they called it a day. This one was owned by a seventy-year-old man who *loved* working with the police and tried to talk their ears off before they could politely excuse themselves.

Back at the station, Laura headed out, as did most of the other detectives. Nick purposely lagged behind, and when the place was mostly empty he did some research.

Robert James Hewlett, aged thirty-three, never married, owned a Silverado truck and a Chevy cargo van. A few minor violations spotted his record but nothing major, and nothing *at all* for the last ten years.

Just for the hell of it, Nick looked up his brother Danny. Daniel Patrick Hewlett, age thirty-seven, wasn't quite as clean-cut. Married twice, he'd also been arrested twice for domestic violence charges, both of which had been filed by his first wife. He owned a Harley-Davidson motorcycle and a Dodge Caravan *minivan.*

Nick laughed. Danny owned the minivan. *Man, did I get that wrong.* The bald biker was the minivan driver. Of course he'd needed some kind of transportation with two kids. He couldn't haul them around on a Harley when they were younger.

Nick hoped like hell the domestic violence stuff was merely a case of two personalities clashing. There didn't seem to be any issues on record with the second woman, but he still had to wonder.

He pushed the thoughts from his mind. *It's none of my business.* The thought niggled at him as he contemplated meeting Rob. If they *were* to get involved, would that make it his business? And what if he witnessed bad behavior by the brother? Would he be able to continue seeing Rob, or would family matters drive a wedge between them?

After shoving himself away from his desk, Nick rose and walked around the bullpen to clear his head. He paused in front of the evidence board and studied the photos tacked to it. *Roger Wilson's killer needs to be found.* Tomorrow, he'd put away all thoughts of Rob Hewlett and focus completely on solving this case. It'd be his number one priority. Tomorrow.

He glanced at the clock. There was time enough to grab a bite to eat, a quick shower and a change of clothes. Feeling his pockets for phone and keys, he sauntered out of the station, whistling.

* * * *

Nick's house was ten minutes from the station in a quiet, older neighborhood. It wasn't large, a three bedroom ranch, but it was plenty of room for him. At nine p.m. he was freshly showered and puttering around to hold his nerves at bay. He didn't know why he was picking up newspapers and straightening pillows, because he had no intentions of bringing Rob back here. He might be horny, but he wasn't stupid. Cops needed to be careful. He needed to take things slowly, and see how it went.

Five minutes later his gut churned and his mind raced, all at the same time. He felt like an idiot. Rob had probably been yanking his chain. He had no intentions of calling, which was probably for the best. Nick had worked the man up pretty highly in his mind. No one could live up to the picture he'd allowed his imagination to paint.

Just as he was talking himself down from the proverbial ledge, his phone rang. He jumped, and fumbled to answer it. "Peyton," he barked.

"Whoa! Still on duty? I figured you'd be taking it easy tonight." Rob sounded amused.

Nick took a breath and tried to calm himself. "Cops are always on edge—but no, I'm not officially on duty. What's going on?"

"I'm just checking to see if you're still up for that beer."

He tried to keep his tone nonchalant, even though he felt exactly the opposite on the inside. "Sure."

"There's a bar called Cubby's pretty close to my shop, have you heard of it?"

"I have. I don't usually frequent gay bars, so I can't say I've ever been there."

"It's nice. My friend owns the place. If you don't like it we can go someplace else. But one beer won't hurt, right?"

"Yeah, that's fine. It'll take me about ten to get there."

"Me too. See you soon." He disconnected the call.

Nick pressed the off button and pocketed his cell. He took a moment to check out his appearance in the bathroom mirror. His hair was short enough he didn't need to worry about it. He'd already shaved. Satisfied there wasn't much else he could do, he headed to the bar.

There were plenty of parking spaces out front. He spotted a dark Silverado truck and wondered if that was Rob's. He parked next to it and entered the dimly lit bar.

It was more crowded than the parking lot would have led him to believe. He made his way through a dozen or so couples and a few single men before reaching the bar. Rob sat on one of the stools, talking to a muscular blond bartender.

"Hey." He approached slowly.

Rob's face lit up. "There he is." He glanced at the hunk who was polishing glasses. "Didn't I tell you?"

"You sure did." The man smiled at Nick. "What can I get you, handsome?"

Nick cleared his throat. "Bud Light, bottle, please."

"Coming right up." He glanced at Rob. "And for you?"

"Same." He spun his stool around to face Nick and widened the stance of his knees. He looped a finger through two of Nick's belt loops. "You looked good in dress clothes but I knew you'd look damn fine in a tight pair of jeans, too."

Nick grinned, and allowed Rob to pull him between his thighs. "Is that right? Well, thanks. So, what did you tell the bartender?"

Rob tugged him so close that their crotches were almost touching. "Only that I had a date with the cutest guy in the bar tonight. He couldn't disagree."

Nick swooned. Any thoughts he had about taking things slow were ebbing away like the tide on a sandy beach.

Rob moved his hands to Nick's hips. "See, this is what I like about a gay bar. Nobody thinks twice if I do this..." He leaned in and placed a light kiss on Nick's mouth. When he pulled back, he smiled. "And if they do notice, the only thing they're thinking is 'lucky son of a bitch'."

Nick smiled. "About which one of us? 'Cause I think I might be the lucky son of a bitch." He kissed Rob back, their lips pressing tighter this time. He could feel the mustache but it didn't tickle like he'd imagined. It felt rough, along with Rob's closely cropped beard, and sexy as hell.

"Here you go, gents." The bartender set two napkins and bottles on the bar.

Nick took that as a cue to break it up, and worked his way onto the stool next to Rob. "Thanks."

"Yeah, thanks." Rob made a face behind the man's back, indicating he was less than thrilled to have been disrupted at that moment.

Nick felt the same way. He raised his bottle with one hand and placed the other on Rob's knee. "Let's drink these and get to know each other a little bit."

Rob lifted the other bottle to his lips. He swallowed the first drink, then smiled. "What don't you know about me? I'd have guessed you looked me up when you got back to the office. Robert James Hewlett, age thirty-three. I've never been married, although I came pretty close right out of high school. I had a cocker spaniel named Misty who used to think she was the boss of me. I drive a Silverado and I haven't had a ticket in over ten years. That's about it."

Nick grinned. "What happened to Misty?"

"Hit by a car. I'll never have another pet. That was gut-wrenching."

"Sorry. And why didn't you get married?"

"She admitted she wasn't pregnant, for one thing. I almost went through with it anyway, because I thought it was what my old man expected of me. But my mom stepped in and saved the day. She'd figured out I was gay, and told me I didn't have to marry Susan if I didn't love her. Once that was out in the open, the weight of the world was off my shoulders. I was the happiest dude on the planet."

"And what happened to Susan?"

Rob tossed back the last of his beer. "She married my brother. *Huge mistake*. They weren't right for each other, and they fought all the time. It got pretty nasty there at the end, calling the cops on each other and all that shit. They finally gave up and got a divorce. Best thing that could have happened. She moved away and we haven't heard from her since."

"Is she the kids' mother?"

"Oh hell no. Margaret was their mother. She was pretty cool at first, until she started drinking. She stuck around until the kids were grown and then she took off. It was the right move for everybody."

"That had to be hard on your brother and his children."

"Harder on the kids, I think. Danny wasn't happy there at the end, and it was a relief when she left."

"Hell of a thing. How did the kids turn out?"

"They're great. Max went to tech college—he's a mechanic. Celia's waitressing right now, but she's smart and she's got a good heart. Our mom's trying to convince her to go to college, so we'll see."

Nick had to grin at that. "Your mom, huh? She live around here?"

"Oh yeah. Made those two kids her life after Dad died. Helping out with them gave her a purpose. The kids love her to pieces. She's cool."

Nick polished off his beer. "What about you? Are they close to their Uncle Rob?"

"Absolutely." He held up two fingers to the bartender. "We're all busy. I don't see 'em that much these days. Weekends, special occasions. But our family is pretty tight."

"Nice." Nick nodded thanks to the bartender and picked up his fresh beer.

"So..." A grin slowly spread across Rob's face. "Does all that info jibe with what you looked up about me?"

"What makes you think I checked you out?" Nick tried to act innocent but he knew he failed miserably at it.

Rob chuckled. "Because I checked *you* out, and I'm not just referring to your tight ass. I Googled you. I'm sure cops are privy to much better stuff. Google barely gave me the basics. Although I did find out that you like to read, and have rated several books recently. Scandalous stuff like that."

"Wow, my secret's out. I live such a boring life that books are my best friends. There you go."

Rob knocked knees with him. "Nah, I like to read, too. I'm not sure I'd want to be with someone who didn't. Knowledge is power, they say. It's always good to keep an open mind."

"I agree. And thanks to the advent of the e-reader, my house isn't overrun by novels. I can keep them all in one tidy spot."

"Ah, but I still love the feeling of a book in my hands. We get boxes of them at the shop. They aren't worth much, money-wise, but they're a lot of fun. I do love digging through a box of old books."

Nick sipped his beer. "Sounds like a good time."

"Not the *best* time I can think of, but not bad. What do you say we head to the back? There's something I want to show you." He tossed some cash on the bar.

Nick reached for his wallet but Rob stopped him. "I've got this. Come on." He made his way through the tables to a back hallway, and finally an office. Rob entered and held the door open.

Stepping in, Nick spotted a desk, an old computer, and some other furniture including a ratty-looking plaid sofa.

Rob closed the door and clicked the lock.

Nick gazed at him for a moment, in time to see Rob reach for him and press his back to the door.

They came together in a passionate kiss, tongues batting as Nick had imagined they would. He groaned when Rob's mouth left his, licking and sucking a wet trail to his earlobe, then his neck. The scrape of his beard was agonizingly sexy. "Oh, God."

"Nope, just me." Rob massaged his chest and started to unfasten shirt buttons.

Nick reached for his hand. "Here? Really?"

"What?" Rob glanced around. "It's private. Stan doesn't work nights, so he lets his closest friends use the office occasionally."

Nick had to laugh. "That's disgusting, don't you think? I wonder what CSI would find if they used the infrared light on that couch?"

"I wasn't going to get *on* the sofa. I was actually thinking of getting on my knees, and seeing if I could make you squirm."

"Oh, I'm sure you could. But not here. Let's go someplace. I'll spring for a motel room."

Rob cupped Nick's crotch and squeezed. "You sure? I could make you real happy, right here and now."

He leaned forward to capture the man's lips in another wet kiss. "I know you could, but it just seems like we might want more time together. I was envisioning a nice, hard fuck. And I'd rather not do that leaning against this door."

"Mmm…" Rob nipped his neck again. "You like top or bottom, or does it matter?"

"Both are equally fine. I've got a condom in my wallet but no lube, which is another reason to get out of here."

"Okay, you convinced me. But we don't need a motel. My apartment is close, and there won't be any unknown DNA on the sofa—or the bed." He looked to the ceiling and scratched his head. "Damn, I can't remember the last time there was even anybody in that bed besides me."

"Good. I'm glad." Nick traced his tongue around Rob's ear. "I haven't been with anyone for a long time, either. I'm clean, by the way. I get tested regularly."

"I knew that." Rob grinned as he cupped Nick's jean-clad ass.

"How'd you know that?" Nick challenged, grinning.

"Read it on Google." Rob gazed into his eyes. "Nah, I just thought you would be. I can't always tell by looking, but somehow I figured that about you. Just like I hope you know it about me, too. And I hope you understand I don't usually do this kind of thing. It's honestly pretty crazy for me. But there's something about you—I can't explain it. Let's just say I wanted this about two minutes after you came into my shop today. Before I even found out you were gay."

"Damn, me too." Nick kissed him, thrusting his tongue deep. They locked lips for precious long moments before he finally drew back. "And no, I don't usually do this kind of thing. It's especially crazy for a cop who knows better. For some dumb fucking reason I trust you, Rob. Please tell me that's not as nutty as it sounds."

Their gazes met. "Not nutty, not crazy. We want each other, we're two clean horny men. Enough said. Let's get the hell out of here, you can follow me to my place. I've got rubbers and all the lube we'll need."

Nick grinned. "I'm right behind you."

Rob turned toward the door and glanced back over his shoulder. "Right where I want you."

* * * *

Nick liked the looks of Rob's small apartment complex. It was in a good area, well-lit, and the common areas were clean. He tried to turn off his detective senses but couldn't quite manage to, until they got inside and he surveyed the place.

Rob unlocked the door and motioned him in. "This is it. Nothing fancy, but it's all I need right now."

"It's nice," Nick answered truthfully. Sharply decorated in shades of black, white and red, the apartment was really quite a showplace. "You do the decorating yourself?"

"Yeah." Rob shrugged. "It's what gay men do, isn't it?"

"Not me, or not so much, I should say. My house is okay, but nowhere near this stylish."

"I'm sure I'll like it. I already know I like you. I'd like you better out of those clothes. Can you manage or would you like some help?"

"Point me toward the bedroom and I'll manage just fine."

"Right this way." Rob led him down the hall. "John to the left, spare room to the right. This is my room." He entered through the last door.

Nick poked his head in the rooms as they passed. Everything seemed neat and pleasant, nothing amiss. He needed to let his guard down and relax.

The bedroom was decorated in a south-western motif with shades of blues and browns. "This is great, Rob. You have quite an eye."

Rob had shucked his clothing the minute they entered the room. "What do you think of the rest of me?" He stood in front of Nick, totally naked, his thick cock bobbing between them.

Nick dragged his gaze from the luscious dick and checked out the rest of the hunk. His muscular chest and arms were covered by a thin layer of light brown hair. Some type of tattoo on the left biceps—*I'll have to look closer, later*—and a fine line of hair trailing down his stomach to all points south. He nearly drooled. "Well, that's a stupid question. I definitely like what I see." Nick dropped to his knees, anxious to get a taste of the man's smooth shaft.

"Oh, no fair. That's what I had in mind."

"Sorry. Me first." He blew on the bulbous head and the cock bounced. Without much fanfare, Nick drew the tip into his mouth and worked his tongue over the slit.

"Christ. Oh, Lord Jesus. I either need to lie down, or you need to back me up to the wall."

Nick grinned. "You can lie down. Get comfortable. I'll do the same." He watched as Rob tossed the covers back and prepared the bed. Nick removed his clothes and when Rob lay down, he grabbed both muscular legs and positioned him where he wanted.

He crawled between them and drew Rob's balls into his mouth. When they were thoroughly wet he released them and returned his attention to the gorgeous shaft. "God, you're amazing. I could stare at this monster for hours."

Rob wiggled his legs. "Please don't, that'd be torture."

Chuckling, he began licking from base to tip until he'd laved every inch. He nipped, suckled and teased until Rob moaned beneath him. Two hands found his head and urged him to go deeper.

Nick obliged and deep-throated until the tip touched the back of his throat. He worked into a steady rhythm, picking up speed according to the body bucking beneath him.

"Fuck, if you keep this up I'm gonna come," Rob muttered through gritted teeth.

"Mmm-hmm," Nick encouraged. *That's the desired outcome, my friend.*

"Not being a very good host. Just making sure that's all right with you."

"Mmm-hmm," Nick repeated with a deeper, more sultry inflection.

"Aw, fuck!" Rob shouted at the same time his cock erupted with thick, warm cream.

Nick swallowed and sucked as best he could to keep up with Rob's gyrations. When the bucking stopped, he slowed his mouth and teased the tiny slit with his tongue as he pulled away.

"Oh my God." Rob reached for him and drew their bodies together, face to face. "Thank you. That was...indescribable."

Nick smiled. "I think we'll find words to describe it, much later, when we're remembering our first time together." He kissed Rob tentatively, unsure if the man wanted a deep kiss after a blow job.

He needn't have worried.

Rob opened his mouth to the caress, and they sucked each other's tongues for what seemed like an eternity. Finally, Rob drew back for a breath and murmured, "First time's not through yet. Rubbers and lube in the drawer right there. Tell me how you want me."

"Stay right where you are." Nick retrieved the supplies and returned to his spot. He pressed Rob's knees up and open. "I like this position so I can see your face."

"And play with my junk."

"That too." Nick squirted some lube into his palm. He eased one slick finger into Rob's anus and watched the expression on his face as he worked it from side to side. "You like?"

"I *love*. More, please."

"Slut," Nick teased, and inserted a second digit. "Damn, you're nice and tight. My cock is gonna love it in there."

Rob's eyes were glazed. "Let's just test the fit, shall we? I'm as horny as the devil."

"Fuck yeah." Nick removed the fingers and greased up his sheathed shaft. That alone nearly caused him to shoot. Seeing the expression on his lover's face added to the intense pleasure. "You ready? Because I sure as hell am."

"Do it," Rob grunted as his ass was invaded. His face tightened then visibly relaxed when Nick was fully seated. "God, yes. Love it. Fuck me. Fuck me now!"

Nick kept one eye on his cock as he pulled back to the edge. He didn't want to come all the way out, but got as close as he could before slamming back in.

Rob jumped, and the rhythm began. Fucking, dancing, blissful joining of two bodies as their skin slapped together making delicious, wet sounds.

Nick held his breath, trying not to come too soon but it finally got the best of him. When Rob's cock twitched back to life and leaked pre-cum, Nick let go. He shattered and did all he could to remain upright as his seed filled the latex and warmed Rob's ass.

"Yeah, baby," Rob encouraged. "Come on. That's good. So good." He massaged Nick's thighs and everywhere he could reach, and when Nick had to lie down, he pulled him into his arms.

"Perfect." Rob kissed his eyelids and face.

Nick gazed at him. "It was, wasn't it?"

"Fucking A. I'm so glad you didn't let us do this at the bar. Being here was so much better. And the best part is, you don't have to leave if you don't want to. In fact, I'm hoping you'll stay."

Nick grimaced. "Sorry, I have to go." His cock plopped free and he grabbed the used condom. Kneeling up, he grinned. "But I'll be right back."

"Praise Jesus!" Rob shouted at the ceiling.

Chuckling, Nick went for a washcloth.

Once they'd cleaned up and were lying in each other's arms, Nick ran the back of one finger over Rob's chin. "This is gonna sound stupid, but I've never kissed a guy with a beard before."

Rob's hand reflexively went to his face. "Is it too rough? I could—"

Nick pressed a finger to his lips. "It's hot as hell. Don't change a thing. You'll have to forgive me if I seem fixated, though. I can't seem to get enough of kissing you."

The lusty, sexy grin he'd seen earlier returned to Rob's face. The handsome hunk rolled on top of him, using one knee to widen his legs. Seductively grinding Nick's groin, Rob pressed a whisper-light kiss to his lips. "No apology necessary. I haven't gotten nearly enough of you, either. I'm afraid it's going to take longer than one night to quench this desire."

Nick reached behind him and tugged at the ponytail holder. "Do you mind?"

"Go ahead."

He released Rob's hair and it fell around his shoulders. "Fuck, yeah," Nick groaned. "I've never seen anyone so hot in my life."

Rob captured Nick's upper lip and nibbled it lightly. "I'd suggest you have your eyes checked, but I'm enjoying myself too much. So I'll let you continue your fantasy."

"In that case...since we're talking fantasies..." Nick paused.

"Name it." Rob gazed into his eyes.

At that moment, Nick realized he could ask the man anything, and he'd probably get what he wanted. The thought sent a thrill and a shiver down his spine. "On your knees."

Rob grinned. "I like where this is headed already." He backed off the bed and knelt.

Nick scooted to the edge and let his legs hang off. "Thinking about those lips wrapped around my cock nearly had me coming this afternoon."

"Hot damn, I'm up for that. I offered earlier, remember?"

"I remember. There was just too much I wanted to do, all at once. But now, the more I think about it, the harder I get."

"Then lean back and watch, stud. I don't know everything, but I know my way around a thick, juicy cock like yours."

Nick dragged the pillows behind his head so he could see as well as feel the pleasure and torment Rob inflicted. Warm breath teased his sensitive shaft, a hint of exciting things to come. Experienced lips drew the head between them and the man's hot mouth suckled him. *Pure joy.* Rob definitely knew his way around a cock. Nick's slit leaked pre-cum after a few short minutes.

The fuzzy feel of Rob's facial hair added to the appeal. Nick gasped when Rob drew him in, nearly swallowing the length of his shaft, then released. Followed by long, languorous licks from base to tip, the occasional rub of his scruffy beard sent Nick to the edge.

"Aw, fuck," he muttered.

"I'll be doing that next." Rob nuzzled his face in Nick's ball sac. "But first, I want all you have to give me. *Need* all you have to give. Come for me, babe. Shoot your wad straight down my throat." He swallowed the head and resumed the potent sucking that would do the trick.

Nick wove his hands through Rob's long hair and fisted handfuls. Pulling ever so gently against the motion of Rob's bobbing head, he closed his eyes. He didn't need to see any more. He could picture the rest of the glorious act in his mind.

He shouted as he came, reveling in the most intense orgasm he'd experienced in...forever. When he'd finally stopped shuddering and his seed was spent, he untangled his hands from Rob's hair and smoothed it gently. "I hope I didn't hurt you."

Wiping the cum from his chin, Rob smiled as he stood. He motioned to his fully erect cock. "Does this look like I'm hurting? Hurts so good, baby. You're gonna have to take care of me, now."

Nick sighed with delight. "Anything."

"Roll over, on your hands and knees. I plan to lube up your sweet ass and fuck you till you scream again."

Drained, but up for one more coupling, Nick flipped onto his belly. He dragged his body up and watched as Rob sheathed his own erection and stroked it with lubricant. "I didn't scream," he muttered jovially.

Moving behind him, Rob grasped Nick's butt cheeks and spread them. "You screamed like a little girl touching a horny toad. And if I do my job right, you'll be screaming again here soon. Open up, big boy. I'm coming in."

Nick felt one finger ream his ass. Initial pain was quickly replaced by intense pleasure, and the immediate need for more. *More fingers, more fullness, more, more, more.* He buried his face in the pillow and held his breath. When the single finger was finally joined by another, he sighed with relief. "More," he said out loud.

"You called *me* a slut." Rob chuckled. "You're my whore, aren't you? You want my monster cock in your ass? Ask for it."

"Please." Nick gasped for air as the words rushed out. "I'm asking—no, I'm begging. And I don't beg for much."

All fingers left his rectum, and nothing replaced them for precious long moments.

"Please," Nick repeated, in sweet agony.

"Tell me what you want."

"Fuck me!" The request was more of a demand. Nick clutched the sheets in anticipation.

Rob nudged his cockhead at Nick's anus, then quickly thrust forward.

"Yess," Nick hissed, feeling the burn. "More."

He held tight as their bodies slammed together. The shaft impaled him in the most delightful way. For a moment when Rob drew back, he feared the luscious cock was leaving altogether, but he needn't have worried.

Rob drove deep quickly, again and again. The pleasure-pain combination was exactly what he'd begged for and Nick thought he might black out from the intensity of it all. Rob had a tight grasp on his hips so there was no worry of falling. He let his lover set the pace and when he could tell the act was almost complete, he felt Rob's hand curl around his own shaft.

Nick couldn't believe he was hard again, but Rob held the proof. And as his lover came, he coaxed another orgasm from Nick's swollen cock. Creamy spunk coated them and the sheets and it felt so heavenly, Nick didn't care when he eventually dropped and lay in it. He'd never been so incredibly, thoroughly used, abused and adored all at the same time. He could die a happy man. If Rob didn't get off and give him some air, he just might. "Um, babe?"

"I know. I just don't want to leave. That was *a-fucking-mazing*."

"I thought so, too. You're not going to kick me out, are you? Because I'm not sure I could walk right now. I'd like to sleep here, even if I am lying in the wet spot."

"I'm definitely not kicking you out. I'm going to get rid of this rubber and clean us up, then find a towel for that wet spot. Then I'm going to hold you in my arms all night long. And maybe, if we set the alarm for early enough, we can do this again in the morning."

Nick smiled. *Nothing could sound better.*

Chapter Three

Nick studied the evidence board the next morning. Two photos of chamber shell casings had been added.

"Abby Walters is going to brief us on her findings." Captain Alvarez tacked up a third picture, much the same as the first two.

"I've got something." Laura joined them. "Eyewitness spotted a white Chevy van leaving the Wilsons' house that night. The kind with no windows in the back — what do they call those?"

"A cargo van," Nick said absently, trying to remember where he'd heard about one of those recently. His head was fuzzy and he felt guilty about it. Lack of sleep didn't put him at his best.

Recalling the reason he hadn't slept caused him to bite back a smile. Given the opportunity to do it over again, he wouldn't change a thing.

He and Rob had made love until the early hours before catching some sleep. He'd woken to another earth-shattering blow job. Returning the favor had nearly made him late for work. Both of them had left the apartment in extremely good moods. He'd run by his place, changed then hurried to the station.

"Yeah, a cargo van." Laura's words drew him back to the present. "It was too dark to read the plates, but we got three numbers and the make, and that's something. I'm running the model through the DMV database as we speak."

Alvarez's expression was grim. "It is something—but I've run listings of vans before. I suspect you'll find several thousand in the metro area. It'll take forever to whittle the list down, even with three numbers."

"Hopefully what I have will help." Abby joined them. "A partial fingerprint on one of the shell casings. Ten millimeter ammo but I can't tell the type of gun. Could be a Colt, Glock, Nighthawk Custom—any one of several semi-automatic weapons."

"I thought you couldn't get prints off casings," Laura said. "Something to do with the heat?"

"Our new equipment allows us to pull images from spent casings. They're only partials, and they won't hold up in court by themselves. But with other evidence to support them, judges have ruled them admissible."

"Excellent." Nick took the sheaf of papers from the ME. "I'll get to work on the print. Nice job, Abby."

His cell rang and Nick glanced at the screen. He didn't recognize the number. "Peyton."

"Good morning." Rob's voice was as smooth as melted caramel. "I was just sitting here thinking about you. More specifically—you, naked, in my bed tonight."

Nick cleared his throat so his voice didn't squeak. "Yes. I believe that could be arranged."

Rob chuckled. "Can't talk? Then I better not mention what else I was thinking. Namely, some slippery shower sex and a game of Drop the Soap."

Nick closed his eyes and willed his face not to turn beet red. "I'll, uh, need to get back to you about that. But it should work."

Another sultry laugh. "I'm sure we can make it work, no problem. But I really did call about business. I think I have a necklace you're looking for. It matches one of the photos, anyway."

"No way!" Nick couldn't believe they had a hit so quickly.

"It looks like it. You might have to haul your handsome ass over here and decide for yourself."

He cleared his throat again. "Yes, *my partner and I* will be right there. If you'll be able to meet with us." He hoped Rob understood his meaning. He wouldn't be coming alone. Rob needed to keep things above board.

Rob's voice oozed sexuality. "Yeah, I hear you, stud. I'll be cool. See you soon." He ended the call.

Nick's cock twitched but he didn't have time to dwell on it. Three possible breaks in the case. They had work to do. He relayed the relevant portion of the call to the captain, his partner and the ME.

Alvarez nodded. "Good news. I think you should take Cameron, though. Let Evans stay here and run the print."

Cameron. Nick sighed. "Sure, I'll call him." He glanced at Laura. "Okay with you?"

"You bet." She reached for the paperwork and he passed it over.

"Happy hunting," Abby called over her shoulder as she left.

"Let's get these guys," Alvarez encouraged.

Nick raised his eyebrows in agreement and pulled out his cell to phone Cameron. He arranged to pick him up outside his office in ten minutes.

On his way, he thought briefly about calling Rob to make sure his sexy new friend behaved himself. Nick dismissed the idea. Rob was a grown man, and he knew there was a time for business and a time for pleasure.

'Pleasure' and 'Rob' in the same sentence brought up all kinds of images.

Do not let your mind go there.

He pulled his Explorer to a stop in front of the Property Crimes office building.

Dean was there waiting for him. "Hey." He climbed in. "Got a hit already, huh? That's good news. Sometimes it means the perps are antsy and in a hurry to dump the goods. In that case, they aren't as careful as they should be."

"What else could it mean?"

"If they're selling the stuff for drug money, they might need a fix, which also increases the odds of their making a mistake or getting sloppy."

"Good point."

Dean smiled at him sideways. "I have a lot of good points, in case you may have forgotten."

Nick cast a quick glance his way and tried not to appear incredulous. He tapped his index finger to his temple. "Mind like a steel trap. Some things are *never* forgotten." He hoped Dean got the message that he recalled the sight of him in bed with another man. He'd chosen not to remember any of Dean's 'good points'.

The fair-haired detective winced. "Yeah, well, like I told you the other day. I'm sorry about that. I made a mistake, probably more than one. But that one was a biggie."

Nick parked in front of Hewlett Pawn and turned off the motor. He pocketed his keys and glanced at Dean. "No biggie. Things are good." He looked straight ahead and smiled.

"You seeing someone, Nicky?"

He mulled the question over for a moment. "Yes I am. He's a great guy."

"I thought so. You look...happy."

"I feel happy. Thanks." He didn't bother to admit it'd only been one time, one day. He had no idea how long the new-found bliss would last—he didn't even want to think about it. For today, he felt happy, and that was good enough.

Plus, three new leads on the case.

Energized, he opened his door. "Let's go see what we've got."

Dean followed him into the pawn shop. Once again, Rob was the only clerk in sight. Nick tried to tamp down the lusty feelings that sprang up when he spotted the handsome man. If he didn't force himself to focus, he's be sporting a raging hard-on in minutes.

Rob glanced up from behind the counter. His eyes flashed for one second then he composed himself, his expression changing to one of indifference.

Nick had seen it, though. The same excitement he felt seeing his lover again. Rob felt it too. He forced his tone to be calm and reserved. "Good morning."

"Morning, Detective." Rob eyed him coolly.

Nick motioned to Dean. "This is Detective Cameron from Property Crimes. Rob Hewlett, the owner."

The men nodded at each other.

"One of the owners," Rob corrected. "My brother and I run the place together. We inherited it from our late father."

Nick bit his lip, recalling Rob's comment about his 'late' ex. But he knew their father had actually passed away, so there was nothing to grin about. It was simply hard *not* to smile seeing the sexy businessman again.

Rob reached under the counter and retrieved a plastic zip-type baggie that held a diamond and pearl necklace inside. He placed a photo of the piece next to it. "Looks the same to me. Once I realized it, I bagged the thing. I can't say I didn't touch it first. So did my brother, when he bought it."

Nick glanced around. "Is he here? We should talk to him."

"No, he went to an estate sale. He'll be gone most of the day."

"An estate sale?" Nick blinked. "I thought people brought stuff to you. I didn't know you went out and bought it yourselves."

Rob shrugged. "Sometimes we do. We both enjoy fixing up old stuff, refinishing furniture, that kind of thing. It sells pretty well here in the store."

Nick studied the necklace. "I thought you told me yesterday that you bought most of the jewelry."

"Usually I do, but we each get some time off. If I'm not here, Danny handles it."

"But you were working yesterday," Nick pressed.

"I was in and out." Rob shot him a pointed glance. "I can't be here every minute. I wish we could afford some minions, but that really isn't an option."

"I see." Nick shoved the bag toward Dean. "What do you think?"

"Looks like a match to me. We'll need to run it by Mrs Wilson." To Rob he said, "Can you give us all the information you have on the seller? We'll wait for your brother to get a description, of course. I assume if we leave you our phone number that he'll call when he returns?"

Rob shrugged. "Assume away. I'll give him the message."

Dean scowled, but didn't say more because Rob pulled a log book out from under the counter and began speaking again.

"Looks like this was brought in last night just before closing at six."

"Any other pieces with it?" Nick asked.

"No, just the one necklace."

Nick whipped out his notebook. "Name and address of the seller?"

"Guy's name was Jack MeHoff. Address twenty-four fifty Grand Boulevard."

Nick stopped writing and looked at Rob. "Seriously?"

Rob glanced up. "What?"

"Jack Me Off?"

Dean frowned. "And he lives at the Crown Center Plaza?"

Rob's face reddened. "Well, shit."

"Don't tell me you fell for that, in your line of work, because that's bullshit."

Nick tried to defuse the situation. "Aren't you required to ask for photo ID before buying something?"

"We are." Rob met his gaze squarely. He didn't offer further explanation.

Nick turned to Dean. "In all fairness, I wouldn't have known that address."

Dean shrugged. "I walked a beat downtown when I was a patrol cop. But the name, really? The oldest prank phone call trick in the book. Call a bar, ask if Mike Hunt is there? Or I.P. Freely?"

Rob raised his hands. "I get it. I don't know why Danny didn't catch the phony business, maybe he was busy. Sometimes it gets cracking in here around closing time."

Dead folded his arms across his chest. "We need to speak with your brother, *today.*"

"I said I'd have him call you. That's the best I can do."

"It's fine." Nick scooped up the baggie and photo from the counter. "We'll expect to hear from him soon. Thank you."

"You bet." Rob caught his eye.

Nick wanted to say so much more, but at that moment, he couldn't. He looked away quickly then headed for the door.

Dean was close on his heel. "What the hell was that? Why'd you let him off so easy? Those guys are required to see photo IDs from anyone selling goods. If they aren't following the law, they could get in a world of trouble."

Nick kept walking. "It wasn't him, it was his brother."

"So he says."

"I believe him." He unlocked the doors of his Explorer and got in. "Look, he said Danny will call us, let's give him a chance." He drove back to Dean's station.

"Yeah, well I'm not holding my breath. I bet he never calls. And if he doesn't, I say we turn these guys in. They aren't above the law."

"Let's wait and see if Danny calls." Nick expelled a breath. He just wanted Dean to get out. He didn't want to think about reporting Rob to law enforcement.

"Danny, yeah, right. You sound like you're his fucking best friend or something." He exited the vehicle. "I'll expect to hear from you." Dean slammed the door and stomped off.

Nick swallowed. He wasn't best friends with Danny, a man he'd never met. He *was* kind of partial to Rob, the man he was head over heels in lust with. He shook his head on the way back to his station.

Last night was a bad idea. He knew it wasn't smart, yet he had no intentions of not showing up again tonight. The thought of not seeing Rob again hurt worse than the idea that he'd made a mistake. *What the fuck ever.* If he'd made one mistake, then surely another one wouldn't hurt that much. *Would it?*

Before he got out he had a second thought, and texted his captain and Laura.

Going to run necklace by Mrs Wilson. Back soon.

He drove to the Wilsons' house. A silver Mercedes was parked in the driveway. Nick pulled next to it, then grabbed the bagged necklace and proceeded to the front door. He rang the bell and waited.

A tall, distinguished-looking man with slick black hair answered.

Taken aback for a second, Nick said, "Hello. I'm Detective Peyton with the KCPD. Is Mrs Wilson at home?"

"Yes, come in." He ushered Nick into the living room. "I'm her brother-in-law, Ashton Wilson." Up the staircase he called, "Ronnie, the police are here."

"I'll be right there," she replied from upstairs.

The man turned to Nick. "I hope you have some news about my brother's murder. Our family is terribly upset."

"I'm sure. Sorry for your loss, Mr Wilson. We've had several leads in the case just today. We've actually recovered a necklace that we believe is Mrs Wilson's. I'd like her to verify for me."

"Excellent!" His smile didn't quite reach his eyes.

Nick studied the man's appearance. Expensive clothes, obviously dyed hair, because his sideburns were pure silver. "What do you do, Mr Wilson?"

He retrieved a glass from the coffee table and took a sip. "I'm in investments."

Purposely vague? Nick glanced at his watch, not yet noon, and the man was drinking?

He seemed to catch Nick's drift. "I'm having whiskey to take the edge off this stressful week. Won't be able to do that when I get back to work, of course. Can I offer you something? We've got coffee or a soft drink."

"No, thank you." Nick glanced around. The house was back in shape after just a few days. Another TV sat where the stolen one had been. It seemed fast for the place to look so...normal. And the brother—he apparently felt right at home, playing host.

Veronica Wilson joined them.

Nick had to look twice. He'd only met the woman once, and granted, it had been a horrible night for her. But she looked altogether different today. Her hair was styled down around her face, more modern-looking than the other night. Her clothes were fashionable and appeared expensive.

Nick remembered thinking she had looked matronly just after the murder. She looked anything but that today. "Mrs Wilson, I'm glad to see you looking so well. Detective Peyton." He extended his hand.

She smiled as she shook it. "I remember you, thanks. I'm getting along with the help of my wonderful family. Ash has been a godsend." She batted her lashes at Ashton.

Nick followed the exchange then held out the baggie. "We had a pawn shop owner phone us today — this was sold at his store last night."

She took the bag and studied the contents. "That's my necklace! Roger bought it for me on our twentieth anniversary. Oh, thank you! May I keep it?"

He shook his head. "Not yet, I'm sorry. We still need to check it for prints and log it into evidence. It'll come back to you eventually, but you may have to be patient."

She handed it back, nodding. "I understand. Whatever we can do to help catch the killer." Rubbing her upper arms, she glanced around the room. "I'm not sure I'll ever feel safe here again. I'm thinking about moving."

"I understand." Nick *did* understand, he wouldn't want to stay where his spouse had been murdered. But the widow seemed cold. Not as torn up as the last time he'd seen her. Perhaps the marriage hadn't been all that great? He made a mental note to follow up on the thought.

"Thank you for keeping us apprised on the case." Ashton stepped next to his sister-in-law. "We've got the funeral tomorrow, then hopefully we can start to put this all behind us."

She beamed at him.

As Nick moved toward the front door he saw them do the same. *Ash* placed his hand on the small of her back, guiding her.

"We'll be in touch." Nick walked out.

They closed the door behind him.

He couldn't shake the funny feeling in the pit of his stomach as he headed back to the station.

When he arrived, another homicide detective was there, just returned from vacation. "Hey, Dix. Welcome back." He patted the man's shoulder.

James Dixon smiled at him. "Thanks, kid. It was great to get away. Virginia is nice this time of year."

"How's your son?"

Dix's face lit up. "He's just great. Really happy we were all there for his promotion ceremony. Not so sure *his mother* was that thrilled…"

Nick chuckled. It was no secret Dix had come out as gay after his marriage had broken up. The son had had a hard time accepting it at first, but the ex-wife had never warmed to the idea.

Dix's KCPD partner Steve MacDonald shook his head. "Did you think she would be? You had some balls hauling Bryan and his girls there for the ceremony. I can just see Sami pumping her fist hollering 'Woot, woot!' when everyone else is clapping."

Dix grinned. "Exactly. But, hey, they're my family now. Jared loves the girls like sisters. Sorry if the ex doesn't approve, but I've stopped expecting her approval."

"There you go." Nick nodded. "Anyway, glad you had a good trip."

Laura joined them. "Did Mrs Wilson ID the necklace?"

"Yes." He pulled the bag from his jacket pocket. "We need to get this entered into evidence and dusted for prints."

"I'll take care of it." Laura took the bag. "What's wrong? You have a funny look on your face."

He scratched his chin. "I dunno. How did Mrs Wilson look to you the other day when you walked through the house?"

She shrugged. "Sad, shaken up, red eyes, the normal stuff."

"That's how I thought she looked, too. Kind of frumpy. She was different today. Hair was attractive, clothes nice, stylish even. She looked good, maybe even a little happy."

"Happy?" Dix raised his brows. "Wonder who she has to thank for that?"

"Her husband's brother was there. Tall, nicely dressed man. Dyed black hair with silver sideburns. Name is Ashton Wilson. She called him 'Ash'. He called her 'Ronnie'." He looked at Dix. "Her name is Veronica."

Laura shook her head. "That doesn't mean anything. Maybe everyone calls them by those names."

Dix raised an eyebrow. "Something feel off to you?"

"Yeah, it did. *Ash* offered me a drink, like someone who lived there might. He was drinking whiskey before noon, by the way. Said it was to take the edge off his stressful week."

"His brother was murdered," Laura reminded.

"When they showed me to the door, he escorted her like this." Nick grabbed Laura's left arm and placed his right hand on the small of her back.

Mac smirked. "Kinda friendly-like."

"It was," Nick agreed. "The whole thing felt really friendly. They mentioned the funeral is tomorrow."

Dix said, "Maybe you two should attend and have a look around. I doubt the person who pulled the trigger will show up, but sometimes we case funerals for that very reason. You might want to observe this one for other reasons."

Nick nodded to Laura. "I think we might. You wanna be my date?"

"I suppose." To Mac, she sighed, "Why are the cute ones always gay?"

He raised his hands. "Don't ask me, I'm happily married."

Nick flicked Laura's arm as he walked by. "Don't you have evidence to process?"

She rolled her eyes. "On my way, slave driver."

He rolled his eyes right back at her, and went to his desk.

* * * *

It was late afternoon when the report came back on the necklace, which had no traceable prints. "Nothing?" he asked the evidence tech.

"Not even a partial. Either everyone who touched it was wearing gloves, or it was wiped clean."

"I'd expect Mr or Mrs Wilson's prints to be on the thing, and probably the pawn shop broker who purchased it."

"One would think so." The tech went on with his business.

Nick returned to his desk. His cell rang and he recognized the number this time. "Peyton."

"Hey, it's Rob. Danny's back if you want to come speak with him."

No small talk, no sweet talk. Nick was happy on one hand, and disappointed on the other. "Yeah, sure. I'll be right over. Thanks."

Rob ended the call without another word.

Nick tried to reach Cameron but he was out on a case, so he drove to the pawn shop alone.

Rob and his brother were both behind the counter. Danny looked much the same as in his photos. Rob's height but twice as wide, burly frame, shiny bald head, mustache and beard.

Neither of the store owners appeared that pleased to see him, which struck Nick as odd, since they knew he was coming. "Hello," he greeted them.

"Hey." Rob's voice softened a little.

Nick could see mixed emotions in his eyes, and his heart lurched. The situation was awkward to say the least.

"Danny, this is Detective Peyton." To Nick he added, "My brother, Danny."

Nick extended his hand and they shook.

Danny smiled. "Sorry about the name in the log book. I had three people in here at once last night. The other two guys had a lot more stuff. I was trying to take care of everything as quickly as possible, 'cause I had someplace to be. Apparently I missed the wisecrack."

Rob said, "I told you it gets crazy in here at closing some nights. It's happened to me, too."

"Sure." Nick gave him the benefit of the doubt, but wasn't convinced Danny deserved the same. "Where did you have to be?"

The man grinned. "Just bought a Harley Super Glide Custom. Wanted to go pick it up."

Nick gave a low whistle. "Those don't come cheap."

"Worth every penny," Danny crowed.

Rob rolled his eyes. "Spending money like he's got it."

Nick could sense a sore subject, so he turned the conversation back to their case. "So what did our friend Jack look like? Can you give me a description?"

"Of course. He was young, maybe mid-twenties. African-American. He wore a stocking cap so I couldn't see his hair, but there was none sticking out so it must be short. The guy was tall, my height, maybe six foot or six one. Skinny as a bean pole, I swear he needed a belt to keep his jeans up 'cause the man had no ass."

"Any tattoos, moles or marks on his face?"

"None that I can remember."

"Besides the stocking cap, what was he wearing?"

"Um, dirty jeans and a T-shirt that used to be white. More coffee-colored now. Expensive sneakers, fancy ones like basketball players wear."

Nick glanced around. "No surveillance cameras in here?"

"Broken," Danny said simply.

Rob cleared his throat. "Been meaning to get that fixed."

"Yeah." Nick read over his notes. "Suppose you could come to the station tomorrow and tell this to a sketch artist?"

"If I have to." Danny shrugged.

Nick gazed at him. "Probably be good, given the mix-up with the guy's name and all. It'd be in your best interest to at least *appear* cooperative."

"I'm being cooperative!" Danny insisted.

"Yeah," Nick repeated. "So let's run through this one more time." He pointed to a necklace in the showcase. "Can you pull that out and we'll pretend it's our stolen piece?"

Rob did as directed and handed it over to Nick.

He held the chain in his hand. "So I'm the seller, I come in here with this. I'd like to pawn it." He placed it on the counter. "What would you do next?"

Danny picked up the necklace and examined it. "We'd check it out, look in the book for comparable pieces, and make you and offer."

"But you'd touch it."

Both Danny and Rob gazed at him. Danny replied, "Well, yeah. No reason to think we shouldn't. We can't assume everything brought in here is stolen."

Nick nodded. "Makes me wonder, then, why the Wilsons' necklace had been wiped clean. No prints at all, not yours, not Rob's. Nobody's."

"Well..." Danny hesitated. "We clean them up before they get put out for sale. Polish them and such."

"But you just took in the necklace last night. It won't go up for sale for at least thirty to sixty days, right? Depending on the term of the pawn agreement?"

"Yes..." Danny sounded shaky. He didn't elaborate.

"But for some reason, this particular piece was polished up immediately. Okay, got it. So what time can you be at the station tomorrow? I'll have a sketch artist ready for you." He handed Danny his card with the office address on it.

"Earlier the better, so I can get out of there before we have to open up. Eight thirty or nine?"

"Eight thirty is good. Just ask for me. We appreciate your cooperation." He turned to leave without making eye contact with Rob.

"We." Danny chortled. "I only see one of you there. Who's 'we'? You and the mouse in your pocket?"

Nick faced him once more. "Me, and the fourteen hundred officers of the Kansas City Police Department."

Danny gave him a mock salute.

Irritation knifed Nick's gut as he walked out. Something wasn't right with Hewlett Pawn. But did that make both of them guilty, or just the brother who was acting suspicious?

He hadn't driven far when the text alert went off on his phone. Once he was parked at the station, he read the text from Rob.

Are we still on for tonight? I could grab a pizza after work.

Nick inhaled then blew out the breath. He typed back —

Wasn't sure we were still speaking.

The reply came immediately.

Of course we are. My place in an hour?

Nick knew the right thing to do would be to end it, not let the relationship go any further. It was definitely a conflict of interest with his current case. He also knew he wouldn't be working this case forever. And the *last* thing he wanted to do was end it with Rob. He typed —

See you there.

Chapter Four

Warm spray from the shower pelted Nick's back. The relaxing sensation was *not quite* as hot as what was going on with his front.

Drenched and apparently unconcerned about the water pelting him from above, Rob knelt before him, sucking his cock for all he was worth. He'd started tentatively by licking, nibbling around the base and nuzzling his face in the wiry hair there. It hadn't taken long for hunger to overcome them both. Nick had jutted his hips forward, desiring more, and Rob had acquiesced.

Nick planted a palm on the stall walls on either side of him for better purchase. His senses on overload, he needed to hang on or fall over before much more time went by. "I'm close," he murmured.

Rob's head bobbed a definite nod as he continued the deep sucking.

"Oh, shit." Nick clutched the walls. His world began to spin, twisting, rolling, gut clenching then releasing as his seed spurted in streams down his lover's throat.

The man didn't miss a beat, taking it all in as he kept up the powerful sucking.

Nick ran a hand over Rob's head. "Thank you."

Taking his clue, Rob drew back and glanced up. "Feel good?"

"Amazing."

He got to his feet and kissed the hollow of Nick's neck. "Good. Tasted amazing. Let's see how much hot water we have left." He adjusted the knob. "Not much. We better rinse off and take this party elsewhere."

Nick grinned. "Aw, damn. I wanted to play Drop the Soap."

"We'll play that in the other room, sans soap."

They soaped and rinsed each other's bodies. Rob's cock was hard and throbbing. Nick had to resist the urge to draw it into his own mouth. He hurried and rinsed then they shut off the water and reached for two towels.

The soft rug in front of the sink was as far as Nick could make it. He dropped to his knees and gently pushed his lover back against the counter. "My turn," he murmured, blowing warm breath on the waving cock.

"Not sure I could have waited much longer." Rob ran his hands over Nick's head. "Suck me. Make me come as hard as you just did."

"My pleasure." He spent a moment licking and teasing but they were both beyond that. Rob's turgid shaft already leaked pre-cum. It wouldn't take much to set his lover off. Nick swallowed the length until the bulbous head hit the back of his throat.

Rob groaned with obvious pleasure.

Nick sucked and bobbed, allowing one hand to slip underneath and rim his guy's tight anus.

"Oh yeah." Rob's words were barely coherent.

Nick grinned around his mouthful. He enjoyed that moment, for himself and for his partner. The moment his lover was so close, right on the edge, but not quite there. He needed a little more coaxing, and Nick was the man to provide that.

His fingertip circled the tight opening. With no lube it wasn't going far, but with enough prodding it went in a bit. *Just enough to tease.* Nick loved that type of torment, both giving and receiving.

"Fuck yeah!" Rob called, still holding Nick's head. "Baby, you do me good."

"Mmm-hmm," Nick agreed, ready for the first course of the evening. Their pizza was in the kitchen getting cold. He knew neither one of them minded. They'd needed this first, to reconnect, touch, feel, taste, devour each other. Dinner could wait.

"Come on," he encouraged. His words were garbled but his meaning was clear. He ached for this as much as Rob did.

"Coming..." His lover gripped the counter with one hand and Rob's head with the other.

Warm spurts of cream flowed down Nick's throat. He closed his eyes and relaxed his gullet, letting the stream seep in. When his lover stopped twitching and released the firm grasp on Nick's head, he pulled back, licking the last drops of cum from the slit.

"Oh, baby." Rob sighed. "You need to register that mouth as a lethal weapon."

Chuckling, Nick stood and pressed their groins together. He placed his forehead against Rob's. "I'm not going to ask you if that felt good, because I can tell it did. It felt good to me, too."

Rob's hands cupped his face and drew him in for a deep, soul-wrenching kiss. Tongue batted against tongue as they grappled, and when they stopped both of their cocks were firming up again. Rob traced the back of one finger down Nick's cheek. "We are fucking amazing together. I'm so happy I found you."

Nick smiled, but he knew his eyes betrayed what he was thinking.

Rob placed the finger to Nick's lips. "All that other stuff is nonsense. There's nothing to it, and pretty soon it's going to go away. Then you and I won't have to see each other for work-related reasons. We can focus on our lives *outside* of work. Trust me."

"I want to." Nick really did. He just wasn't as confident the 'other stuff' was going to go away that easily.

"Just trust me." Rob handed him a dry towel. "Wrap this around you, and we'll go eat some dinner. No reason to get dressed, I'll be stripping you naked again before long."

Nick grinned. "I like your way of thinking." He did as directed, and followed Rob down the hall.

"But you still don't trust me." Rob glanced over his shoulder, smiling.

"I do."

Rob handed him a plate, his glance skeptical.

Nick laughed. "Okay, I'm working on it. That's the best I can do right now."

"I'll take your best, any time of the day or night. For now, let's eat this cold pizza. You can nuke yours in the microwave if you want."

"This is fine." They grabbed a couple of beers and headed for the sofa in the living room.

Rob settled in, leaning back against the cushions as they ate. "I guess I don't have to ask how your day was, since I saw you twice today."

Nick finished a slice and shrugged. "It was okay. We developed a few new leads to pursue, so it wasn't a total loss."

"I hope my brother isn't one of the leads you're pursuing. He's not guilty of anything besides a bit of negligence. Please tell me you realize that."

"I'd like to believe it, I really would. I just have to follow the evidence as it comes in. I hope *you* know I'll be as accommodating as I can within the bounds of the law."

Rob tossed a half-eaten slice on his plate and set it aside. "Wow, is that cop lingo for 'You're screwed, buddy'?"

Nick rolled his eyes, and set his plate down. "No, it means I don't want to talk shop anymore. I don't want to talk about your brother, or my case. In fact, I really don't want to talk at all."

Rob smiled. "How are we supposed to get to know each other, if we don't talk?"

Nick clasped him around the waist and dragged Rob onto his lap. "There are other ways to get to know one another. For instance, I know you like it when I rub the underside of your balls. And you like it when I swallow your monster cock so deep I can feel it against the back of my throat."

"No, I *love* that. What I'd *like* is to learn more about you. I've told you all there is to tell about me. I work every damn day and when I'm not working, I look for things to do, like refinishing furniture to sell. My mom, my brother, and his kids are my only family. I have no idea about your hobbies, or relatives."

Nick gazed at him. No wonder Rob was so protective of Danny. He really hoped they were able to solve the case without implicating Rob's brother. "Well." He nuzzled Rob's neck. "Both my parents are still around. Mom's a high school math teacher and Dad's a contractor. I have a married sister and two nephews in elementary school."

Rob bent his head to allow better access. "They live around here?"

"Not far. St Joe."

"Nice. Close enough to visit, but not so close that they're all up in your business."

Nick laughed. "You got that right. Still, my sister and my mom are always on the lookout for eligible bachelors to set me up with."

Rob caught his gaze. "You can tell them to stop doing that."

Nick's heart lurched at the intensity of his stare. "Oh yeah?"

"Oh...yeah." Rob pressed their lips together and when Nick responded, he opened his mouth to deepen the kiss. He caressed everywhere he could reach, fingers playing lightly over Nick's skin. "I want to be inside you," he murmured, lips touching.

Nick's breath caught. "Oh God, I want that too."

"Let me grab some supplies and I'll be right back." Another kiss, more heated as anticipation built. "I'm gonna bend you over the back of this sofa and ball your brains out."

"Please," Nick gasped. Nothing would make him happier.

"Only problem," Rob managed between hungry kisses. "You're going to have to let me up."

Nick exaggerated a sigh. "If you insist." He released his grip.

Rob stood, giving a firm squeeze to Nick's engorged cock, which poked through the towel. "On your feet. I'll be back in a flash."

"I'll be ready." Nick removed his towel and spread it over the back of the sofa. When his lover walked by he grinned and yanked Rob's towel off, placing it on the floor beneath their feet.

"Good man." Rob set the lube and foil-wrapped condom off to the side, within reach. "Now bend over. I'm feeling impatient."

Nick did as requested and gasped as Rob's hands spread his legs, then his ass cheeks. He felt the same way. The barest minimum of foreplay was fine with him. He was primed and ready to go.

Rob inserted a greased finger into his anus and stretched it from side to side. "So hot. So tight. God, I love your ass." He kissed Nick's back and neck.

"*I* love what you're doing to my ass. More. *Please.*"

A seductive chuckle, then another finger wedged into his hole.

Nick moaned, so turned on he could barely stand still. "I'm ready, babe. Need to feel you inside me. Filling me up. Fucking me with all your energy."

"I am so there." The fingers slipped out.

Nick heard the rustle of the foil wrapper, then felt the head of Rob's cock at his entrance. "Yes."

"My kind of man." Rob pressed forward. "Hot and tight, like I knew you would be. Perfect." He sank in fully and paused while they both acclimated.

They sighed in unison.

"Damn," Nick muttered.

"Hang on, lover." Rob pulled back then plunged in again. *And again.* He repeated the arousing motion and picked up speed until their sweat-slicked bodies made juicy sounds slapping against one another.

Rocking, bucking together, they seemed totally in tune with one another. Nick couldn't imagine a better feeling until Rob reached around and clasped his turgid cock. Curling his fingers around the shaft, he pumped in time with his thrusts.

"Oh fuck, yes!" Nick didn't mean to shout, he just couldn't help it.

Rob's throaty chuckle sounded in his ears. "That's it, baby. Ride the wave. We're getting close, so close."

"I'm there," Nick muttered through gritted teeth. He couldn't hold back any longer, and didn't try. Shattering, his world exploded in a flash of light and color before he couldn't see anything at all. He collapsed against the sofa, and realized from Rob's ragged panting, he was right there with him.

"It's...better," Nick whispered.

"What?" Rob rose up. "Am I hurting you?"

"No. I said—or tried to say—it just keeps getting better."

Rob laughed. "I think so, too, hot stuff. I've never felt so connected to anyone in my life. Now, having said that..." He pulled back and his cock slid out.

Nick turned to look at him. "I've never been so fucking head over heels in lust before. We haven't cleaned up from the last time and I want to do it again."

Rob ran a smooth hand over his back. "That's why you're spending the night, and the weekend, if I can talk you into it. I want to do it again, too. And again." He kissed a spot between Nick's shoulder blades. "And again."

Nick could only smile.

* * * *

The routine was getting comfortable. Nick woke at Rob's apartment and showered, then dashed home to change clothes before work. Friday morning, he dressed conservatively for the funeral, and grabbed a cup of drive-thru coffee before hitting the station.

Danny arrived at his scheduled time and Nick put him in a private room with Officer Jenkins, one of the department's sketch artists.

"Hope this doesn't take long," Danny grumbled. "I have places to be."

"Yeah, me too." Nick looked at him. "I'm going to Roger Wilson's funeral this morning."

Guilt flooded the bigger man's face and he glanced down.

Guilt for complaining, or something else? Nick wasn't at all sure.

He returned to his desk and did paperwork until it was time to go. He drove Laura to the church and they sat in the back where they had a good vantage point.

"You look nice today." He made small talk as they waited for the service to begin.

"I hate wearing a dress," she muttered. "But thanks."

He smiled, and observed.

Nothing particular caught his eye at the church. When they got to the cemetery, he pointed out Ashton Wilson to Laura. They both watched the man's protective behavior toward his sister-in-law. She sat in the first chair and he stood behind her, his hand on her shoulder.

"They seem chummy," Nick commented.

"He's being supportive. She just lost her husband."

"She doesn't seem that broken up."

"Well," she hesitated. "You're right about that."

Before the minister began, Nick spotted Ash staring at someone off to the side. Not simply staring—*glaring*. Ash did not seem happy. He leaned down and spoke in Mrs Wilson's ear, then slipped away.

"Let's go." Nick motioned to Laura to follow him, and they moved in Ash's direction, staying on the fringes of the crowd. "Try to figure out what he's up to."

The grieving brother approached a sandy-haired man who wore faded jeans and a denim work shirt. His complexion was pock-marked. He appeared out of place with the other mourners.

"Wonder who his friend is?" Laura mused.

The two men whispered for a moment, until Ash's face reddened and his hushed tone grew louder.

"Not so sure they're friends," Nick commented.

Ash motioned toward the parking lot.

"He obviously doesn't want the guy here."

The stranger muttered something before turning to leave.

"And he's going." Nick continued to watch. "You want to trail him, see if you can get his vehicle make and tag number? I'll stick with our friend Ash."

"You bet."

They went their separate ways. Nick kept his gaze on Ash and Roger's widow during the brief service. When it was over, they spoke with a few well-wishers, then hurried off to their waiting car.

Nick met up with Laura.

She looked at her notepad. "He was driving an old blue Ford truck, tons of rust around the fenders. I got all but the last two numbers on the license plate. He pulled out too fast. Sorry."

Damn. "It's okay. Hopefully this will get us something. Just might take longer. Let's go. I think we've got all we're going to get here."

He drove back to the station in a foul mood. Something didn't sit right with the Wilsons, and he couldn't put his finger on what it was.

The captain met him in the bullpen, where he held up a sketch. "Here's what your pawn shop guy came up with."

Nick frowned. *He's not 'my' pawn shop guy. My pawn shop guy is one hell of a lot cuter and doesn't lie. I think. I hope.* Then he frowned for a different reason. "This could be any black man in the metro area."

"Exactly what I said. Jenkins mentioned the guy wasn't particularly helpful. Said it seemed like he was pulling stuff out of the air, maybe making it up as he went along."

Nick snatched the drawing and slapped it on the evidence board. "That's just fucking terrific. Every one of our leads has crumbled to a half-assed possibility this week."

"Get anything from the funeral?"

He shook his head. "One out-of-place character. Mrs Wilson's brother-in-law obviously didn't want some guy there, asked him to leave."

"Plates?"

Nick scowled. "Half-assed."

Alvarez nodded. "Keep at it. It'll all fall into place eventually. It always does."

"Almost always," Nick mused. His gut churned at how the case had gone sour so quickly. He was glad it was Friday, for more reasons than one.

* * * *

At the end of the day, he threw a couple of changes of clothing into a bag and met Rob at his place.

His lover greeted him at the door. "I got Chinese takeout."

"Sounds good."

"I wasn't sure what you liked."

Nick tossed his bag on the sofa. "Anything is good. I'm easy."

Rob grinned. "Is that so? Good to know."

Nick guffawed. "You haven't had much trouble with me, have you?"

"No, actually, I haven't. But now we've got a whole weekend to ourselves. What would you like to do? We don't have to stay in, we could go to a bar or a club. Tomorrow we could go antiquing, shopping, to a movie or to the races. Hell, we could go to Worlds of Fun if you're into that sort of thing. I have no idea what you like to do."

Reaching for the buttons on Rob's shirt, Nick began to unfasten them. "Sure you do. And staying in is fine with me. I think we could have a world of fun right here." He tugged the shirt off and tossed it aside.

"Okay, if you really want to. Don't say I didn't try to bring a little joy into your life."

Nick laughed. "Are you kidding? You've brought *a lot* of joy into my life. More than any one man deserves, probably. But I don't need to go out. I'm more than content to hunker down right here with you for the weekend."

Rob raised an eyebrow. "Or maybe you just don't want to be seen out with me."

"That's not true." Nick's voice didn't hold much conviction. He was sure who he was trying to convince, his handsome stud, or himself.

"It's okay." Rob ran his hand over Nick's shoulders. "This is new, and touchy given the way we met. But it's all going to be all right. Pretty soon you'll solve your case and we won't have to hide anymore."

"We're not hiding!" Nick insisted.

"Of course not." Rob removed Nick's shirt. "And we're not fixing to have sweaty butt sex, either. Tell yourself whatever you like. Just remember, if it walks like a duck and quacks like a duck..."

"Quack, quack." Nick grinned, tired of making excuses. Maybe he *was* trying to keep their relationship on the down low. It was the appropriate thing to do for now. He cupped Rob's jean-clad crotch. "Chinese food first, or sweaty butt sex?"

"Oh my God." Rob thrust his groin into Nick's hand. "If those are my two choices, I'll always take the sex. The food can wait. Not sure I can."

Nick leaned in and kissed him passionately. "I can't get enough of you, either. I just want more, more, more..."

"Good." Rob smiled, then turned and tucked a finger through the belt loop on Nick's pants. "Right this way. Let the weekend begin."

* * * *

Waves of pleasure washed over Nick. His cock was buried balls-deep in Rob's snug anus. His thrusts had worked his lover into near frenzy. Rob jerked and bucked backwards against him so hard, he knew neither of them would last much longer.

"Ah, God." Rob's groan was guttural. On his hands and knees atop the bed, his head hung down.

Nick spotted him watching their coupling between his legs. "Like the view?"

"You know I do. I always enjoy looking at you, but watching you fuck me is about the hottest thing ever."

"We need mirrors on the ceiling," Nick chuckled.

"Maybe we need a little less talk and a lot more action. You gonna finish this thing, or what?"

Nick reached between them and felt for his lover's cock. "Oh yeah?" he teased when he found Rob's hand wrapped around his own shaft.

"I'm getting serious here. You can either come with, or step off, dude."

That was all it took. Nick closed his eyes, imagined his man milking his rod, and shuddered. He let go, his warm seed filling the latex in his partner's ass. Glancing down through glazed eyes, he saw Rob's semen spurting onto the towel beneath them.

He leaned in and kissed Nick's back. "I was going to do that. You beat me to it, so to speak."

Rob glanced back at him, grinning. "You were busy and I had a free hand."

Nick couldn't help but laugh. "What the fuck ever, man." He pulled out and took a moment to dispose of the condom before dropping back onto the bed.

He rested his head on Rob's arm, feeling melancholy. They'd not only stayed in all of last weekend, they'd enjoyed it so much they had followed suit the next week. Their second weekend together was almost over. "I hate Sundays. I mean, I love my job, but Sunday means I won't get to stay in bed with you all day tomorrow."

Rob ran a hand over his face. "That probably wasn't going to work for much longer, anyway, babe. We've spent the last two weekends—and every week night in between—hibernating, doing nothing but making love."

"Are you complaining? We came up long enough for air and food. What else do we need?"

"Personally, I'm cool with it, but my mom is wondering where the hell I've been. Your family might be thinking that, too."

Nick shrugged. "I guess I've been greedy, keeping you all to myself. I didn't want to let the real world in."

Rob gazed at him lovingly. "Let's go at this from another way, shall we? How about bringing our relationship into the real world? We could do the things we need to do, like grocery shop, clean house, visit our moms—but maybe we could do them together. It's just a thought."

Nick smiled. "Point taken. Okay, starting this week we'll do one productive thing each evening before we fall into bed. I'll admit my house could use a good cleaning. It's mostly dusty because I haven't been there much."

"I can dust." Rob waggled his brows.

Nick hadn't taken Rob to his home yet. He knew he was being overly cautious. After everything he and Rob had shared the past two weeks, it was time. He was ready. "Fine. Tomorrow night we go to my place. You can have a look around and I'll do some much needed laundry."

Rob grinned. "Can I bring some clothes, too? Sounds better than the coin-ops down the hall."

"Of course you can." Nick felt bad he hadn't thought of it before. His whole house was larger, and would provide them more room to spread out. "If you want, we can spend the night there. See how you like it."

"Oh, you know how I like it, big boy." Rob batted his lashes. "But sure. I'd like to see your home. And I'm sure it'll be just fine."

* * * *

Nick was shuffling through a stack of paperwork when he heard Laura whoop on Monday morning.

"Finally!" She hurried toward him, waving a sheet of paper in her hands. "It took nearly two weeks, but we finally have a hit on the shell casing fingerprint."

"No way." Nick had about given up hope. Two weeks was a *long* time to get a match.

"Yes, siree, look right here." She slapped the sheet down in front of him. "Samuel Morgan, age twenty-eight. He's done three stints in the pokey for petty theft, larceny and driving under the influence—more than once."

"Hmm." Nick studied the face. Caucasian, light brown hair, and his upper body was heavily tattooed. "This doesn't look anything like the perp Danny Hewlett described."

"So, maybe there was more than one guy involved. Odds are there were at least two. And get this. Samuel Morgan has a white Chevy cargo van registered in his name."

Nick looked at her. "No fucking way."

"Yes way." She made a face at him. "He's falling into our lap, Peyton. Not sure what you're gonna do about it, but I think I'll go pick him up for questioning."

He rose, patting his pockets for phone and keys. "I believe I'll go along. Want me to drive?"

"Nope, I've got it." She glanced smugly over her shoulder and headed toward the door.

He could only smile and follow.

"Check it out," Alvarez called after them. "If it looks suspicious at all, call for uniformed back-up."

"Yes, Cap'n." Nick waved and went after Laura.

She unlocked her Jeep and they climbed in. "He lives in a crummy neighborhood."

"Yeah." Nick read the rap sheet as she drove. "Looks like he's married. His wife Jill drives an old Ford beater."

A few minutes later, Laura turned onto their street and slowed to read the house numbers. Most were peeling off, along with much of the house paint. "Crummy is an understatement."

Nick agreed. "These houses would need an upgrade to be considered crummy." He pointed. "Is that it? White cargo van, old green Ford being held together with bumper stickers."

She parked and they peered in the vehicles as they walked past. "Both of them are. The van's not much better."

He walked behind it to check the license plate, but there wasn't one. "Well, shit."

"They could have removed it." She shrugged.

He pointed to the back passenger side tire, which wasn't inflated. "And flattened the tire?"

"Might have just gone flat."

He grinned at her as they approached the rickety front porch. "Ever the optimist, Mary Poppins."

"Damn right. And fuck anybody who doesn't like it." She took the two steps gingerly.

"Careful, this is rough." He pointed to a rotten board.

"Another understatement. If the inside's anything like the outside, this place should be condemned." They paused and she looked at him.

He nodded.

Laura knocked on the door. She unfastened the snap on her gun holster.

Nick did the same.

She waited a full minute, then knocked again.

A petite, blonde woman with a toddler on her hip answered the door. "Can I help you?"

"We're looking for Samuel Morgan." Laura flashed her badge. "I'm Detective Evans and this is Detective Peyton of the KCPD."

The woman's brow furrowed. "What do you want with Sam?"

"We just need to speak with him. Is he here?"

"He's sleeping. Can you come back?"

Nick and Laura exchanged glances. "No." She shook her head. "We need to speak with him now. I'm afraid you'll have to wake him."

The woman took a step back to allow them in. "He ain't gonna like it. He works nights, and just got to sleep a little while ago."

"Sorry." Laura winced congenially.

"Where does he work?" Nick glanced around the cluttered little house. Much of the free space was taken up by baby equipment—a swing, playpen and bouncer. Toys littered the floor.

"At the Shop Mart over on Tenth Street. His shift is from eleven to seven in the morning, five days a week." She moved down the hall. "I'll go get him."

Nick stepped closer to her but remained in the living room. He listened to hear any exchange between the couple, but they were quiet.

On the far wall of the room he noticed a nice flat screen TV. He glanced at Laura. "What size TV did the Wilsons' have?"

"Forty-two inch."

He nodded. "What size do you suppose that one is?"

She eyed it. "Looks about the same as mine at home, which is forty-two inch."

He raised an eyebrow and she mimicked him. *Interesting.*

Chapter Five

A small, shaggy-haired boy peered around the corner at Nick. His eyes were wide and curious.

Nick gave him a tiny wave.

Laura smiled. "Hi there."

He didn't speak, just clutched a toy to his chest.

"What do you have?" she asked.

He still didn't reply.

"Looks like an expensive video game," Nick muttered under his breath. "One of those handheld systems. Last time I checked, they were upwards of two hundred dollars."

"Interesting." She continued to smile at the child.

The woman returned. "He'll be out in a minute." She shifted the little girl in her arms from one hip to the other.

"Thanks," Laura said pleasantly. "How old are your children?"

"One and a half, and three."

Nick noticed the little girl was holding a smartphone. "Is that your phone?" He smiled at the child and held his hand up to his ear in a 'telephone' gesture. "Hello? Can you say 'hello'?"

The little one gave him a slobbery grin and held the phone to her ear. "Hewwo."

"Yeah!" He laughed. "Hello."

A man appeared in the doorway and drew Nick's attention. He was several inches shorter than Nick, unshaven, and appeared to have just woken up. He didn't seem happy about it, either. "Help you with something?" He scratched his head.

Nick showed his badge. "I'm Detective Peyton with the KCPD. This is Detective Evans. We have some questions we need to ask you, but given the circumstances, I think it'd be best if we did it at the station." He glanced at the two children watching them.

"What's this about?" The man didn't seem to understand Nick's discretion.

"We'd rather not go into it in front of the children. Please, just put some shoes on, grab your wallet, and we'll drive you down there."

"How's he gonna get home?" the woman asked.

"We'll bring him back once the questioning is over," Laura told her.

"I don't know about this." Morgan acted confused. "Do I need a lawyer or something?"

"Not at all," Nick reassured him. "Just a few simple questions. It shouldn't take long if everything checks out." He watched the man carefully as he went for his shoes. No signs of bravado. Nick wasn't sure the guy had it in him. He seemed more like a whipped pup than an aggressor.

One eye on the man, Nick continued to check out the house. A sparkling pearl and diamond necklace around the woman's neck caught his eye. It looked very out of place with her jeans and plaid shirt. "Where do you work, Mrs Morgan?"

"Jill," she said. "I'm a waitress at Pete's Pancake House."

He nodded. "Good pancakes."

"The best," she agreed.

Nick half turned so he could get Laura's attention. He touched his neck and nodded toward Jill.

Laura gave a small nod. She moved to the woman and remarked, "That's a lovely necklace."

"Thanks." Jill smiled and fingered it absently. "Sam's always giving us gifts, toys for the kids, and nice things for me."

Nick wondered for a moment if he brought them much food. The children were scrawny and Jill had very little meat on her bones.

"Ready." Sam joined them.

Nick led him to the back seat of Laura's car. He fastened his holster and got in the back, taking care to keep Morgan on his left side, away from the gun.

The guy still hadn't shown any signs of aggression. He'd been more than cooperative.

Laura slid into the driver's seat and glanced back at them. "All set?"

"Yep," Nick replied.

She took them to the station, where Nick led Morgan into one of the interrogation rooms. "Have a seat. Care for something to drink? We have soda, coffee or water."

"I'd take a diet pop."

"Coming right up." Nick left him and went to the hallway where the captain stood with Laura and Dix.

"I'll get his drink," she offered.

"Thanks." He knew they'd all observe his questioning, and as soon as Morgan said anything useful, someone would go check it out.

Dix said, "Get him talking about his job. If he says he was working the eleventh, the night of Roger Wilson's murder, I'll call his employer for verification."

"Will do." Nick took the can Laura returned with and headed back into the interrogation room. He handed over the soda and loosened his tie before he sat. "So, Sam, we're investigating a murder that took place on Mason Avenue a couple weeks ago. The victim's house was robbed and he was shot."

He shook his head. "I never heard anything about it."

"Your wife says you work nights."

"I do, from eleven to seven in the morning."

"What nights?"

"Usually Tuesday through Saturday. Sometimes it changes, but that's my normal schedule."

Nick glanced at the calendar on the wall. "Tuesday the eleventh, you worked that night?"

"Yeah. Yeah I did."

"Do you drive your van to work?"

"What, that piece of crap? No, it ain't run for months. I take the car."

As if that car is much better. Nick nodded. "How does your wife get to work?"

"She doesn't go in until I get home. She takes the kids to her old lady's then works the ten to six shift." He smiled. "So you see, we only need the one car."

"Handy." Nick heard a knock on the two-way mirror. "Excuse me." He rose and stepped out of the room.

Dix looked at him. "Morgan's boss says he was canned two months ago for missing too much work.

Hasn't seen or heard from him since he picked up his last pay check."

"Two months ago?" Nick blinked. "How's he feeding his kids?"

"Getting by on the pancake house salary?" Dix shrugged.

Laura frowned. "Barely getting by. The kids were none too over-fed. Rent is probably cheap in that neighborhood but they still have to pay something."

"Probably higher than you'd think," Alvarez offered. "Slum lords squeeze every last drop of blood from their low income tenants."

Nick asked Laura, "Can you check and see if they receive government assistance?"

"Already did. Nothing."

"He's getting money from somewhere."

"And stuff," she added. "That baby was slobbering over a two hundred dollar smartphone. And you guessed the video game the boy held was at least that much."

"Wife had a nice necklace, and they had a big TV. Lots of other *stuff*. Their tiny living room was full." Nick turned to his captain. "Maybe we need to get Mrs Morgan in here and have a chat with her. We should probably call Cameron and have him bring photos of other recently stolen items."

"I'll go get her," Laura offered.

"I don't want you going alone," Alvarez said. "Dix, you and Evans go to the restaurant and bring the woman back here. I'll have Mac call Cameron, then get some lunch in here for everybody."

They all nodded, and Nick went back into the small room.

"What's going on? I'm tired, and I want to get home to bed." Morgan yawned.

"Gonna be a long day, pal." He pulled out the sketch Danny had described. "Do you know this man?"

Morgan studied it. "Could be one of a hundred guys that came into the Shop Mart. I don't know."

Nick pulled the sketch back. That's what he thought, too. *Time to get serious.* "We recovered a shell casing from the scene of the murder, and your fingerprint was on it."

"No fucking way!" Morgan yelled, his face reddening. "That just ain't possible. I told you I was working that night."

"Yes, but your employer told us he fired you two months ago for missing too much time. So where were you working, Sam? Or should I say, who were you working for?"

Morgan shook his head. "He's a lying sack of shit. Trying to get back at me since I complained about the lousy conditions at the Shop Mart. Fucking filthy."

"Regardless, you weren't at the store on the eleventh, so where were you, Sam? Who were you working for? We've got the van and the fingerprint, that's enough to bind you over for trial. You can go alone, or you can cut yourself some slack and tell us who your partner was. Maybe it was more than one person. Might as well spill it, since we have you, now."

He set his jaw. "I got nothing to say. In fact, I probably need a lawyer."

"Sure, if you want one. But keep in mind, I'm trying to help you, here. If you ask for a lawyer I'll no longer be able to do that."

"How exactly do you think you're helping me?"

"The judge will go much easier on you if we tell him you cooperated with the police."

"Yeah, well, I'm innocent, so I'm not looking for a plea bargain."

"That's the problem, Sam. We have you. You're already fucked for this thing, murder one, life in prison or at the very least, twenty-five to life."

"I didn't kill nobody!"

Nick slapped the table between them. "Your fingerprint was on the shell casing! We got you, man. And right now, we have a Property Crimes detective coming with pictures of recently stolen items. We're going to see how many we can match to the stuff in your house. Hope that pretty necklace your wife was wearing doesn't show up. Or the smartphone your daughter was playing with. And possibly the worst thing, I'd really hate to take the video game away from your boy. But if it was stolen—"

"Leave my family out of this!" he shouted, face red again.

"Too late, man. They're bringing Jill in right now. We have a search warrant for your house and vehicles. The crime scene guys are going there to search. Of course, you know, if we find anything, Jill will be implicated, too. I hope Grandma wants to raise those kids, because the two of you are going away for a long time."

"No! No..." Morgan buried his face in his hands. "Things were never supposed to go down this way."

Nick softened his tone. "How were they supposed to work, buddy? Just a few simple burglaries, sell the stuff, and everyone would be cool? But you didn't sell your share, did you, Sam? Didn't you stop and think about what might happen if you got caught red-handed with the goods?"

"He wasn't offering enough. It killed me to pawn things for pennies on the dollar. I made out better by keeping the shit."

Nick's heart leaped. *Now we're getting somewhere.* "I don't blame you. You acquired some nice items. The TV was worth a couple thousand, probably. Who knows what the necklace was worth?"

"Fucking pawn shop bastard! Tried to cheat me. I was tired of it."

Nick nodded. "Absolutely. So which pawn shop was it? Did you use the same place each time, or spread it around?"

Morgan sighed. "Spread it around so it didn't cause suspicion. The arrogant bastard didn't want me coming to his shop. He had the balls to suggest I go as far as St Joe to unload the stuff. Like my car would make it to St Joe and back."

"You've got a point. So who is this guy? What's his name, which shop does he work at?"

"He doesn't just work there, he *owns* the place. Greedy son of a bitch."

Nick's stomach clenched. He'd been worried Danny was involved. He wondered if Morgan had any evidence to back up his accusations. "You must know his name if he was helping you get rid of the goods."

"Helping me?" Morgan chuckled sourly. "It was all his idea. He told me what an easy scam it would be. Take a few things, the homeowners would report it to their insurance and they'd get paid back. A victimless crime."

Nick frowned. "Until Roger Wilson."

Morgan suddenly looked nervous. Like he had just realized he'd copped to the burglaries, and now there was an elephant in the room to deal with. *The murder.* "I didn't kill him."

"Who did?" Nick stared at him. "I need a name, or it's going on you."

"That Hewlett fucker. It was all his fault."

Nick swallowed. "You're not saying Danny pulled the trigger?"

"Danny, who's Danny? I'm talking about Rob Hewlett. Long brown hair, usually wears it in a ponytail, mustache and beard."

Nick swooned as if he'd just been socked in the gut. He clutched the table for support while trying to show no emotion whatsoever.

Rob.

It can't be Rob.

He'd only known him for two weeks, but they'd been together every minute they weren't working, so they'd gotten to know each other pretty well in the short amount of time. He'd even spoken to Rob's mom on the phone once, when she'd bugged her son to let them talk. She'd been great. He was looking forward to meeting her.

It can't be Rob.

Property Crimes was investigating a series of burglaries with the same MO. The last one had taken place when Roger Wilson had been killed. There'd been no other cases in the two weeks since then. *Two weeks.*

Nick's heart lurched. He closed his eyes, then opened them and looked at Morgan. "You're saying that Rob Hewlett pulled the trigger?"

"Fuck no. Bastard wouldn't get his hands that dirty. He's the boss, though, and he gets minions to do his bidding."

"Minions." Nick remembered Rob using that word about hiring help at the shop. Every clue that added up felt like another knife to his ribcage.

"His word, not mine. He has the white van you're looking for, too."

White cargo van. Nick recalled seeing that in Rob's file. The tag number would be there, too. He could see if it contained the three numbers their eyewitness spotted. "Fuck." He stood and headed for the door.

"Where you going? Can I get out of here since I cooperated with you?"

Nick glanced back at him. "Get comfortable, dude."

Without a word to anyone, he stomped to his desk and looked up Rob's van tag number. To his chagrin, it contained the three digits that the witness could read. "Fuck," he repeated. For a moment he thought he might be sick.

"Jill Morgan is in interrogation room two." Laura stood next to him. "And there are sandwiches in the break room."

His stomach still churned, he couldn't think about eating.

"What's wrong? You look like someone kicked your puppy."

Nick couldn't reply. Brushing past her shoulder, he went straight to the second room and walked in. "Jill, we've got a problem."

She sat in her waitress uniform, twiddling her fingers nervously. "What's wrong?"

He leaned against the door. "Sam's confessed to several robberies over the past few months. In the most recent one, a man was murdered. His fingerprint was on the shell casing."

"No, it can't be Sam's! He works every night. He—"

Nick shook his head. "He lost his job a couple months ago and didn't want to tell you. He's been robbing houses for money and loot. You and the kids were awarded some of the prizes."

She fingered the chain around her neck. "No, please, no. He said he was buying the stuff."

"You didn't question why none of the gifts were new, in boxes? Or why he barely had enough money to buy food but he was bringing home expensive 'gifts'? Not sure I buy that, sister. We've got a search warrant and the techs are going through your house as we speak. You're very possibly going to be implicated as an accessory to these crimes."

"No!" Her cry was sincere. Tears flooded her face. "I wasn't— I never would do something like that! Maybe I should have questioned where the stuff came from, but it was easier not to. But I swear to you, I wasn't involved. Please, you have to believe me. I've got two small children. They need me."

He shrugged. "Sam said your old lady can take care of them."

"What? No way! He's not trying to drag me down with him, is he? I was *not* part of it."

Nick got in her face. "Who was? Sam didn't act alone. Who did he work with?"

Jill shook her head frantically. "I don't know."

"Then it must have been you. Anything you want me to tell Grandma about the kids? Hope they have enough clothes and their special blankies for sleeping."

She slammed a hand down. "Terry Franks. I don't know him, but I've heard Sam mention his name."

"Terry Franks," Nick repeated. "What else do you know about him?"

"Nothing, I swear." Tears rolled down her cheeks. "I'm telling you the truth. Please don't take away my babies."

"We're going to investigate your story. If everything you told me checks out, we might release you. But, Jill, don't leave town. You're treading on thin ice. One more mistake, and I can't promise you Child Protective Services won't get involved."

She nodded and he left the room.

Dix waved a sheet of paper at him. "Terry Franks has a record as long as my right arm. This shit is right up his alley."

Nick glanced at the information. "We have an address on him?"

Dix grinned. "Oh, yeah. Would you like me and Detective MacDonald to go pay him a visit?"

"*Oh, yeah,*" he repeated. "Bring him back for a nice cup of coffee, will you?"

"We will." He turned to go.

Nick smiled. "Isn't the expression 'a record as long as my dick'?"

Dix glanced over his shoulder. "That'd be one hell of a record my friend." He winked, and walked out.

Laughing, Nick went to guzzle some coffee himself. Time dragged and everything slowed to a crawl when they went to haul in someone else. The interminable day was winding down, and it promised to be an even longer night.

He didn't want to talk to Rob. The very idea made him nauseated. Nick grabbed his cell and texted—

Looks like duty calls tonight. Might not be done until late. Can I call you tomorrow?

He waited, and soon a reply appeared.

You're fucking kidding me. Come over when you're done. We can go to your place and do laundry another time. Just come here to sleep…and…

Nick bit his lip. It hurt too much to think about what the 'and' involved. He tried to choose his words carefully. If Rob was truly guilty, and he got wind that they were cracking the case, he might skip town.

Sorry, can't tonight. I'll explain tomorrow, I promise.

I'll miss you, but I understand. Good luck.

Thanks. Have a good night.

A few moments later, Nick received one more text.

I miss you already.

He pocketed his phone. No truer words were ever spoken. He refilled his coffee cup and headed back to the interrogation area.

Laura met him with a big smile on her face. "Guess who Mac and Dix brought in?"

He blinked. "Um, Terry Franks?"

"Duh." She motioned to the third interrogation room. "Check him out."

Nick moved in front of the two-way mirror and gazed at the man with light brown hair and a bad complexion. "I don't know him— Wait—no! Are you for fucking real?"

Her grin widened. "Ash Wilson's funeral buddy, or should I say, the uninvited guest?"

He looked at her then at their captain. "What the hell is going on here?"

"I don't know." Alvarez shook his head. "But my sense is it's all unraveling. You just need to get in there and figure out which strings to tug."

Nick marched into the room and let the door slam behind him. He'd been patient with Sam Morgan, less so with Jill, and by now his patience had all dried up. "Terry Franks. Detective Nick Peyton. Thanks for coming down."

"Did I have a choice?" The man stared at him coolly.

"No, you're right. Then thanks for coming along peacefully, and not shooting anyone on the way. Do you even still have the gun, or did you dump it someplace?"

The comment didn't seem to faze him. "What are you talking about?"

"The gun you used to kill Roger Wilson. I assume it was you who pulled the trigger. Sam Morgan said it wasn't him, and it was just the two of you there."

"Sam who?"

Nick stood, pounding a fist on the table. "Cut the crap. We know you were there. We've got eye witnesses and two people have positively ID'd you. Morgan's writing down everything he knows as we speak." He paced the room, wondering just how far to push it. He calmed his tone as he continued, "Honestly, Sam appears to be a decent guy but he's no brain surgeon. I don't see him as the mastermind behind any of this, which leaves you."

"I think you're blowing smoke. I don't know Sam Morgan, and you can't prove I do."

"But you did know Roger Wilson. You were at his funeral, anyway."

The first hint of nervousness flickered in Franks' face, but he blinked it away quickly. "I was his plumber, did some work at the house for him and the missus. Nice folks. I read about his death in the paper, and wanted to pay my respects."

"You didn't stay long. I watched you talk with Wilson's brother and then leave shortly after."

Franks didn't comment.

"You weren't dressed very nice, either. Jeans and a work shirt don't say 'respectful' to me."

The corners of his mouth twitched. "Some of Wilson's relatives wore jeans. Half the kids there did."

"Yeah, well, that's a different generation and teaching respectfulness is their parents' problem. Until they get to be an adult, at which time it becomes my problem." Nick allowed a small smile.

"Wilson's brother didn't think I was dressed right either. That's why I left. I didn't want to cause a fuss."

"Really." Nick thought about that as he paced. *Bullshit.* "I think you left because he told you to get the hell out of there. What I'm trying to figure out is *why*. Why wouldn't Ashton Wilson want his brother's plumber at the funeral?"

"Beats me."

"Okay, enough of this. I've got my witnesses, that's all I need to keep you tonight. If you aren't going to say who hired you to pull these jobs then I have to assume you're the man in charge. We'll leave it for the jury to decide if Roger Wilson's murder was an unfortunate by-product of the home invasion, or a planned, cold-blooded killing. Make yourself comfortable. Someone will come and take you to Central Booking soon."

"Wait!" Franks shouted as Nick walked out.

He didn't stop, just kept going.

"You going to send him to Booking?" Alvarez asked. "We don't have anything solid on the guy."

"*Yet.* I know it. I'm letting him think we do, and hopefully he'll stew about it. We need to get Morgan to Booking and whenever Cameron's done with her, send Jill home."

"Cameron's been here and gone. He ID'd the necklace she was wearing and bagged it. He went to their house to look for more stolen property."

Nick nodded. "Good. Let's cut her loose for now."

Terry Franks had walked to the two-way mirror and was now pounding on it. "Get back in here! I need to talk to you, you motherfucker!"

Nick exchanged glances with his captain.

Alvarez rolled his eyes. "I'll take care of Mrs Morgan. Be careful in there. Restrain him if you need to."

He opened the door to Franks' room. "You need to sit down, and calm down. Another outburst like that will get you in cuffs."

"I didn't kill Roger Wilson. I might have been involved in a few thefts, but those are victimless crimes."

"Yeah, yeah, insurance companies pay back the homeowners—I've heard the song and dance. Tell it to Mrs Wilson."

"That was an accident." Franks eyes widened, and his lips closed in a firm, straight line.

"So you were there. If you didn't do it, and Sam didn't do it, who shot him?"

Franks shrugged. "No idea."

"But you were there."

"Never said that."

Nick placed the sketch in front of him and watched the reaction. "You know this guy?"

"Hmm, yeah. Isn't that Morgan Freeman? Or Samuel L. Jackson? I always get those guys mixed up."

He snatched the sketch back. "We're through. They'll be in to get you soon." Nick stood.

"I want a lawyer."

"You'll need one. A good one." He opened the door.

"Hewlett. The pawn shop guy. He cased the houses, told us when one would be empty. We used his van, and took the loot back to him. He kept what he wanted and we divided up the rest."

Nick froze. He turned, pulling the photo of Mrs Wilson's necklace from his papers. "What about this, from the Wilsons' house? Did Hewlett keep this piece?"

Franks looked at the photo. "Yeah, he kept all her jewelry. Morgan took the TV and we split the other electronic shit."

"Mr Wilson wasn't supposed to be home, was that it? He surprised you? If the shooting was an accident, that puts it in a whole different category to a premeditated murder."

The man looked down. "It was an accident."

Nick's heart leaped, but he forced himself to remain calm. "I understand. Stuff happens, right? What'd you do with the gun?"

"We wiped everything clean and ditched the gun in an alley behind the pawn shop, when we returned the van."

Shock rumbled through him. *Could it be that easy?* "Was it hidden pretty well? Do you think it might still be there?"

"I tucked it into a crevice. I bet it's still there."

Nick spoke slowly. "So Wilson surprised you, and you pulled the trigger?"

Franks hesitated but must have decided he'd all but admitted it anyway. "Yeah."

"Thank you." They'd solved the murder, but the events surrounding it were still messy. "Back to the pawn shop guy. You said he was the ring leader. What was his name again?"

"Hewlett. Rob Hewlett."

Franks put the twist on the imaginary knife Morgan had inserted into Nick's ribcage. "Can you describe him?"

"Long brown hair, usually wears it in a ponytail, mustache and long beard."

Long beard? Nick blinked. The wording was the same Sam had used, except for the beard part. Anyone who knew Rob wouldn't say he had a 'long' beard. It was neat and closely cropped. *And it felt heavenly when Rob nuzzled his neck, the small of his back, and...other...places.* Nick sighed.

"I'd like you to ID him." He glanced at his watch. Too late to put a line-up together tonight, it'd have to be tomorrow.

"Whatever."

"For now, you're going to be booked and held. We'll figure out the charges once we get more details. It might be manslaughter if your story holds up."

"I'm telling you the truth." Franks looked weary.

"I hope so." Nick walked out. His captain was the lone man watching the interrogation.

"I believe about half of what he says," Alvarez admitted. "Haven't figured out which half, yet."

"No shit. I need to go look for that gun, though."

"We'll get him transferred out while you do that. Take someone with you, then you should call it a night. It's been quite a day. You solved the murder, Peyton. That's huge."

"Thanks, Cap. It doesn't feel finished yet, though. Too many loose ends. I'll be happier when the stolen goods gang is sorted out."

"It'd be nice, but it's not really your concern. You did your job. Let Cameron do his."

"I need to bring the pawn shop owner in for a line-up tomorrow. We've come this far, I'd really like to do this. Can I schedule it first thing?"

Alvarez frowned. "I suppose. You can have one more day on this clusterfuck. After that, turn it over to Cameron. We have other cases to solve."

"Thank you." Nick breathed a sigh of relief. Hopefully, one more day would be all it took.

As the captain prepared to go home, Nick wandered into the break room and found some extra sandwiches in the fridge. He hadn't eaten lunch, and suddenly felt famished. He took the food and a cup of coffee back to his desk. The bullpen had cleared out, and he could eat and think in silence. He still needed to go look for the gun, but he wanted to make sure everyone was gone from Hewlett Pawn before he went.

"Hey." Dix appeared from out of nowhere. "You should cut out while you can. It's been one hell of a day. Good job, Detective."

"Yes it has." Nick smiled. "Thanks, but I couldn't have done it without all of you. Team effort."

"For a guy who just solved a case, you don't look very happy."

Nick waved a hand. "It's nothing. You should get home to Bryan."

He dropped into the chair next to Nick's desk. "Actually, Bryan is working late. I'm grabbing a carryout pizza. You look like you could use someone to talk to. What's going on?"

Nick leaned back in his chair. "Personal life stuff. It would bore you."

Dix glanced around. "I doubt that. Look, there's no one else here. Truthfully, I might understand your 'personal' stuff better than anybody. Why not give me a try?"

His smile was so genuine, Nick could only grin back. "Yeah, I guess you might. But you probably never did anything stupid like mixing business with pleasure."

"Don't be so sure. What are we talking about here, another cop? Who is it, that sexy Jeff Taylor over in Vice? Before I found Bryan, I seriously considered looking him up. Might be a bit young for me, but he's perfect for you."

Nick laughed. "No, it's not him, although now that you mention it, he is hot. And no, it's not another cop. Been there, done that, and it didn't turn out so great. I learned my lesson real quick in that regard."

Dix simply stared until Nick caved. "Okay, I'll give. It was Dean Cameron, and it was a while back."

"Cameron? No fooling?" Dix waggled his brows. "Not bad."

"It was pretty good for a while. Then it got bad. I'll spare you the details, but he has some commitment issues. He's not into monogamy, and I definitely am."

"Sorry. Want me to trip him the next time I see him?"

He laughed. "Nah, we're cool now. This was the first case we've worked together since, but it was okay."

"So if it's not another cop..." Dix folded his arms across his chest.

"It's a pawn shop owner."

"Fuck me!" Dix jumped up and circled the desk. "One of them involved with this burglary ring?"

"I don't know. I mean, I didn't think so. Of course I didn't think so, or I would never have started anything. Oh, hell, I guess I just didn't think."

"Who is it? I was running all kinds of rap sheets while you were interrogating people today."

Nick hesitated, but knew he needed to admit it. "Rob Hewlett."

"Hewlett—is he the bald brother, or the long-haired one?"

"Long hair. But, you see, both Morgan and Franks described him exactly the same way, almost like it'd been rehearsed. Except Franks added that Rob has a long beard and he doesn't, it's a very closely cropped beard. Why would he describe it as 'long' if he knows the man?"

"Interesting point. You're thinking he doesn't know Rob, and they're framing him?"

"That's exactly what I was thinking. Then I started second guessing myself, wondering if I was making shit up because I *so do not* want him to be involved."

Dix returned to the chair. "Listen. When I met Bryan, it was because someone who'd been killed had been seen the night before in his bar. I didn't know for sure he wasn't involved. We moved ahead pretty quickly—unbelievably fast, as a matter of fact—but it all worked out in the end. He wasn't guilty of anything, but, if you recall, his cousin was."

"I remember that case."

"So I'm just saying, even if Rob's clean, his brother might not be. You should prepare yourself for that possibility."

"Are you kidding? I'm trying to prepare myself for what's going to happen tomorrow. I have to go to the pawn shop and pick up Rob, and stick him in a line-up. I'm not sure he'll ever speak to me again after that, whether he's guilty or innocent."

"That's a tough one. Mac and I could go get him, if that would help."

"No, thanks. I need to do it. Somehow, I have to try to explain."

Dix slowly glanced up. "You're *not* going to see him tonight, are you?"

"I couldn't handle that. I think I'll just stay here and work straight through. I still need to run over and look for the gun Franks said he hid in the alley."

"You waiting until you're sure everyone is gone from there?"

Nick shook his head, chuckling. Dix was a sharp cookie. "Possibly."

"I'll go with you." Dix slapped his thighs then stood. "So what do you like on your pizza?"

Chapter Six

Nick found the gun where Franks had said it would be. He bagged the Glock and on the way back to the station, Dix picked up a pizza. They signed the gun into evidence then talked while they ate. Dix finally left around nine, but Nick worked until midnight when he couldn't keep his eyes open any longer.

He drove home and fell into bed, not bothering to read the dozen text messages Rob had left for him. He read some of them in the morning after he'd showered and was preparing to go back to the station.

Lying here thinking about you.

About what we'd be doing if you were here.

I'd peel your clothes off, and since I know you like a shower after work, we'd start there.

Nick couldn't read any further. Images of Rob and thoughts about what he had to do made his heart hurt.

He shoved his cell in his pocket and drove to work, stopping along the way for five lattes to share.

"Thanks," Laura smiled as she accepted hers. "Get any sleep?"

"Not much." He passed coffees out to his captain and Mac, giving the final cup and a grateful smile to Dix. "Morning."

"Thank you. Good morning. How you doing?"

"Hanging in there. I need to speak with the DA and Central Booking first thing. I want to get the line-up going asap."

"If you need anything, just ask."

"Thanks." Nick smiled appreciatively. Talking to Dix last night had made him feel better. He knew he wasn't the first guy to fall into bed with someone on the first date, but it helped knowing other cops had made similar 'thinking with the wrong head' moves. Things had worked out well for Dix and Bryan. He just couldn't see them working out as well for him and Rob. The man was going to be pissed off, no matter what the outcome of the line-up.

He made the necessary arrangements and DA Steve Royce would meet him at Central Booking at ten. Nick dragged his feet until nine, then sucked it up and expelled a big breath. *Time to get the show on the road.*

He drove to Hewlett Pawn and was surprised to see Danny there instead of Rob. He'd made all the plans without ensuring Rob would even be there. His thinking was still screwed up.

"Detective," Danny greeted him suspiciously. "Something I can do for you?"

"I was looking for your brother, actually. Is he around?"

Danny turned his head and yelled, "Robby! Someone here to see you."

Rob appeared in the doorway from the back room. His face lit up when he spotted Nick. "Hey."

Nick's stomach did flips but he tried to tamp down the emotions rushing through him. "Hey. We have a problem, and I need your help." He'd given lots of thought to the way he'd word his request. He longed to tell Rob that he didn't believe the men who had fingered him, and this was just a formality to clear his name. Disclosing that much information, though, would be a definite no-no.

The smile slid from his face. "What's up?"

"We got the shooter in the Roger Wilson murder. Unfortunately, he was just the trigger man. Someone else is calling the plays."

"Okay. And you're telling me this because?"

Nick steeled himself. "Both men we apprehended pointed to the same guy as the ring leader."

Rob sighed. "You're fucking kidding me. Look, I know my brother has been in some trouble in the past, but he's been clean for a lot of years. He's—"

"Rob," Nick interrupted.

The handsome hunk stopped talking and stared.

"They named you."

An expression of utter disbelief washed over Rob's face. "Excuse me?"

"No way!" Danny hollered. "That's bullshit!"

"I agree," Nick said calmly. "I think it is, too. We have to go through the formalities, though. I need you to come to the station for a line-up."

"A line-up?" Rob's voice cracked. "Are you serious? Do I need a lawyer?"

"Look," Nick tried to calm him. "We have reasons to believe the men are lying. This is just a way to prove that." He'd already said more than he should have. His cop instincts were warring with the instinct to protect the man he cared very deeply for. "You shouldn't need a lawyer. Unless you won't come with me, then we'll have to arrest you so you'll have no choice but to submit to the line-up. If that happens then, yeah, you'll want to retain an attorney."

Rob looked at Danny. "Fuck me. I'm totally screwed on this one."

"I'm calling a lawyer." Danny reached for his phone.

Nick raised one hand. "I'm telling you, I firmly believe this is going to be okay. Just come with me and get it over with."

"What if they finger me?" Rob shouted. "I'll be behind bars and it won't matter what the fuck you believe."

"They aren't going to," Nick insisted.

"How do you know that? They're obviously liars. If they stick to their story and continue to lie, I'm screwed. You won't be able to help me."

"I'm not going to let that happen."

Danny moved to his brother's side. "Don't trust the fucking cops, man. He doesn't give a shit about you."

Nick and Rob exchanged glances. They both knew that wasn't true. Neither of them said anything.

Nick finally murmured, "Trust me."

Rob sighed. "I do. Not sure why I do." He glanced at his brother. "If this doesn't go well, you'll be my one phone call. You better fucking answer."

"Want me to go with you?"

"No, just stay here. Don't close the shop unless things go bad."

"I'll be right here, waiting to hear from you." He cast a scornful glance at Nick then turned away.

Nick studied Rob's face. "You ready?"

"No."

Nick smiled. "Come on." He led them out, and they got in his Explorer.

"I can't fucking believe this," Rob muttered.

"Come 'ere." Nick reached for him and hugged Rob over the console. "It's going to be okay, I promise it will."

"This isn't happening." He pulled back and glanced at Nick. "Is this why you didn't come over last night?"

"The case broke open. I worked until midnight."

Rob moved close to the door, away from his reach. "I sent you all those stupid texts while you were preparing to arrest me."

"Nobody's arresting you. I'm bringing you in for a line-up. Once you're cleared, you'll be free to go."

"Why would they pin this on me? Who are these guys? I should have a right to face my accusers."

"Not yet. Let's just do this and get it over with."

"Fuck," Rob muttered, and stared out of the window the whole ride.

At the station, Nick led him into a small room where four other men had been assembled. They all had long brown hair and different lengths of moustaches and beards.

"What is this?"

Nick smiled. "Two cops, and two husbands of cops. These guys fingered someone with long hair and a beard. They need to take it one step further and finger you. I don't think they can."

"What if they do?" Rob's eyes widened.

"Is there something you need to tell me?"

"Fuck no! I told you, I didn't do anything."

"Then have some faith that the system will work. I'm leaving you with Officer Lyons, here. She'll explain what to do. I'll be in there, with the suspects."

He pointed to the room behind the mirror. "I'll see you after."

Rob still didn't look happy. Nick had never seen him so frightened. He couldn't blame him. A lot was riding on the words of two admitted liars and thieves.

He went to the next room where the District Attorney stood with Laura and Sam Morgan.

"They won't be able to see you," she told Morgan. "Just take your time, and let us know which man has been running the stolen goods ring."

A knock on the window indicated that the line-up was ready.

Nick looked at Sam. "You good?"

The man nodded.

Nick raised the blinds, and the five bearded men came into view. He studied them along with Sam.

The department didn't have enough long-haired cops to fill out the line themselves. Husbands of officers often came into play when they matched the description. He looked at their faces, noticing the hardened expression Rob now wore. Number four. *Please don't pick number four.*

"Do you see him in there?" Laura asked.

Sam studied the man a while longer then nodded. "Yes, yes I do."

"Which number?" the DA prodded.

Nick held his breath.

"Number three. It's definitely him. Three." Sam nodded.

Nick exchanged glances with Laura and Royce. His heart was soaring, but he didn't say a word.

"Thank you." Laura led him out, then brought in Terry Franks.

"Take your time," Royce told the man. "Let us know if you recognize the man who gave you your orders the night of Roger Wilson's murder."

"I see him." Franks looked at the DA. "Number two. Rob Hewlett. Long hair and beard, just like I told you."

Nick could have kissed the man. His heart thumped wildly as he glanced at the guy he really wanted to kiss, number four. The real Rob Hewlett.

"Thank you." The DA watched as Laura led Franks out, then turned to Nick. "Okay, so both of your defendants are lying sacks of shit. We may never know who was calling the shots, but I don't believe it was that guy. Let the pawn shop owner go. Pray there's a print on that gun, or we wait until one of those two scumbags decides to come clean."

"Which is bad, because Mr Big is still out there. He'll lie low for a while, then find a couple new scumbags to do his dirty work."

Royce shrugged. "Like it's the first time that's ever happened. Such is life, my friend. Call me if you get any new evidence."

"Will do. Thanks." He returned to the room where Rob waited, toe tapping nervously.

Nick smiled. "It's all good. You're free to go, just like I told you."

Rob didn't return the smile. "Yeah, well, you told me a lot of things." He brushed past him through the door.

"I'll take you back to the shop."

"Don't bother. I'll catch a cab." Rob hurried through the station.

"Rob, wait." Nick followed.

Outside on the sidewalk, Rob faced him. "Don't. Don't say anything, don't do anything, just don't. I'm really pissed off right now, and I need some time to work through it."

"I understand. But at least I can take you back to work. Your truck is there."

Rob glared at him. "I can't be with you right now. I'll walk for a while, maybe hail a cab."

Nick started to protest.

Rob raised a hand. "I mean it. Don't." He turned and, taking long, angry strides, hurried off.

Nick felt horrible. He couldn't blame Rob—in fact he'd known the man would be ticked off. He'd called that one right. Hopefully, time would heal all wounds. He went back to work, feeling sadly deflated.

* * * *

After lunch, Laura brought him the report on the gun. "It's a Glock Model G20 and it uses ten millimeter auto ammo. Ballistics is a match to the spent casing we found."

"It's definitely our murder weapon."

"Yes. It's been wiped clean, of course. Franks admitted that."

He nodded. "It's nice to have, but it's moot since Franks admitting pulling the trigger." He considered the gun again. "Is the Glock registered to anybody?"

"Not an individual."

He gazed at her. "That's strange wording."

Laura shrugged. "I was just thinking, if it was ever pawned, wouldn't it be in the pawn shop database for weapons?"

"Should be."

She smiled. "I'll go check that."

"Don't hold your breath," he called after her. "Too many 'shoulds' in this case."

"Shoulda, woulda, coulda," she tossed back.

Grinning, he phoned the DA. "Peyton here. We got the murder weapon. No prints, of course. We're still tracing it through the system, but it's not registered to any one person."

"Okay, keep me posted. What did you get from the van?"

"The van?" Nick blinked, and his mind started spinning. *Shit.* He hadn't followed up on Rob's white cargo van. He needed to have it inspected *now.* "Have to get back to you about that." The call ended and he met Laura halfway between their desks. "We need to get the techs out to inspect Rob Hewlett's cargo van."

She waved a computer printout. "While we're there, let's ask him about the Glock. It was logged in at Hewlett's three months ago. They never logged it as sold. But I don't think it's still there."

"Probably not, since it's here." He put his hands on his hips, thoughts still whirling. How could he go back and face Rob yet again? It was relationship suicide, if the thing wasn't dead already.

Dix leaned back in his chair. "Want me to run over there? Mac and I don't mind, do we, Mac?"

"Whatever." Mac waved a hand.

Nick looked at him appreciatively, but shook his head. "I need to do it. But thanks." To Laura he said, "Let's put the CSI on alert that we may be calling them soon. We'll make sure the van is there before we drag them over."

She went to make the call.

On the way to the pawn shop, Nick tried to process the possibilities. "Something is funny at Hewlett Pawn. If it's not Rob, it has to be Danny."

"He seems like the obvious choice."

"Would he throw his brother under the bus? If Morgan and Franks worked for Danny, would the man have instructed them to accuse his brother rather than him?"

"They could have done that on their own. Maybe they like Danny for some reason."

He pulled into a parking space and looked at her. "Or maybe Danny has something on them. Something big enough that they're willing to lie for him."

"They're both in the pokey now, what could be worse? It'd have to be something huge for them to keep his secret and protect Danny."

They got out and walked in. "Something huge, huh?" He couldn't fathom anything that big, other than somehow protecting their families.

Danny was behind the counter again. He looked up, then shook his head. "What the fuck? You guys got nothing better to do than harass us?"

Nick was in no mood to play. "We haven't begun to harass, yet. If you'd like to see true harassment, that could be arranged. I hope your books are worthy of scrutiny."

"Suck it, cop. What do you want this time? And if you're looking for my brother, too fucking bad. He was so worked up when he got back, I told him to take the rest of the day off. He's not here."

"We'd like to see the Glock Model G20 with this serial number. You logged it in here several months ago."

Danny took the piece of paper and read it. A strange look crossed his face as he studied the number.

"Can you get it for us, please?" Laura asked.

The store owner didn't reply.

Nick looked at her. "I don't think he can."

"Nope," she agreed. "Not surprising, really, since we have it at the station. Submitted as evidence in the murder of Roger Wilson."

"Nothing to say?" Nick watched Danny. The man seemed to know he was cornered, and men in that frame of mind can be dangerous. He pressed on. "Then I'll keep talking. Next we'd like to see the white Chevy cargo van registered to Rob. We understand it's kept in the garage here."

"He hasn't driven that thing in months."

"Then he shouldn't have a problem with us looking at it."

Danny shrugged. "Keys are back here." He went through the storeroom door.

Nick followed and was immediately whacked in the face with a metal storage rack. "Fuck!" He shoved the thing out of his way and spotted Danny running out of the back door. "He's running," he yelled to Laura.

"I'll call it in!"

"Try to head him off." Nick didn't take time to aim, just tossed his Explorer keys on the floor at her feet.

He raced into the alley and glanced both ways. Danny could be seen rounding the corner to a connecting alley, and he took off after him. The man had at least fifty pounds on him, and Nick closed the distance quickly. "Stop, Hewlett!"

"Fuck you." Danny shoved a row of metal trash cans between them and kept running.

Nick spotted Laura in his Explorer as she pulled into the alley ahead of them. She stopped and jumped out, raising her gun. "Freeze, asshole!"

Danny was caught between them. He paused, bending over to catch his breath, hands on his knees.

"Hands in the air," Laura commanded.

He didn't comply, just remained where he was.

Panting, Nick approached with caution. "Hands in the air, Danny."

"I said 'fuck you'." The man rose and Nick saw a flash of silver.

"He's got a gun!" Laura screamed.

Nick dropped as a bullet whizzed by his shoulder. Another shot rang out, then two more. He looked up to see Laura standing over Danny, who was obviously dead.

Her hands started to shake.

Nick scrambled to his feet, the wail of sirens filling the air.

He approached his partner from the side. "Give me the gun."

She let it dangle from her hand, and he grabbed it.

"Oh my God!" Laura backed up, her face ash white.

Nick grabbed one arm and drew her into a hug. "Thank you. You saved my life."

"I didn't— I've never— Oh my God..."

Two patrol cars appeared at either end of the alley, followed by a dark SUV. Nick saw Dix and Mac running toward them. "You two okay?"

"Yeah." Nick held a sobbing Laura in his arms. "She told him to freeze, ordered him to put his hands in the air, and he didn't respond. He pulled a gun on me, and she took him out."

Mac held out a baggie. "Give me her weapon. We need to do things by the book, here."

Nick dropped it into the bag.

"What the hell happened?" Dix asked Nick as he checked Danny for a pulse.

"He got real quiet when we questioned him about the Glock. But when we mentioned the van, he bolted. Anything?"

Standing, Dix shook his head. "He's gone. I guess we know who Mr Big is."

"Was." Nick glanced at the body of his lover's brother. His ex-lover's brother. There was no coming back from something like this, he knew it now, for sure. "I need to notify his next-of-kin."

"No, you do not," Dix said firmly. "Alvarez is on his way here to take charge of the scene. You and Evans need to give statements. Mac and I will take care of notification."

"The pawn shop is unattended. Maybe you should go there and call Rob to come down. He'll need to lock the place up."

Mac added, "After Property Crimes and CSI go over it with a fine-tooth comb. That place will be closed for a long time."

"A very long time," Dix agreed. "Come on," he said to his partner. They paused long enough to fill the captain in, then went to call Rob.

Alvarez walked toward them. "Evans, you okay?"

She pulled away from Nick and nodded, wiping her eyes.

"She saved my life," Nick offered.

"I've shot a man before." She stared at the body. "I've never killed one, though."

"You did what you had to do." Alvarez placed a hand on her shoulder. "There's going to be an investigation, lots of questions and paperwork, mandatory counseling sessions, that kind of stuff. But it'll be okay. Evans, you did what you had to do."

Nick turned away. He had things to do, too. But first, unanswered questions nagged at him. He hoped he knew where to find the answers.

* * * *

Sam Morgan was brought into the interrogation room in handcuffs. The accompanying officer locked him to a ring on the table and left the man alone with Nick.

"Thanks," Nick said as the officer slipped out. "How you doing?" he asked Morgan.

"Been better. I guess you reap what you sow."

"I guess. I thought you should know, Danny Hewlett is dead."

Sam blinked. "Danny? I told you it was Rob we dealt with."

"Yeah, and you told me you didn't have anything to do with the crime ring, either. Now that Hewlett's gone maybe we can get past the lies and uncover the truth."

"I don't know what you want me to say, man."

"For starters, I'd like to know why you framed Rob instead of Danny. Did someone tell you to do that?"

He seemed flustered. "I don't know —"

Nick snapped and pounded the table. "Cut the bullshit, Sam! You do know, and you're going to tell me the truth right now. Did Danny have something on you? Did he threaten you or your family?"

Sam nodded slowly. "I met Terry at the Shop Mart, we used him for plumbing stuff. We had a run of crapper problems, and he was there a lot, for several nights in a row. He and I got pretty friendly. We talked about our shitty, low paying jobs. His was shittier than mine, of course." He grinned. When Nick didn't smile, he went on, "One night, he suggested a way we could make some extra cash. The next day he introduced me to Danny Hewlett. Danny had the burglaries all worked out."

"He just used you to do the dirty work."

"Yeah. After the first job he passed around a couple necklaces we'd heisted, and showed us two guns he seemed real proud of. We passed the stuff between us like first class idiots. Once we'd touched everything, Danny bagged it and told me and Terry that he was going to lock it all away in a safe place. If we ever got caught and fingered him, he said he'd plant the stuff in our houses where the cops would find it, to seal our guilt. He also said he'd do things to our wives and kids. Bad things." Sam shuddered. "I couldn't take the chance."

Nick frowned. For the first time, he believed every word Sam spoke. "What a prick."

"I can't believe he's dead. It's over." Sam appeared relieved.

"Yeah, it's over. Danny Hewlett can't hurt you or your family anymore, Sam. There's just one more thing that's bothering me. I saw Terry at Roger Wilson's funeral, talking to Wilson's brother. The brother didn't seem happy to see him there. Terry left shortly after."

Sam shrugged. "I dunno. Maybe he felt guilty?"

"I just need to be sure. Did you know Roger Wilson was going to be home that night when you went there?"

"Huh?" Sam's face contorted into a mask of disbelief and fear. "Oh, hell no! You think we went there to off him? Hell no! I didn't know nothing about that!"

"I believe you." Nick did. He wasn't convinced Terry didn't know, and didn't figure the man would fess up too easily. "Thanks for answering my questions. I'll make sure the DA knows how cooperative you were."

"Yeah, do that. Thanks, man. Anything else you need to know, just ask."

Nick smiled as he left. Sam was cooperating like a contortionist now.

He walked down the hall and gasped when he spotted Rob and a woman who had to be his mother pass in front of him, escorted by an officer. The woman was distraught, sobbing. Rob wasn't, but he didn't look good. He glanced up and caught Nick's eye.

Nick froze.

Not a flicker of recognition. He'd dismissed him as easily as that.

If only it were that easy to dismiss his memories of Rob. He couldn't focus on that now. He had one more loose end to tie up.

At his desk, he pulled financial records for Ashton Wilson and Danny Hewlett. What he found was enough to warrant a visit to Mr Wilson. He checked his watch—it was after five. Dix was the last detective in the office. He rushed past Dix's desk, planning to go with or without him. "I need back-up, you game?"

"Hang on, I'm coming." Dix followed.

Nick clued him in on the way. He guessed where he might find Ash Wilson, and his hunch proved correct.

At Mrs Wilson's house, Ash answered the door. "Hello, Detective. Here about a break in the case, I hope?"

"I am. I definitely am." Nick stepped inside. "This is Detective Dixon. We have two men in custody and one is dead. We think we've got it all figured out."

Mrs Wilson joined them, clutching Ash's arm. "A man is dead? How awful."

"I guess he chose not to go to prison with his cohorts. What do you think about that, Ash? Is that a choice you could make?"

The man chuckled, but didn't look happy. "I hope I never have to find out."

"Well, hope springs eternal. We don't always get what we want."

Dix added, "Maybe you should make that, we don't always get what *we think* we got."

"Excuse me?" Ash blinked.

Nick waved a paper in his face. "I'd like to know about the twenty-five thousand dollar withdrawal you made from the bank on the tenth of this month."

Ash looked decidedly uncomfortable. "It was a transfer to my money market. Nothing unusual."

"Good. Then you can show me where the funds were deposited. Because I have a receipt from Danny Hewlett's bank showing he put that exact amount of money into a brand new bank account he just opened, on that very day."

"Who?" Beads of sweat formed on Ash's temples.

"I didn't see any unusual activity in Terry Franks' account, and certainly none in Sam Morgan's. I don't believe Sam knew about the deal, but after seeing Terry at the funeral, I think he did. You mentioned knowing him. He did some plumbing work for you?"

"What deal?" Mrs Wilson looked at her brother-in-law.

"This is fabricated," he insisted.

"I don't think so." Nick turned to the woman. "I think Ash paid Danny Hewlett twenty-five thousand dollars to have your husband killed."

"His brother," Dix added.

"No!" She swooned, and leaned against the wall. "You promised me you wouldn't go through with that!"

Nick and Dix exchanged glances. *We got him.* Nick looked at the widow. "You discussed a murder plot?"

"Of course not! Not seriously, anyway. We were tipsy and joking around about it one night. I never thought—"

"That's a hilarious thing to joke about," Nick scoffed.

Dix added, "You never thought when your husband came up dead that your lover had something to do with it? You expect us to buy that, lady? You're both under arrest."

Ash raised one finger. "Wait. She didn't know. Please, leave Ronnie out of this."

Nick rolled his eyes at Dix. "They discussed offing her husband, but when it happened she never gave their conversation a second thought. Right. We're all going down to the station, *Ronnie* included. The truth will come out." He reached for his cuffs.

Dix grabbed his own set. "It always does."

* * * *

The press had caught wind of the story and had run with it. Reporters had hounded the station hoping for tasty morsels of the juicy scandal. Nick had managed to avoid them most days. His heart was heavy. The case had been solved and all the guilty parties were in custody.

Cameron was happy as hell. Much of their stolen property had finally been accounted for. He had thanked Nick profusely and offered to buy him a drink.

Nick had declined. He hadn't felt like celebrating.

He was filling out paperwork a few days later when he glanced up and spotted a man wearing cap and sunglasses walking toward him. He looked again, then blinked. His jaw dropped open.

Rob removed the glasses. His hair was very short, his face clean-shaven.

Stunned, Nick asked, "What the hell happened to you?"

"It's the only way I can get around without an entourage these days. The media hasn't recognized me yet."

"Sorry about that. Shit, Rob, I'm sorry about so many things."

He held up a hand. "I'm not here for this. I just wanted to drop off your things." He set a bag on Nick's desk. "I think I got it all. You didn't leave much."

Nick's heart felt like it could burst. "Rob, please. We need to talk. I was giving you some time and space, but—"

He flashed the hand again. "Not enough time, not enough space. We're trying to plan a funeral for my brother and the press is making it damn near impossible. That's all I can think about right now. Mom and the kids need me."

"I'm sure they do. I'm so sorry, Rob, about everything."

"Yeah." He stared into Nick's eyes for a moment.

Nick stared back, at a loss for words. There was really nothing left to say.

Epilogue

Three months later

"Detective Peyton, some people are here to see you," the clerk at the front desk called.

He raised his hands in a shrug. "Send them over." To himself he muttered, "Since when does anybody get announced? People have been in and out of here all damned day."

The couple he saw walking toward his desk appeared very unsure of themselves. The woman was young, thin, with bleached blonde hair and multiple piercings, including one on the side of her nose.

The man was also young, muscular, with short dark hair and grease-stained jeans. He looked like he may have been a mechanic.

Nick blinked.

"Detective Peyton? I'm Max Hewlett. This is my sister, Celia." He extended a hand.

Still shocked, Nick shook it, then Celia's.

"Is there someplace we could talk?" Max asked.

"Sure." Nick led them to a small conference room off the bullpen. He motioned them in and closed the door. The three of them sat around one corner of the large table. "How are you?" he asked. "How's your grandmother?" He wanted to ask about Rob, but couldn't bring himself to do it.

"We're doing okay." Celia nodded. "It was awful at first, but things have settled down now."

"I'm sure it was. I hope the worst is over."

"It's hard." Max looked at his hands. "Dad's birthday was last month, that was rough. We never dreamed we'd lose him, never thought about life without him."

Celia dabbed at the corner of her eye. "Never imagined in a million years that he could do what he did."

There was a box of tissues in the middle of the table. Nick reached for it and pushed it toward the girl. "They say the first year is the hardest. The first one of everything, Thanksgiving, Christmas, all that stuff."

She took one and dried her tears. "Yeah, the holidays are going to suck this year."

Max frowned. "We haven't quite gotten over what he did. That part makes no sense. We didn't have a lot growing up, but we had what we needed, and it was enough. I'm not sure why he thought he needed so much more."

"Like that new bike." She made a face. "It was the first thing Uncle Rob got rid of."

Nick sighed. "I'll bet. It's hard to know why someone does a certain thing. We can never really understand, especially when he isn't here to explain himself."

"Grandma is taking it hard," Max said. "Like she failed as a parent or something. Uncle Rob spends a lot of time reassuring her that she didn't."

"It wasn't her fault," Nick agreed. He wanted to add that Rob turned out fine, but didn't.

"And Uncle Rob, oh geez." Celia wiped her eyes again. "He's been a mess. He closed the pawn shop, you know. He hasn't been working. He's super depressed."

"I didn't know." Nick knew that the pawn shop hadn't reopened, but he hadn't realized it was permanent. Since he'd stood in the back of the funeral home at the small service for Danny, he hadn't seen Rob at all.

Max gazed at him. "Uncle Rob is a total mess. That's actually why we're here. He talked about you to Grandma. He was so happy. She was excited to meet you. Then all this stuff with my dad happened."

"Yeah, well..." Nick didn't know what to say.

"The thing is..." Celia added. "We don't understand why the trouble with my dad had to break you and Uncle Rob up. One thing's not connected to the other."

Nick looked at her skeptically. "Other than the fact that I uncovered the crimes your father was committing, and I was there in the alley the day he died."

"You didn't kill him." Max shook his head.

"I would have, had the situation been reversed and he was aiming at my partner. She had a very hard time with the shooting, I hope you know. None of us wanted things to go down that way."

"I hope she's okay," Celia said softly.

Nick smiled. "She's a tough one. She'll never be the same, but she's starting to be okay."

"That's pretty much where we're at," Max said. "Not the same, but slowly, things are becoming okay again. Celia's in school."

"Really?"

"Beauty college. I'm going to be a cosmetologist. The Victim's Assistance Fund helped pay for my tuition." She grabbed another tissue. "I didn't realize they'd help us out, too. I never thought about us as victims."

Nick knew about that, because he'd helped arrange it. "You two and your grandma and your uncle were victims just like all those people who got burglarized. None of this was your fault."

Max laid a hand on the table. "Do you think you could tell our uncle that? He needs to hear it from somebody besides us. And I think he needs to hear it from you."

"He doesn't want to see me."

"Oh, yes he does." Celia nodded.

Max continued, "We understand why you might not want to see him. But please, for his sake, think about it? He really is in bad shape."

Nick looked away. It wasn't that he didn't want to see Rob. He couldn't believe Rob might want to see him. "I'm not sure."

Max rose. "Just think about it. He needs you." He looked at his sister.

Celia stood. "He misses you, I know he does."

Nick joined them. "Thanks for stopping by. It was good to see you, and hear how well you're both doing."

They each shook hands with him, and before Celia left she gave him a quick hug. They hurried out.

Nick reached for the box of tissues.

* * * *

After his shift had ended, he drove to Rob's apartment complex and sat in the parking lot for twenty minutes. The Silverado was there, so he guessed Rob was home. His stomach was doing flip-flops, but he finally forced himself to get out and walk inside.

He knocked on the door.

It took a couple of minutes, but Rob finally answered.

Nick's throat clutched and he wasn't sure he could speak. The man looked as gorgeous as ever. The mustache and beard were back, and his hair had grown to shaggy collar-length. "Hey," was all Nick could manage.

Rob's eyes widened. "Hey. What are you doing here?"

Nick shrugged. "I have no idea. I just needed to see you, I guess."

"Come in." Rob stepped back and motioned him inside.

Nick glanced around. The living room was filled with packing boxes. "Where are you going?"

Rob sauntered to the fridge and pulled out two beers. He shoved stuff off two chairs and handed one bottle over. "Well, I lost my pawn shop and now I've lost my apartment. I can't afford to pay the rent, so I've been asked to move."

"I'm sorry." Nick twisted the lid off and took a swig from his bottle. The cold liquid burned going down, but it felt good. Just feeling *something* again was good. "The shop is gone?"

"As good as. Cops took half my inventory as stolen goods." He laughed bitterly. "God, I was a fool. I knew Danny made some shady deals, I won't lie to you. The fake name thing happened more than once. But I swear to heaven, I had no idea how deep he was involved. I would never have gone along with *anything* like that. I hope you believe me."

"Of course I do. And I hope you believe that I never wanted things to happen the way they did. When I questioned him about the van, he said the keys were in back. I followed him, and he bolted. I was shocked as hell."

"We all were." Rob looked at his beer bottle. "I let him use the van for shop business, since I had a truck and didn't need it. I had no fucking idea what he was really using it for. Damn, I was a fool."

"No you weren't. You were his brother. You trusted him."

He laughed again. "Big mistake there."

"You weren't his keeper, Rob. None of this was your fault."

He set his bottle down, stood and moved across the room. "I couldn't even look at you. Couldn't begin to imagine what you thought of me. I was so ashamed."

Nick took one more drink then set it aside and rose. "I never thought any of it was your fault. *I* felt ashamed that I had a role in his death. I assumed you'd hate me for that, probably for the rest of your life."

Rob faced him. "Damn. Well, you know what they say about assuming. The problem is, I could never hate you."

Nick's heart skipped a beat. *Is he saying what I think he's saying?* He took a step closer, afraid to utter the actual words he so wanted to say. "I could never hate you, either."

Their gazes locked. Before Nick could make another sound, Rob was in his arms.

"I'm sorry! I'm so sorry for everything." Rob's lips pressed against his.

Nick wove his fingers through the shaggy hair and pulled the man closer. Their mouths crushed together and that first kiss tasted sweeter than anything he could have imagined. When they pulled apart, tears streamed down both their faces.

Using his thumbs, he wiped Rob's cheeks. "No more 'I'm sorry's. It's time to move on."

Smiling, Rob brushed the tears from Nick's face too. "There's one thing I need to say. *I love you*. I've loved you since the day we met, but I knew it was too soon to spring it on you. I was biding my time... But then my time ran out."

Nick grinned. "I love you, too. From day one, no doubt in my mind. I didn't know what might happen with us—if anything could be salvaged. I hoped if I gave you enough time and space—"

"Too much time. Too much space. I need you, Nick. I don't want to live without you. I was just trying to work up the nerve to come and tell you." He kissed Nick again, more insistently this time. Hungrier. Needier.

The same emotions flooded through Nick. He opened his mouth and reveled in the play of their tongues against each other. It'd been too long. *Much too long*. But finally they were back where they needed to be. He pulled away slightly to smile. "I need you too, babe. Starting right now, for the rest of my life." He glanced around. "Where are you taking this stuff?"

"To my mom's. She said I could stay there until I get back on my feet. I've taken one truckload over already."

"Good. Then I can finally meet her when we go to pick it up."

Rob stared at him questioningly.

"Unless you don't think she's ready to meet me?"

"Of course she is, but I need to a place to live."

Nick rested his hands on Rob's hips. "How about moving in with me? I've got plenty of space, I think you'll be comfortable there."

Rob smiled. "As long as I'm in your arms, I'd be comfortable in a ditch."

Nick laughed. "It's a little nicer than that. We'll get along just fine. I even have two weeks' vacation coming to me, so I can help you move. I've been so surly lately, they'll be glad to get rid of me."

"Two weeks sounds amazing. Let's see, it'll take us about a day to move everything, so that leaves thirteen days to spend in the sack. I assume you have a nice big bed?"

"Like it matters if I don't? But yeah, a king-sized bed. I'm sorry you haven't seen the house. We'll take care of that tonight."

Rob slid his arms around Nick's waist. "Sure, but later. We've got something else to take care of first." He walked Nick backwards into the bedroom.

"Ah, your bed is still here. Good."

Rob grinned. "Like it would matter if it wasn't?"

"You're right." They rolled onto the bed kissing, and when they stopped Nick was on top. "I love you. I guess I already told you that."

"Tell me again. Every day, for the rest of our lives."

"I promise."

Rob touched his face. "Promise to help me figure out a job, too? I was thinking about maybe opening a thrift store with the stuff left at the pawn shop, and adding to it. No pawns, just buying and selling furniture and things."

"Sounds workable, if that's what you'd like. Whatever you want, I'll help you make it happen."

"Damn, I love you. I'm so glad you're here."

"We have Max and Celia to thank for that. They came to see me today."

Rob's jaw dropped open. "Max and Celia? No kidding?"

"Apparently they love you like I do."

"I love those knuckleheads, too. Pretty sure they'll be getting good Christmas presents this year." He unfastened Nick's trousers and slid his hand in. Curling his fingers around the aching shaft he found there, Rob squeezed.

Nick gasped. Pure pleasure zinged through him. "Um, yeah. Really good presents. From me, too."

A wicked, lustful grin spread across Rob's face, and he squeezed again.

Nick's eyes rolled back in his head, and he smiled.

About the Author

Jenna Byrnes could use more cabinet space and more hours in a day. She'd fill the kitchen with gadgets her husband purchases off TV and let him cook for her to his heart's content. She'd breeze through the days adding hours of sleep, and more time for writing the hot, erotic romance she loves to read.

Jenna thinks everyone deserves a happy ending, and loves to provide as many of those as possible to her gay, lesbian and hetero characters. Her favourite quote, from a pro-gay billboard, is "Be careful who you hate. It may be someone you love."

Jenna Byrnes loves to hear from readers. You can find her contact information, website details and author profile page at http://www.totallybound.com.

Totally Bound Publishing

CPSIA information can be obtained at www.ICGtesting.com
Printed in the USA
LVOW07s1107140615

442423LV00001B/99/P

9 781784 302054